WICHITA MANHUNT

WICHITA DETECTIVE
BOOK TWO

PATRICK ANDREWS

ROUGH
EDGES
PRESS

Wichita Manhunt
Paperback Edition
Copyright © 2022 Patrick Andrews

Rough Edges Press
An Imprint of Wolfpack Publishing
5130 S. Fort Apache Rd. 215-380
Las Vegas, NV 89148

roughedgespress.com

Paperback ISBN 978-1-68549-154-3
eBook ISBN 978-1-68549-153-6
LCCN 2022944092

Dedicated to
Boo and Willy
A couple of good ol' Wichita boys from my youth

WICHITA MANHUNT

"Dwayne, your sense of morality is tempered by a levelheaded dash of malfeasance."

– Peter Van Dyke, former captain of the U.S. Army Military Police Corps

CHAPTER 1

Dwayne Wheeler, a licensed private investigator, sat on the passenger side of the 1941 Packard sedan's front seat. He was in the company of his temporary employer A.J. Kessler. A.J. was a well-groomed and most fastidious dresser with thick black hair and a handlebar moustache that curled up on the ends. He was also a little person, standing about four feet tall.

The vehicle the pair sat in was specially-built and designed to accommodate A.J.'s physical requirements. A couple of sofa pillows on the seat, along with a built-up accelerator, clutch and brake pedals enabled A.J. to drive safely and efficiently. He used a walking stick to reach the floor starter.

Another unusual feature of his automobile was the lack of handles on the inside of the rear doors. This arrangement had been installed to prevent passengers from being able to get out of the car by themselves. Most of these individuals were not voluntary riders; they were, in fact, prisoners of their diminutive driver. A.J. Kessler was a bail bondsman, and he went after jumpers with a vengeance. And when he caught one, he took them to the county jail in that atypical Packard as they sat fuming helplessly in the back seat, also restrained by handcuffs.

That afternoon, with Dwayne at his side, A.J. was about to move in on a fugitive by the name of Johnny Mason. Mason had used the bail bondsman to get him released from custody prior to his trial on charges of commercial burglary. The bail was five thousand dollars and A.J. had posted ten percent of that amount with the court. Normally he would have required some sort of collateral from the prisoner, but he and Johnny went back several years and A.J. had developed a trust for the professional criminal. After all, he had dealt with him on nearly a dozen occasions. Johnny was always present in the courtroom when the judge's gavel banged down to open the proceedings of the trial.

But this time it was different.

Johnny Mason had skipped town, meaning that if he didn't show up for his trial date as promised, A.J. would have to fork over four thousand, five hundred dollars to the court. He went to a skip tracer, but nothing came from that. Then a month later word from the street revealed that Johnny was back in town. At that point A.J. hired private detective Dwayne Wheeler to track Johnny to his Wichita hideout.

Dwayne was a native Wichitan with experience on the streets that went back to his teen years. The slimly muscular shamus had contacts among bootleggers, bookmakers, fences, hookers, rummies, and other local criminals, thus he began his search making inquiries among those less than sterling denizens of the city. It took him only three days to find out where Johnny Mason was holed up, and now A.J. and Dwayne were keeping an eye on a house in southeast Wichita, ready to move in and grab their prey.

A.J. glanced over at Dwayne. "What do you think?"

"I think he's in the house," Dwayne replied. "That's where his ex-wife lives. They may be divorced, but I know for a fact they're still hot for each other. Johnny prob'ly figgers we won't look for him there. I don't know what brought him back to Wichita, but he's sure to lay low and prob'ly get some of his pals or family to run errands for him. That way he wouldn't have to venture out into the open."

"Yeah," A.J. said in agreement. "How do you want to do this?"

Dwayne reached under his jacket and patted the .45 Colt semi-automatic pistol in his shoulder holster. He also had a pair of handcuffs in his rear trouser pocket. He glanced over at A.J. "You got a sap?"

"Look in the glove compartment."

Dwayne opened the door, reaching in to grab the shot-filled leather pouch. "Okay," he said. "Since I'm acting as a bail bondsman's agent, I don't need a warrant. So I'll walk up to the door, knock, then bust in. Meanwhile, you pull up to the curb over there and wait for somebody to come running out the back way. It'll be Johnny and that's how I figger it'll go down."

"I agree," A.J. said. Like Dwayne, he was also armed. His semi-automatic handgun, however, was a Beretta Model 1922 nine-millimeter. This compact weapon fit A.J.'s smaller hand quite well. Additionally, he had a self-designed telescoping baton made of stainless steel. Its one foot length could be doubled by the quick flick of a spring-loaded release button. The little man practiced constantly with the device, and could wield it fast and effectively against larger opponents. "I'm ready," he announced.

"Let's went," Dwayne said, getting out of the car.

He sauntered across the street as A.J. started the Packard. Just as Dwayne stepped up on the curb, the little bail bondsman eased down on the accelerator, and pulled slowly around to a spot by the backyard.

Dwayne went up the walkway to a small concrete front porch. He checked the screen door and was pleased to note it was not latched. He rang the doorbell and waited. A moment later a plump woman with mousey brown hair opened the door. She looked at the caller and stood somewhat defiantly at the entrance to the house with her arms crossed over her large breasts.

"What the hell do you want, Dwayne?"

"Now, Lucy, is that any way to talk to an old friend?"

Her attitude softened somewhat due to a fondness she had for the handsome detective. "What can I do for you?"

"I'd like to see Johnny."

She gave the caller a look of suspicion. "Just what makes you think he's here?"

That tipped off the private eye that her ex-husband was inside. If not, the reply to his request would have been a simple "He ain't here."

Dwayne quickly pulled open the screen door and charged inside the house, knocking Lucy to one side. He had the sap in his right hand as he rushed through the living room into the kitchen. A bedroom door opened beyond that and Johnny Mason came out. He was ready for a fight. Dwayne obliged by swinging the sap at the man's head.

Johnny was a scrapper whose fighting style was backed by lightning quick reflexes. He ducked the private eye's attack and managed to latch onto the wrist controlling the sap. A quick twist and the weapon sailed across the kitchen, smashing into some dishes and cups on a shelf, sending shattered shards of glass flying. Duane threw a left hook at the exact moment that Johnny shot a straight left punch. Both blows connected simultaneously, causing the two combatants to stagger sideways in opposite directions.

At that point Johnny figured a retreat was in order, and he spun around toward the back door. Dwayne was shook up by the blow to his jaw, and it took him a couple of beats to recover. As he rushed after the bail jumper he failed to notice that Lucy had appeared on the scene with a baseball bat. Luckily, by the time she swung it at Dwayne's head, he had just taken two quick steps at the beginning of his pursuit and the Louisville Slugger bounced off a door jamb.

Johnny Mason almost knocked the backdoor off its hinges as he stormed through it. He leaped across the small stoop and hit the lawn just in time to have A.J. Kessler confront him with the fully extended baton.

Johnny bellowed, "Get the hell out of my way, A.J.!"

The little man charged with the heavy flexible weapon, and Johnny scampered to one side. A.J. pursued him as the fugitive continued to dodge and dart, avoiding the whistling device being whipped at him. But a moment later A.J. scored a hit across Johnny's knees.

"Oow!"

A.J. struck again twice, and his victim went down. The bail bondsman took a quick glance at Dwayne noting that Lucy was running at him with the ball bat raised over her head.

"Duck, Dwayne!"

Dwayne caught sight of the woman just in time to move sideways. The bat missed, and she turned her attention to A.J. who was standing over her former, but still beloved spouse who was groaning piteously on the grass. Lucy launched her attack to save Johnny, but quickly stopped. She stood panting, and dropped the bat to the ground.

"Aw, hell, A.J.," she said. "You're such a cute little sumbitch, I can't hit you."

Dwayne walked up and picked up the bat, flinging it up on the roof of the house. Lucy, knowing her cause was lost, stepped back a couple of paces to indicate she was withdrawing from the fray. Johnny sat rubbing his sore knees, knowing he was too injured to run fast enough for an effective escape.

"I'm taking you in," A.J. said to him. "You jumped bail on me, Johnny, you son of a bitch."

"I'm really sorry about that," Johnny said. "Honest I am, but things just went topsy-turvy. I had to settle a couple of scores down in Tulsa." He pulled up his pant legs and looked at his swollen, battered knees. "Damn, A.J.! You oughta use your pistol more. One of these days you're gonna kill somebody with that goddamn baton."

Dwayne walked over and helped Johnny to his feet, quickly snapping the handcuffs around his wrists. The prisoner leaned on the private eye for support as the bail bondsman preceded them over to the car.

"Hey!" Lucy yelled after them. "Who's gonna pay for my busted dishes?"

"Oh shit!" Dwayne said. "I got to go back in the kitchen and get that sap."

———

BY THE TIME JOHNNY MASON WAS TURNED IN TO the county lockup and all the paperwork was finished, it was evening. A.J. paid off Dwayne in cash for his services. The agreement was that the private investigator would be paid five percent of the bail along with five days at twenty-five bucks a day for tracking down the bail jumper. Dwayne earned a respectable $375 for the job.

He rode with A.J. from the jail to his bail bond office where Dwayne's 1935 Pontiac Coupe was parked. A.J. pulled around to the back of the building and stopped. Dwayne got out, pulling his car keys from his pocket. "Well, be sure and give me a call when you got another job."

"Will do," A.J. said, jumping down from the seat. "Thanks for your help."

"Anytime," Dwayne said. He checked his watch. "I got to roll. See ya."

Normally, Dwayne ate at the Jayhawker Restaurant on West Douglas in downtown Wichita where his sweetheart Donna Sue Connors worked as a waitress. The Jayhawker was really more of a diner than a regular restaurant with tables and booths. The establishment's business was heaviest in the mornings and at noon when downtown workers dropped in for breakfasts and lunches. Since most went home around five p.m., the eatery closed anytime between four and six, depending on how many customers were in the place. Because the bail bond caper had finished so late, Dwayne had to go to the Continental Grill farther down on Douglas to grab a bite of supper.

Donna Sue was attending night school to prepare herself for a high school diplomacy examination. She went to class on Monday, Wednesday and Friday from seven p.m. to ten p.m. The school was within walking distance of the restaurant, so after work she went there by herself. But it was a lot farther back to her apartment, and Dwayne always picked her up to drive her home. It wasn't safe for a woman to be traipsing about the streets that late. There was a dearth of people out at that hour in the area near the Big Arkansas River, and a few good-for-nothings were always lurking in the shadows.

After eating his supper, Dwayne still had a couple of hours to kill, so he drove over to East Douglas to amuse himself at some of the penny arcades. Actually Dwayne would have preferred to pass the time in a bar, but the State of Kansas was dry with its own homegrown style of prohibition.

The arcades featured pinball machines and other mechanical games along with short picture shows in viewing apparatuses that cost a nickel. These showed women disrobing; the catch was that to see her continue stripping down, the viewer had to put in another nickel for the next segment. However, these were not very popular with adult males, because the last scene never got her out of her brassiere and panties. High school kids, however, never seemed to get enough of the semi-strip teases.

Dwayne ceased his pinball games at 9:45, and went outside for the drive to the Board of Education building. He found a parking spot in front, and pulled up to the curb to wait. He glanced up at the second floor where the lights glowed in the various classrooms. He shuddered inwardly. Dwayne always disliked school and the culture of education. The untimely death of his father when the old man was run over by a taxi while drunk had resulted in the boy having to drop out of Wichita High School East at the age of sixteen to help his mother out. But even after he came home from the war in Europe in 1946, he never had a desire to go back for a diploma.

Dwayne sat slumped in the coupe's seat, daydreaming, and was shaken back to wakefulness by the sounds of people leaving the building. He watched for Donna Sue, and caught sight of her coming down the steps with her books cradled in her arms. She hurried over to the car and got in.

"How'd it go?" Dwayne asked.

"Not bad," Donna Sue replied. She was curvy and pretty with blond hair and freckles. "In fact, I got some good news. Mr. Goodwin said I was doing so well that he thought I should give the high school equivalency exam another try before I finished the course."

"Well," Dwayne said, remembering that she had failed it on the first go-round. "You was always a fast learner."

"You should say, 'you *were* always a fast learner'," Donna Sue corrected him.

Dwayne chuckled. "I'm getting an education myself since you started going to them classes."

"*Those* classes."

"Yes, ma'am!"

"It doesn't hurt to use good grammar, Dwayne."

"Yes, ma'am!" he repeated.

"I'm surprised at getting straight 'A's'," she said. "I haven't been inside a classroom since my last day of the eighth grade. That was—let me think—almost twenty years ago."

"I always thought it was a shame you had to quit school so early," Dwayne remarked. "At least I lasted until my junior year at East High."

"Yeah," she agreed. "But there wasn't much choice in the matter with my daddy running off and leaving us."

"It was a shame that you got laid off at Boeing when the war ended."

Donna Sue shrugged. "They did that to all us women." She sighed. "I was really earning a big salary, too."

"And back you went to slinging hash at the good ol' Jayhawker Restaurant."

"Yeah," she said. "But if I get that high school diploma I can get into business college. It won't be as much as I made welding on B-17 bombers at Boeing, but it'll pay better than being a waitress." She impulsively turned and glared at him. "I wish you'd stop wasting your money betting on the goddamn horses so I could work as your secretary after I finished."

"Is it bad grammar to swear?" he asked.

"Don't change the subject!"

They rolled westward on West Douglas until reaching North Water Street where her apartment house was located. Dwayne whipped the old Pontiac to the right and went up a couple of blocks. When he pulled to the curb, he cut the lights and the engine. "I wish I could go up with you."

"You know the rules," Donna Sue said. "Mr. and Mrs. Greeley don't allow the girls' boyfriends in the place after ten p.m."

Dwayne peered at the apartment house. The landlord and landlady occupied the right front of the building. "I'll bet the old lady is looking out at us right now."

"Probably," Donna Sue said. She leaned over for a kiss, then opened the door. "Can you give me a ride to the board of education tomorrow afternoon? I want to take that test after the noon rush at the restaurant."

"Sure," he said. "How much is that business college gonna cost?"

"I don't know," she said. "I would imagine so much an hour."

He reached into his inside jacket pocket and pulled out the money A.J. had paid him. He peeled off some bills. "Here's a hunnerd bucks."

"Why thank you, sweetie!" she said. "I don't need it. I'm going to use some of the money I saved up while I was working at Boeing." She paused. "But why don't you go ahead and give it to me. I can hold it for you."

"What's that all about?"

"For a very good reason," she said, getting out of the car. She shut the door, and looked back at him through the open window. "That way you won't throw it away on those goddamn horses!"

"I still say swearing is bad grammar."

"Good night, Dwayne."

CHAPTER 2

It was the morning after the apprehension of Johnny Mason, and Dwayne had just finished off the last of his favorite breakfast—eggs over-easy, link sausage, rye toast and French fried potatoes—at the Jayhawker Restaurant. He got off the stool with his empty cup and went behind the counter for a refill at the coffee urn. After returning to his eating spot, he settled down to slowly sip the strong brew and smoke a Lucky Strike cigarette.

Donna Sue and her waitress partner Maisie Burnett were busy clearing off the dishes left from the last of the breakfast crowd. Arnie Dawkins the fry cook stood in the kitchen door, leaning against the jamb, drinking a glass of ice water to cool down after slaving over the hot grill for a frantic hour and a half.

"We made money this morning," he announced to no one in particular.

"And the tips was good," Maisie said.

Donna Sue fought down a desire to correct her friend's grammar as she stacked the last of the dirty plates and flatware. She glanced over at Dwayne. "So what's on your agenda for today?"

"The only thing I got to do is take you over for that test after lunch," he replied. He glanced through the front window at the OK Barbershop across the street. "And I might wander over to say hello to my friends."

"You mean make some bets," Donna Sue remarked with a frown.

The dishwasher, one of the many who rotated in and out of the restaurant, had just come out of the kitchen to carry the dishes back to his work station. He was a tall, skinny guy from Texas called Slim who had a room at the Salvation Army shelter. "Hey, Dwayne, how's about making one for me? I got ten bucks to put on the number three horse to show in the fourth race at Saratoga."

Dwayne took the money. "Gotcha, pal. Ten bucks on the number three in the fourth at Saratoga. To show."

Even Maisie disapproved of the gambling. "When are you guys gonna wise up? You gotta be so far behind in them bets that you'll never get even."

"All it takes is one big win," Dwayne said.

Donna Sue smirked. "Well, you're certainly not going to do it with a bunch of little bets. Especially when you win at a rate of only one in twenty or thirty times."

"I don't keep records."

"Maybe you should," Donna Sue suggested. "It'd probably wise you up to all your losses."

"Could be," Dwayne allowed. He took a last gulp of coffee, and ground out his cigarette in a nearby ashtray. He got to his feet, picking up his copy of the *Racing Form*. "Nothing ventured, nothing gained. See you folks later."

He left the restaurant and jaywalked directly across Douglas to the barbershop. His late father had been employed in the establishment at the time of his death, and the owner Ernie Bascombe let Dwayne hang out in the place and even take phone calls when he was behind in his rent and locked out of his office. When Dwayne walked in, Ernie looked up from cutting hair in the first chair. "Hey, Dwayne," he said. "How's it going this morning?"

"I'm feeling lucky," Dwayne said.

"Feeling lucky is a bad sign," Ernie opined, lathering up the back of his customer's neck for a shave. It was common knowledge in Wichita that bookies operated in the barbershop, but the cops left the place alone because many of the clientele were influential locals; a couple were even well known at city hall and the courthouse.

Dwayne continued toward the back of the shop where two bookies by the names of Longshot Jackson and Ollie Krask conducted their business through a couple of telephones. There was also a short wave radio where race results from all over the country could be picked up.

Longshot, a dapper guy who dressed zoot suit style and sported a pencil thin moustache, looked up at Dwayne as he approached. "How's it going?"

"Pretty good," he replied, and nodded a greeting to Ollie. "I want to put fifty bucks on the nose for the number two horse in the fifth at Santa Anita. And Slim across the street wants ten bucks to show at Saratoga. Number three in the fourth."

Ollie, an extremely corpulent man who was munching on an O Henry candy bar, chuckled from his special wide, reinforced chair. "You figger California's lucky for you today, huh, Dwayne?"

"Yeah," Dwayne replied. "And unlucky for bookies."

"Now that's mean, Dwayne," Longshot said. "You know how tickled I am when you win."

"Uh huh," Dwayne said. "I recall how you roll around on the floor and howl with glee."

Ernie Bascombe's voice sounded over the other noise in the shop. "Dwayne! You got a phone call."

Dwayne handed the money for the two wagers to Longshot, then hurried up to the front. He picked up the receiver. "Yeah?"

"Dwayne, this is A.J. I tried your office but no answer. So I figgered you to be at the OK."

"You figgered right," Dwayne said. "What's going on?"

"I got another job for you," A.J. said. "And it might take some time and trouble. I thought this one was gonna be easy, but it's turned itself upside down."

"I'm on my way." He hung up the phone, glancing back at Longshot Jackson. "Have my winnings ready for me when I get back."

"Sure!" Longshot said. "I'll order a Wells Fargo armored truck."

———

A.J. KESSLER BAIL BONDS WAS A CEMENT BLOCK building down on Main Street a little south of the police station and jail. Dwayne drove around to the rear to park beside A.J.'s Packard. He walked to the front, entering where the diminutive bail bondsman's young secretary Jill Stuart kept her desk. She had recently graduated from Wichita High School North, and the job in the bail bond office was her first.

"Hi, ya," Dwayne said. He looked around. "Where's A.J.?"

"He's in his private office," she replied. Then, in a lower voice, she added, "And he's in a bad mood."

"That could just be the pressures from running his own business," Dwayne remarked with a grin. "He's gotta figger out how to spend all that money." He strode over to the door and knocked, then stepped inside. "What the hell's going on, A.J.?"

"Sit down," A.J. said. "There's a guy you got to find for me. I got the word he's still in town, but nobody knows where. It's a nothing case about one lousy bad check, so I don't see what his motives are for laying low. And to top it off, his lawyer has already made a deal with the D.A. for him to go on probation for a year."

"It sounds like he don't have a record."

"He don't," A.J. replied. "All he's got to do is cough up twenty bucks to cover the bad paper."

"What mouthpiece are we talking about here?" Dwayne asked.

"Carl Banter," A.J. answered. "He should be some help...well, a little help at least."

"I know him," Dwayne said. "Who's the jumper?"

"Fritz Harrigan," A.J. replied. "Here's his mug shot."

Dwayne took the police photo, and his eyebrows raised. "I know this guy. I went to Willard Elementary with him. Also Roosevelt and East High." He thought a moment. "That'd be back from 'twenty-six to 'thirty-six. Ten years."

"What do you know about him?"

"A nice little guy," Dwayne said. "Very artistic. He used to draw pitchers that was put up in the liberry and the halls. He made all the 'Beat North' posters when we played those bastard Redskins."

"Okay," A.J. said. "I think he went out of town for awhile during the war. He'd always been kind of sickly, so evidently he was 4-F and didn't get called into the Army."

"Does he still have family here in Wichita?"

A.J. nodded. "I understand his mother is alive. She's got a home on Poplar just north of Lincoln."

"I know the place," Dwayne said. "It's only a block from my old house on Green Street."

"Were you guys playmates as kids?"

"Not really," Dwayne said. "Now and then we'd walk home together in grade school, but we drifted apart in junior high and high school. Sometimes bigger guys picked on him 'cause he was kind of odd. I stepped in when I could to put a stop to the bullying. Fritz was quiet and smart." He chuckled. "And I was loud and dumb."

"You ain't all that dumb, pal," A.J. said sincerely. "Go get the fucker. Same deal as always. Twenty-five bucks a day and five percent of the bail." He shrugged apologetically. "It's five hunnerd dollars, so mathematically you'd get twenty-five, but we agreed your minimum would be fifty bucks."

"You don't have to remind me, Honest John," Dwayne said with a wink. "That ain't a lot of money for you to be worrying about."

"The dough is my second concern," A.J. pointed out. "A bail bondsman's got to pertect his reputation. Otherwise the court can get reluctant to let him post bail."

"Understood," Dwayne said. "I'm heading out."

He left the building, after giving Jill a wave. The girl watched him leave with a sweet pain in her heart. She harbored fantasies about the handsome P.I. breaking up with his girlfriend then asking her out.

———

CARL BANTER, ATTORNEY-AT-LAW, HAD HIS office in the Central Building. It was located at Main and Douglas, about three blocks north of A.J.'s place of business. Dwayne found a parking place across the street, and broke the jaywalking ordinance for the second time that morning, going through the front entrance to the elevators. When he arrived on the fifth floor, he went down to the office he sought and opened the door without rapping on the frosted glass. The lawyer's secretary looked up at his entrance, and treated Dwayne to a pleasant smile.

"Well, Dwayne Wheeler!" she exclaimed. "Our hero who saved us from a gang of Kansas City criminals!"

"Hi, Judy," he said. "I can take all that hero stuff and a nickel and get a cup of coffee."

Judy Miller was an ash blonde with bright blue eyes. As an attractive divorcee with exposure to some of the wealthiest men in the city, she attended many local social events on the arms of various posh admirers. "I saw your picture in the *Eagle*," she said. "You looked like a hard-boiled private eye."

"I'm soft-boiled actually," Dwayne said. "Can I see Carl without an appointment? It's about Fritz Harrigan."

"Oh!" she said. "In that case he'll be glad to talk to you." She pressed down the transmit lever on the intercom. "Carl, Dwayne Wheeler is out here. He wants to talk to you about Fritz Harrigan."

In less than a beat, the door to the inner office was flung open. "Hey, Dwayne. Get in here, pronto."

Dwayne nodded his thanks to Judy, then walked past Banter into his bailiwick. The lawyer was dressed in a western style suit and cowboy boots. An expensive blocked Stetson hat was hanging on his coat rack. "Sit down, Dwayne," he invited as he went around behind the desk.

"A.J. Kessler has hired me to track down Fritz," Dwayne said. "I thought you might have some info on the guy to start me off in the right direction."

"I gotta tell you something," Banter said. "I can't for the life of me figure out what the kid is up to. He wrote a bad check for a lousy twenty bucks. First offense. I didn't have a goddamn bit of trouble making a deal with the D.A. He'd see that Fritz got nothing but probation if he paid off the bad paper. Wipe the slate clean, y'know? I even offered to loan him the money, but he said he could raise it easily, and would get back to me. Then he goes off and I haven't see hide nor hair of the little pecker head since."

"I went to school with him," Dwayne said. "And I know a little bit about Fritz, but I ain't seen him since before the war. So I don't know who he's hanging around with. I do recall he was an artsy guy."

"Yeah," Banter said. He pointed to a frame print on the wall. "He gave me that picture. It's made from an engraving he'd done. It's numbered and signed."

Dwayne got up and walked over to look at the piece of art. It was an image of an old barn and abandoned farm implements surrounded by weeds. "Man! That's good!"

"Yeah," Banter agreed. "He uses a combination of fine and thick lines spaced out so they appear as different shades of gray from a distance."

Dwayne went back to the chair. "So the charges against him ain't serious, huh?"

"The so-called crime was such a simple unimportant thing," Banter explained. "I figured on wrapping things up in a couple of weeks. Then, when it comes time for him to appear, he doesn't show up. The judge chews my ass out and all I can do is shrug and ask to be let off the case. The judge says 'Hell, no!' and I'm stuck."

"A.J. told me he's staying at his mother's house," Dwayne said. "If he's still living at home he must not be doing too good. That's prob'ly why he wrote the rubber check."

"I wish I could give you more to work with," Banter said. "Maybe his mother can help you."

Dwayne stood up, looking at his watch. "I'll drop by there later. I've got to take my girlfriend over to the Board of Education to take a test to get a high school diploma."

"Is that the cute gal at the Jayhawker?" Banter asked.

"The same."

"Sometimes I go over there for a cup of coffee and piece of pie after I have my hair cut at the OK Barbershop."

"And make a bet on the ponies, right, Carl?"

"Why Dwayne Wheeler!" Banter exclaimed with a laugh. "You know that's against the law."

"If you ever get arrested, give me a call," Dwayne said. "I'll try to find you a good lawyer."

"Do you think you can find one in Wichita?" Banter asked.

Dwayne laughed and waved a goodbye. He left the office and went out past Judy's desk. "It seems all I've been doing all day is waving bye-bye to secretaries."

"Come and see me anytime," Judy said with a wink.

"I ain't got the dough for an expensive date like you," Dwayne said.

"If you ever do, give me a call," Judy invited. "You'll find me worth it."

"Be still my heart!" Dwayne said with a quick intake of breath.

———

DWAYNE WHEELER WAS A STICKLER FOR HABIT when it came to his meals. He had a favorite breakfast, and for lunch he always insisted on a grilled cheese sandwich, Orange Crush soda pop, and—of course—French-fried potatoes. Supper could be anything as long as French-fries were included.

Now, after eating and washing the sandwich and fries down with the pop, he relaxed at the counter of the Jayhawker. He glanced over at Donna Sue who was going through the routine of bussing the dishes. The lunch crowd, as usual, started out with a rush and subsided just as quickly leaving the eatery empty as the customers hurried back to their places of employment. Only Dwayne and another guy who was reading a magazine while slowly consuming a piece of pie, were in the place.

When Donna Sue walked past him to get some more dirty dishes, Dwayne asked, "What time do you have to be down there for the test?"

"Two o'clock," Donna Sue replied, stacking the plates. "And I'd like to get there at least fifteen minutes early."

Dwayne lit a Lucky Strike. "That's up to you. I'm just a-sittin' and a-waitin'."

Maisie Burnett, with no customers to take care of, glanced over at her waitress partner. "When're you coming back?"

"Around four or four-thirty."

"Okay," Maisie said. "That won't be so bad. It should be kind of a slow afternoon."

Dwayne got up and walked around the counter, getting himself another Orange Crush from the pop cooler. He found a comfortable spot between the coffee pot and the bread toasters where he could lean up against the wall. "I got all afternoon, but A.J.'s hired me for another bounty hunter job, and I got to give it a lot of my attention starting tomorrow morning."

"What's the bail?" Donna Sue asked.

"Five hunnerd bucks."

"You're not going to make much money on that."

"I might," he said. "The guy's dropped into a pretty deep hole and I get twenty-five bucks a day hunting for him."

"Just remember the rent on your room and office first when you get paid," Donna Sue said. "Then the phone bill."

"Yes, ma'am!" he said, saluting her.

"I'm serious, Dwayne," Donna Sue said. "You're always one step ahead of a complete financial disaster. That's why you couldn't get a loan from the bank to expand your business."

"I'll get there," he said. "Eventually."

Slim the dishwasher came out and began putting the dirty dishes in a deep plastic bussing pan to take them back into the kitchen. "Hey, Dwayne," he said. "My horse placed and paid fifteen bucks."

"Way to go," Dwayne said. "I almost forgot them bets. I'm gonna run over and see Longshot to find out how I did."

"Save yourself the trouble," Slim said. "Your nag was way back in the pack. You should bet 'em to show. That way you get a little bit if they come in the money."

"There ain't much of a thrill in that," Dwayne said. "And a hell of a lot more money can be made betting on a winner."

Donna Sue took off her apron, looking at Dwayne. "It's pretty dead here. Let's go over for the test now."

Dwayne nodded his acquiescence and watched her go to the backroom for her purse. Suddenly he had a feeling of apprehension about a nameless something or other. It was a puzzling sensation, and he didn't know where it had come from. When Donna Sue came back to the counter, the mood subsided.

———

DWAYNE SAT IN THE HALLWAY ON A BENCH across from the testing room in the Board of Education Building. He had been waiting for forty minutes, and was on his fourth cigarette. The first three were stuffed into the sand pot beside him. He was about to put the last one in to join them when Donna Sue came out. She walked over and sat down beside him without saying a word.

"How d'you think you did?" he asked.

She shrugged.

"If you pass, what're you gonna do?"

"I don't want to talk about it," Donna Sue said. "It's bad luck."

"Okay," he said. "How long will it take to get it graded?"

"The man said they can do it quickly," Donna Sue replied. "I was the only one taking it, and they have a form with holes in it to lay over the multiple choices to see if the right one was marked. And the written answers aren't very long. Each one just takes a few moments to read."

Neither said a word for the next twenty minutes. A couple of times Dwayne was tempted to make a remark, but Donna Sue's demeanor was one of serious, almost angry silence, so he kept quiet.

A man stepped out the door into the hallway, and Donna Sue got to her feet, her face solemn and hopeful. He smiled at her, saying, "Miss Connors, you passed. You are now officially a high school graduate. Congratulations."

"Thank you!"

"In fact, you did quite well," he said. "Ninety-seven percent. When your teacher said he wanted you tested, I was hesitant since you hadn't finished the prep course. But it was obvious he knew what he was doing."

Dwayne stood up. "I knew you could do it."

The man said, "A certificate will be mailed to you within the next couple of days. Again, congratulations." He ducked back into the room and closed the door.

Dwayne gave her a hug, knowing how much she wanted to succeed. "Is it all right now to ask what you're gonna do?"

She laughed and kissed him. "I'm going to the Keystone Business College and enroll in their secretarial course. And when I finish that, I'll look for a job in an office somewhere." She nudged him hard. "And if you save your money and move to a nicer building, I'll work for you."

Once more Dwayne experienced that perplexing sense of dread. This time it didn't slip away quite so fast.

CHAPTER 3

D wayne started out the new day from his rooming house on Estelle Avenue at about nine o'clock. He drove south down to Kellogg Street and made a right turn. His destination was the fugitive Fritz Harrigan's boyhood home on Poplar Street, but he turned off one block before it on Green. A left turn took him down that street where he had lived his life up to the age of sixteen. He had only visited the area once since returning from the war, and the experience had been so emotionally painful, that he never wanted to do it again. But now, after eighteen months had passed, he felt a desire for another look. He was beginning to feel that the more confrontation he had with his unhappy past, the sooner he could conquer all those old ghosts that haunted his memories and reveries.

Dwayne slowed to fifteen miles an hour as a mood of sweet sadness swept over him. The sights of the modest homes on the street with unattached garages, the mowed and trimmed lawns, and sidewalks buckling in places brought back memories of his parents and carefree days he had enjoyed as a boy. He and the other neighborhood kids played on that same street, turning the placid environs into an imagined wild west or battlefields as they acted out the parts of cowboys and soldiers. When they got older and developed a collective interest in sports, they went down to the open field at Lincoln and George Washington Boulevard across from the Sundrug Store to play pick-up games of baseball and football. Other kids from Willard Elementary and Roosevelt Junior High joined in the casual athletic events.

When he reached the old house, Dwayne came to a stop and looked over at it. It was the same white color with the green trim, though obviously repainted, and a familiar crack on the front steps up to the porch was still there. The driveway was actually two strips of cement with grass and weeds in between. He remembered his father arriving home in the Model A Ford after a day of cutting hair at the OK Barbershop. He could also vividly recall his mother watering the flowers around the front of the house in the summertime, giving the plants loving care. And there was the backyard where he had played with his toy soldiers in the dirt. It had been a quiet secure life that he took for granted as happy children always do.

All that came to an end when his hard-drinking father staggered in front of a speeding taxi downtown on a Saturday night and was instantly killed. With the breadwinner gone, he and his mother had to turn to Sedgwick County for help, and they ended up being lodged in a small hotel room on East Douglas after the bank foreclosed on their house. To get by she had to work for a pittance in a laundry and they turned to the Salvation Army for handouts. Four years after that, she died from cancer, and Dwayne was left alone. He enlisted in the Army, thinking he might never return to Wichita.

Now Dwayne sped up the old coupe, going to Lincoln for a right turn. Another quick right took him onto Poplar and he went up to the middle of the block, pulling to the curb. Memories stirred here, too, and when he glanced up at the house he sought, Dwayne remembered little Fritz Harrigan who had been his classmate for all his eleven years of schooling.

Dwayne got out of the car and walked up to the porch, crossing it to the front door. He pressed the bell and waited. A lady answered the summons, and as he looked at her, he could recall a younger version beneath the present-day exterior of middle-age.

"Hello, Missus Harrigan. D'you remember me? I'm Dwayne Wheeler."

"Oh, for heaven's sake!" she exclaimed. "It *is* you, Dwayne. Please come in."

She opened the door and he went inside to the living room. She followed after Dwayne, and gestured him to a seat on the sofa. She took an overstuffed chair across from him. "Well, Dwayne, what brings you here?"

"I'm looking for Fritz," he said in a direct way.

Her face clouded over. "I'm afraid I don't know where Fritzie is, Dwayne. I...well, I...I just don't know where he is." Then she paused and said, "I think I saw your picture in the *Eagle*, Dwayne. Something about catching some criminals. You're a policeman, aren't you?"

"I'm a private detective," Dwayne said. "And that's why I'm looking for Fritz, Missus Harrigan. He's skipped his bail and the bail bondsman wants me to find him."

"I believe that is Mr. Kessler," Mrs. Harrigan said. "Or is it Banter?"

"It's Kessler," Dwayne said. "Banter is his lawyer."

"I see."

"I'm not gonna make any trouble for Fritz, Missus

Harrigan," Dwayne assured her. "I hope to help him out by bringing him in."

"I believe you, Dwayne," she said. "I remember how kind you were to Fritzie when you were both youngsters. He told me about the times you kept bigger boys from picking on him."

"I always liked him," Dwayne said. "He was a nice little guy. And right now ever'body is confused about him dropping out of sight. Mr. Banter had arranged for a year of probation after he paid for the check. It was only for twenty dollars. That ain't much at all, and Fritz wasn't in serious trouble."

"I know for certain that Fritzie was going to pay off the check," Mrs. Harrigan said. "He even took his engraving set to a pawn shop. He said he could get more'n fifty dollars for it."

"An engraving set?"

"Yes, Dwayne," Mrs. Harrigan replied. "You see, Fritzie wanted to be an artist and he went to New York City to find a school. He had an art scholarship to Kansas State after he graduated from East High, but he thought he would learn more back east and get his career started faster. Fritzie learned a craft where he engraved pictures in metal, then printed them off. The artists that do that don't make many copies and they sign and number them. After that they destroy the engravings. Fritzie said that made them more valuable."

"I never heard of that," Dwayne said. "Mr. Banter showed me one Fritz gave him. And I remember that Fritz could draw really good."

"He's even better now," Mrs. Harrigan said. She got up and went to the back of the house. When she returned, Mrs. Harrigan had a cardboard box with her. She down beside Dwayne on the sofa, and pulled out some drawings. They were pen-and-ink sketches of still landscapes and people. All were sketched with the same technique as the drawing in Carl Banter's office. At the bottom right of each were neatly printed block letters spelling out **FRITZ HARRIGAN**.

"He's really good," Dwayne said. "Fritz should be able to set himself up pretty nice as an artist."

"Yes," Mrs. Harrigan agreed. "But all I know now is that he took his engraving tools to a pawn shop to get the money, and I haven't seen him since."

"How long ago was that?"

"Two or three weeks, I guess," she said. "And he never came back home or showed up for his court date."

"Do you have the pawn ticket?"

She shook her head. "Fritzie kept it in his wallet. As soon as he got all the charges settled, he was going to get a job somewhere, then earn the money to get his tools back."

"So he gave ever' indication that he was going to court?"

"Yes. He didn't say a thing about running away."

"Can you think of someplace he might go?" Dwayne asked. "Did he have any special friends he would stay with?"

"No," Mrs. Harrigan answered. "He never hung around with other kids like most boys did. I guess you remember that."

Dwayne got to his feet. "D'you know which pawn shop he went to?"

"No," Mrs. Harrigan said. "He never told me."

"Well thanks for the information, Missus Harrigan," Dwayne said. He fished in his jacket pocket for a business card. "If Fritz shows up have him call me. I've written a couple of other numbers on the back where he can reach me. Be sure and tell him I want to help him with this problem. And so does Mr. Banter."

"I'll tell him, Dwayne," she promised. "And thank you for coming by."

————

EAST DOUGLAS AVENUE BETWEEN WASHINGTON Avenue and the Canal was not the classiest neighborhood of Wichita's downtown. It consisted of rundown buildings and businesses that mostly dealt in loans, second hand items and salvage. It was also a place where it was easy to locate pawnshops. For that reason, Dwayne drove into the area and pulled off onto a side street to park. He knew of three nearby pawnbrokers, and thought his best course of action would be to begin his hunt for Fritz Harrigan's engraving tools at those shops.

He went first to where he and his mother used to go to get loans on belongings left over from happier times. This was an old establishment called Wallek's Pawn Shop, and was run by Joe Wallek and his sons. Their front windows were filled with cameras, optical instruments, watches, office machines and other quality items people left off for money. A clothing section occupied one side of the building, and jewelry was behind a locked door toward the rear.

When Dwayne walked in he saw Joe's oldest son Henry behind the counter. Dwayne walked up and they renewed their acquaintance with handshakes. Henry asked the usual question of, "Whatcha got?"

"I got nothing to pawn," Dwayne said. "Actually I'm looking for a set of engraving tools."

"Oh, yeah?" Henry remarked. "I had one for a short time."

"Was it brought in by a little guy?"

"Yeah," Henry answered. "One of them artsy-craftsy types. A sissy, if you know what I mean. It was a nice set. I gave him seventy-five bucks for it."

"You said you had the set for a short time," Dwayne said. "When did he redeem it?"

"He didn't," Henry answered. "Another guy came in with the pawn ticket. He took it with him."

"Another guy, huh? Can you describe him?"

"I'd say he was around six feet, slim build and spoke in a kind of uppity way like he was from back east."

"Did you ask him how he got the ticket?"

Henry shrugged. "He had the ticket, I gave him the tools. Things are that simple in this business. Some customers sell their paper if they can't get enough money to redeem it."

"How was the guy dressed?" Dwayne inquired.

"Pretty snazzy," Henry said. "A nice suit and tie. Expensive hat. Diamond tie tack. Nice watch. I'd've allowed him a hunnerd bucks for the whole set."

"Okay," Dwayne said. "Well, thanks, Henry."

"Hey! I seen your pitcher in the *Eagle*. My dad showed it to me. So you're a gumshoe, huh? Is this one of your cases?"

"Yeah," Dwayne said. He produced a business card. "Give me a call if something comes up. I've written down a couple of another numbers on the back where I can be reached."

"Sure will, Dwayne."

"Say hi to your dad for me."

———

DWAYNE'S NEXT STOP WAS A.J. KESSLER'S BAIL bond business. When he walked in, the little man was in the outer office making arrangements to bail another guy out. Dwayne recognized the man who was going the bail. It was Delmar Watkins who owned a billiard parlor uptown. Dwayne walked up to the pair. "Hi ya, Delmar."

Delmar turned, slightly irritated, then relaxed when he saw who it was. "How're you doing, Dwayne?"

"A.J.'s keeping me busy," Dwayne said. "Who're you bailing out? Anybody I know?"

Delmar shook his head. "It's my youngest kid. He's only sixteen and he tried to steal a car."

"Sorry to hear it."

"Yeah," Delmar said. "My other two boys have never caused me any problems. But this youngest one is turning into a reg'lar hellion."

A.J. looked up. "They're treating him as an adult. He's got a hell of a rap sheet as a juvie, and the judge has had it with him." He finished his paperwork. "Okay, Delmar. I'll meet you at the police court at three. Bring the paperwork on your collateral, and we'll seal the deal with the judge. Your kid will be able to go home with you."

"All right," Delmar said with a sigh. He turned to go, then stopped. "Hey, Dwayne, that was a hell of a write up on you in the *Eagle*. Pitcher and all, huh?"

"Yeah," Dwayne said. "Did you find a bookie to take over where Arlo Merriwell left off?"

"Not yet," Delmar said. "The cops've been keeping an eye on my place since all that trouble with them Kansas City pricks, so I can't get another bookie to move in. Now this shit."

"Well, things will get better soon."

"They sure as hell can't get much worse," Delmar muttered.

After Delmar left the building, A.J. leaned back in his chair. "You got any news for me?"

"The only news I got is no news. Fritz Harrigan has performed what is known as a mysterious disappearance."

"It don't make sense," A.J. commented.

"Well, the bail was only five hunnerd bucks, and if I start looking for him under these circumstances, my fee will eat all that up," Dwayne said. "I'm not gonna charge you nothing for what I done today. All I found out is that Fritz pawned some artist tools and hasn't been seen since."

"Can't you have the pawn shop guy call you when he shows up to get his stuff?"

"Nope," Dwayne said. "Because the goods have already been claimed. And it wasn't Fritz that fetched 'em."

"Jesus!" A.J. exclaimed. "Maybe he got robbed. Fritz might be laying dead someplace after some son of a bitch killed him and stole the ticket."

"According to the pawnbroker, the guy that got the tools was dressed real snazzy in an expensive get-up," Dwayne said. "That ain't hardly the type that would rob somebody of a pawn ticket worth seventy-five bucks."

"Yeah," A.J. agreed. "But I wonder why a guy like that would have any interest in artist brushes and stuff."

"Actually it was an engraving set according to Fritz's mom," Dwayne said. "I don't know what that is exactly."

"Me either," A.J. said. He sighed. "It looks like I'm gonna be out five hunnerd smackers, not to mention the damage to my reputation."

"Yeah," Dwayne said. "I'm gonna go ahead and spend a few days looking for Fritz. My time's free for awhile."

"Let me pay you for today and two more days at least."

"If I find something meaningful, okay?" Dwayne said.

A.J. chuckled. "Sometimes you're too nice a guy for your own good."

"This is kind of a personal thing," Dwayne explained. "After seeing his mom and remembering how I used to keep bigger guys from bullying him, I'd really like to help Fritz." He checked his watch. "I got time for lunch then I'm taking Donna Sue over to a business college. She's gonna enroll in a secretarial course."

"Tired of slinging hash, huh?"

"It seems that way," Dwayne said. "See you later."

"Stay in touch."

Before leaving the office, Dwayne stopped by Jill's desk. "Hey, sweetie, where'd you go to secretarial school?"

"I didn't go to one," the young woman replied, happy to have a chance to talk with the man she was falling in love with. "I took business courses at North High."

"Well, kid, that's the advantage of having an advanced education, I guess."

"I'm not a kid, Dwayne," Jill said with a pout.

He smiled. "Sorry."

Dwayne walked from the office, and Jill sighed, feeling the sweet pain of her crush.

CHAPTER 4

The lights in the basement were all turned off except in one corner where Fritz Harrigan sat on a high stool, hunched over a draftsman's table. He worked slowly and painstakingly engraving a portrait into a small rectangular steel plate. He was a small young man, with unruly black hair and a thin build. Fritz was copying from a mirror that reflected his subject backward; this was necessary in order that when the plate was printed, the items on it would appear the correct way.

Fritz had no idea what time it was or how long he had been confined to work at his craft in the underground room. His watch was mysteriously missing, and he had no knowledge of how he had gotten to that particular location.

He looked up to rest his eyes and stretch, then turned his full attention back to his task.

———

IT ALL BEGAN WHEN HE LEFT THE PAWN SHOP after dropping off his engraving tools. His memory of the event was vague and confused, but he did recall a woman asking him to escort her to her car since the neighborhood was rundown and seedy. She was dressed quite well, but he couldn't recall her features. It seemed they walked down a street, past an alley, and then he was suddenly grabbed from behind. He immediately felt a sharp pricking sensation in his buttocks. After that everything was a blank in his mind, except waking up on a bed in this same basement. He was surprised to find his pawned tool set beside him, and he couldn't remember redeeming it. As his mind slowly cleared he became aware of a man sitting in a chair next to him.

"How is it you are feeling?" the stranger asked in a heavy foreign accent.

Fritz had to struggle to sit up. He gazed at the individual, noting the fellow was large and muscular; just the type of guy who could scare hell out of little Fritzie Harrigan. "Am I in jail?"

The foreigner shook his head. "You are not in jail."

Fritz pointed to his tools. "I pawned these to get money to pay off a bad check. I'm out on bail, and I'm supposed to show up for court."

"You forget all about that," the man said. "Everything it is taken care of." He held out his hand. "My name is Karlis."

"I'm Fritz. What am I doing here?"

"You are chosen for a secret government project," Karlis replied. "You are to be doing engraving jobs. Because is covert, you must stay here."

"What kind of project are you talking about?"

"I am sorry I cannot be telling you," Karlis replied.

"But when finished is your work, you will be give freedom and much money."

"How much money?" Fritz asked.

"Is also a secret," Karlis said. "But it will be very, very much." He got up from his chair and went to a door. He opened it, hollering, "Lotte!" This was followed by some words in a foreign language. With that done he returned to Fritz's bedside. "You are to be meeting somebody most special. She will be for to make you happy."

"My mother?"

Karlis laughed. "Oh, no! She is not your mother, be believing me!"

"But why should the woman make me happy?"

"Because we are wanting you to like it here."

A few moments later a knock sounded, and Karlis went over to the same door. When he opened it, Fritz noted there was another portal just beyond it. Karlis opened it, and a blonde woman appeared. She walked over to Fritz's bed as Karlis relocked the entrances.

"Hello," the woman said in an alluring voice. "My name is Lotte." She had a curvy sexy body with an attractive but somewhat hard face. Her features were not unlike a tough, sexy bar gal in a detective movie. "I am going to be your special friend while you stay here with us."

"Hello," Fritz said, trying to be subtle as he admired her ample breasts that were well exposed by the low-cut blouse she wore. He also noted that, although she had a foreign accent like the man, she spoke perfect English with all the words in the correct syntax.

Karlis walked up. "We must be leaving you now. There is food in the refrigerator for you to be snacking. Also drink. Make yourself to home. We will return."

Lotte winked at him, then followed after Karlis. They

exited the basement through the double doors, and Fritz got to his feet a bit unsteadily and stood studying the basement. The living quarters were pleasant under the circumstances; there was a comfortable double bed, a bathroom with a shower showing through an open door, an easy chair, and what was obviously a dining area. A game table with a chess set and board was also available for his use. Fritz thought that perhaps it was for him and Lotte to pass the time.

Next, the young artist investigated the refrigerator and found it stocked with pop, cans of Hershey's chocolate syrup, and chopped pecans. He opened the freezer and saw a quart of vanilla ice cream. A wave of dizziness swept over him, and he began to feel slightly unsteady. Fritz went back to lie down on the bed.

It didn't take him long to doze off into a light slumber, and he was awakened by the door being unlocked. He opened his eyes and sat up to see Lotte walking toward him. She smiled and winked. "How are you feeling, Fritz?"

"Kind of shaky," he admitted.

"I am here to make you feel better," Lotte said. "But I think you have a girlfriend or sweetheart?"

"No."

She reached out and patted his cheek. "But I think you like girls."

"Yes. I like girls pretty good, I guess."

Before Fritz went to New York City to study art, he would have been confused by such a question. But he had seen several of his male artist friends show an inordinate amount of affection for each other. He hadn't been fully aware of the implications until he'd walked into the apartment he shared with two of them. Both were naked in bed with their arms around each other.

Fritz repeated, "Yes. I like women and girls better than men."

Lotte asked, "Do you think I am a pretty woman?"

"Well...yes...yes, I do. I think you are very pretty."

"I am so glad, Fritz."

Then without another word, she calmly began undressing. He watched her, unable to believe his eyes. When she was completely naked, she reached down and took his hand, gently pulling him to his feet. Lotte kissed his lips, pushing her tongue teasingly into his mouth as her hands worked buttons and zippers to get him out of his clothes.

Fritz was a virgin with absolutely no experience with the opposite sex. The only naked women he had actually seen were not up close. They were models in some of his art classes, standing on daises at the front of the room.

At that time in the basement, he was timid as Lotte began the procedure, but his initial shyness was quickly overtaken by carnal desire. Then she pushed him back on the bed, and joined him. For the first time in his life Fritz had a woman's body available for his pleasure. He could feel and kiss her all he wanted. Lotte's breasts were his to examine to his heart's content, and he kneaded the mounds of warm flesh like soft dough.

After a few minutes, she pulled him into position. Pure instinct guided the young man as he began his first experience with sexual intercourse. He humped away until he finished, going so limp he almost collapsed on top of her.

Lotte kissed him again before getting off the bed. She dressed rather quickly and blew him another kiss before going to the door and knocking. He presumed it was Karlis who opened it, and when it closed he sat still for a moment, his mind reliving the wonderful experience.

Obviously this captivity or whatever it could be called wasn't going to be too bad.

An undeterminable amount of time passed and once more the door opened. Fritz had dressed, but he was ready to take his clothes off again. Unfortunately it was not Lotte; the visitor was Karlis. He had a piece of paper with him and a packet. He handed it to Fritz. "Take a look at this."

Fritz studied the small sheet. It was tan colored and six by three inches in size. Green and red printing was on it that consisted of complicated scroll designs, numbers and words in a foreign language. He turned it over and saw almost the same thing with the exception of a man's portrait in an oval wreath in the middle of the motif. The man was Adolf Hitler.

"What in the world is this?" Fritz asked. "Is it some kind of money?"

"You do not worry," Karlis said. "Maybe it is money or stock certificate or something else." He handed him the packet. "These are steel plates. You take tools and copy what is on this paper onto the steel plates."

"You mean this is to be printed?"

"Yes."

"There are three colors," Fritz explained. "That means I must make a separate plate for each color. And they must register."

"You can do this, I am told."

"Yes," Fritz said proudly. "I am very good at this craft."

"Each plate will have different numbers," Karlis explained. "You are making one, five, twenty-five, fifty and one hundred. Are you understanding?"

"Yes," Fritz answered. "But what about the serial numbers in the box?"

"Not for you to worry."

Fritz knew that meant an automatic numbering machine would be used. "This would be easier if I had a small mirror to look at the model backward. It has to be reversed for the plate or it won't print correctly."

"I get you mirror," Karlis said. He pointed to the stool and draftsman's table in one corner. "There you work."

That was how Fritz learned what he would be doing. Shortly after he began the work he discovered that he would not be given a lot of supervision. He would work at the task until his eyes grew tired, then he could stop and rest. Anytime that Karlis appeared when he was relaxing, nothing was said.

A routine began in which he worked, and food was brought to him at what seemed to be regular hours. He was surprised to find that the meals were his favorite dishes, and he couldn't figure out how his hosts or captors or whatever they were, knew about those preferences.

Lotte continued her visits at various times. Those moments of ecstasy were worth dying for as far as the horny young man was concerned. Fritz was consumed with curiosity about this delightful creature, but any inquiries outside of her name were met with silence and a wiggling of a finger indicating he was not to ask questions.

Aside from Lotte, his only other human contact remained Karlis who brought him food and would check in on him from time to time. The man obviously appreciated Fritz's engraving skills, and gave him what appeared to be sincere compliments and praise. Karlis seemed to know this was exacting work, demanding the utmost in concentration and dedication. If Fritz were truly upset or frightened, there was no way he would be able to perform the tasks they demanded of him.

———

NOW, WORKING ON THE PORTRAIT'S FACE, FRITZ cut into the plate with the graver tool, skillfully leaving hair-thin lines exposed on which the ink would adhere during the printing process. His copying was exact and accurate, and the final result of this plate would show the same shadowing as the original. He guessed he had probably been in the basement ten days or so, basing this estimate on the amount of work he had completed so far.

The basement door opened, and Fritz took the jeweler's glass from his eye. He had already noticed that this door was an inner one, and another, located some twelve feet away, was an outer one. By locking each in its turn, there was no way the prisoner—if that's what he was—would be able to rush past Karlis or Lotte and get out the other side. This time the visitor was Karlis, and he carried a tray.

"It is time for to eat," Karlis announced. "And it is good food I am bringing to you. Is everything you are liking. You have fried chicken, and the potatoes mashed, and gravy and green beans. For to drink there is cold tea with ice and much sugar. And a red apple. Also there is bread and butter. Cherry pie there is also."

Fritz slid off the stool. "How'd you know what I like to eat best?"

"You talked to us in your sleep. So you do not remember."

"That's strange," Fritz commented.

"Is not for you to worry."

Fritz noticed the repasts he was getting were plentiful and healthful, giving him strong indication that they wanted him hale and hearty. He had gotten to the point he looked forward to those meals, but not as much as he did Lotte.

Fritz walked over to the dining table, settling down and pulling the cloth off the tray. The chicken, consisting of a thigh, breast and drumstick, was fried golden and crispy. He picked up the thigh and took a bite; it was delicious. He wondered who did the cooking. The cook certainly knew his or her way around a kitchen. Perhaps it was brought in from someplace else, but Karlis and Lotte didn't seem to be the types who would want to have much to do with a catering service.

———

It was Saturday afternoon and Dwayne leaned against his old Pontiac coupe where it was parked at the curb. He was in front of the Keystone Business College on North Broadway, waiting for Donna Sue to come out of her secretarial class. The neighborhood was a combination of residences and businesses where downtown grudgingly gave way to homes and apartment houses.

This was her first day of the twenty hours of instruction that would earn her a diploma from the school. When she finished the course, she would be proficient in skills such as filing systems, correspondence, billing, telephone courtesy and other procedures, including how to operate a switchboard and perform as a receptionist. If she desired to advance her skills further, there was a much longer and more complicated course that taught the Gregg shorthand system.

She had enrolled in a special Saturday afternoon class designed for young women who had full time employment elsewhere. The only prerequisites were a high school diploma and a typing certificate of at least forty words a minute.

She learned her classmates were mostly salesgirls and typists who wanted better jobs. In her opinion some of the students were a bit on the ditsy side, but Donna Sue thought she might have formed that opinion because she was some ten years older than they.

Dwayne, standing impatiently outside, smoked incessantly, almost nervously as he inhaled and exhaled rapidly. He checked his watch, noting it was five minutes to five, almost the time for the four-hour session of instruction to come to an end. The secretaries-to-be began leaving the building ten minutes later. They came out carrying books and notepads, and either scampered toward cars waiting for them, or hurried to the bus stop at the end of the street. When Donna Sue appeared, Dwayne waved at her. She waved back and walked rapidly to the car.

"How'd it go?" he asked, opening the passenger door for her.

"Pretty good," she said getting into the coupe.

Dwayne went around to the other side. He settled behind the wheel and went through the chore of starting the car's stubborn engine. This required a careful manipulation of the manual choke in coordination with pressure on the floor starter. After a whining grind that lasted five full seconds, the motor coughed and caught to settle into a rough putt-putt sound. Dwayne put the automobile into gear and pulled away from the curb to head south on Broadway.

"Did you learn much?" he asked.

"Well, we had an hour for enrollment and getting our books. But the last three were interesting. We began with filing systems."

"What's the big deal?" he asked. "You put folders in a file drawer by alphabet, right?"

"In most cases," she said. "But if there are a lot of categories, each one has a number. For example, if I was a secretary at a construction company, each project would be given a numerical identification. Then everything that had to do with the work would be filed numerically and alphabetically."

"I see."

"If I worked for a finance company, I would use a different system."

"Yeah."

Donna Sue could tell he wasn't really interested, so she fell into silence. After a couple of minutes, she said, "Dwayne, you got to stop betting on those damn horses."

He gave her a glance of irritated surprise, then turned his attention back to the street.

"You must stop wasting money," she counseled. "If you don't start saving and planning, you'll spend the rest of your life in that crummy office. And you won't be able to hire a secretary."

"Meaning you, right?" he asked with a grin.

"Do you want me to work for you or not?"

"Sure, honey. Just like my hero Sam Spade."

"Forget that silly radio program!" she snapped. "If you're going to be a businessman, then be one! A *real* one."

"Where do you want to go tonight?" he asked, desperately wanting to change the subject. "How about Western Danceland."

"I have some things to do," she said. "We have a reading assignment and they're giving us a test on it in the next class."

"That's a whole week away," he protested.

"Dwayne," she said in a strained voice. "What I'm doing is something I take very seriously. I want that diploma and I want to get a job as a secretary so I can stop waiting on idiots across the counter in the Jayhawker."

Dwayne felt a surge of anxiety like he had at the restaurant before giving her a ride to take the high school equivalency test. He knew that it wouldn't be long before his relationship with Donna Sue went through a big change. It was almost like she was on a one-way trip and each day was moving farther away from him.

"What do you say to a quick bite to eat at the Continental Grill?"

"As long as it's quick," she replied.

He took a deep breath and let it out slowly, thinking, *This ain't good.*

CHAPTER 5

When Dwayne and Donna Sue reached her apartment house after leaving the Continental Grill, he went upstairs with her. If she preferred doing her reading assignment to going out on a Saturday night date, he at least hoped she would be willing to have sex, even if it was only a quickie.

But when he made his moves, she stepped away from him. "Honey," she said in a weary voice, "I'm just not in the mood right now. I have a lot on my mind with this secretarial course, and...well, I don't want to."

Once more the melancholy mood emerged and he felt more sadness than anger. At first he didn't know what to say, but after a moment he muttered. "Okay. I'll call you later."

When he left the apartment he had the distinct feeling that she was glad to see him go. He drove away in a gloomy mood, experiencing a peculiar sort of loneliness. For the first time in about a year it appeared he would be spending Saturday evening alone. He drove back to his rooming house, and went upstairs to his small living space.

When he walked in, he took off his jacket and draped it across the back of the only chair in the room. He went over to the sink and turned on the faucet, filling a water glass. As he drank, Dwayne glanced at his reflection in the mirror. A sad face gazed back at him; his features showing the frustration of having the person he cared for the most in the world give him the cold shoulder.

"Fuck it!"

He set the glass down on the sink, went over to the chair, grabbed his jacket, and left the room.

———

ELMER PETTIBONE, WICHITA'S PREMIER bootlegger and a good friend of Dwayne's, had a small nightclub just beyond the northern city limits on Arkansas Avenue. The name of the place was the Road-house, and was well known to a select clientele. Most of these people bought their liquor from Elmer, and were at the top of Wichita's social register. The building was set off far enough from the road to guarantee privacy to those visiting the place, and there was ample parking. Now that new cars were being manufactured since the war ended, many of those vehicles in the lot that evening were the latest models.

No neon sign blazed with the name of the nightspot nor was there any other identification posted on the building. A couple of burly doormen named Jack Wallace and Denny Tarball manned the front entrance, and they knew all the members by sight. If a stranger showed up, they checked him out carefully, inquiring about any connection with a regular. If a refusal of entry was necessary, which happened about ninety-nine percent of the time; it was issued in a polite, but resolute sort of way. Any person who was unwise enough to protest the rejection was immediately grabbed and frog-marched from the door to his car.

————

DWAYNE WHEELER PULLED OFF ARKANSAS Avenue into the Roadhouse parking lot. Although he wasn't a member of the local society's *crème-de-la-crème*, he was given access to the club since he had served a good number of Wichita's first citizens in his business as a private investigator. The bootlegger owner Pettibone was also grateful to the shamus for thwarting the takeover of Wichita's underworld by Kansas City thugs.

After finding a spot for his car, Dwayne went up to the door and smiled a greeting at the two guardians of the gate. "Hey, guys."

"How you doing, Dwayne?" Jack said. "We ain't seen you for awhile." He was the spokesman for the duo, and Denny nodded with a slight grin.

"Oh, I been around," Dwayne said.

"We seen your pitcher in the paper," Jack said. "You're a hero, huh?"

"That shit don't last long."

"Well, it must've been good for your business," Jack opined.

"Not much really," Dwayne replied. "Well, I'll see you guys later."

"Enjoy your evening," Jack said.

Dwayne went through the door without looking around for acquaintances. A small jazz combo made up of four black men was playing in one corner of the club. The musicians sported a string bass, guitar, saxophone and piano. The small dance floor was semi-crowded, and the music was excellent. The combo also provided a pleasant background for quiet conversation and drinking.

The main part of the room was filled with tables, complete with tablecloths and centerpieces, and the serving staff were tastefully dressed and hired for their well-mannered behavior and distinguished appearances. Although no meals were served, snacks were available from the small grill in the kitchen located in the back. A bar was located along one wall, and that was Dwayne's destination. He found an empty stool and settled down. Harry Land the bartender walked up with his hand extended. "Hi ya, Dwayne. Long time no see. Where's Donna Sue?"

"She's studying," he explained, shaking hands. "She got tired of the Jayhawker and is going to secretary school."

"How about that?" Harry remarked. "What's your pleasure?"

"Soda water," Dwayne replied, pulling a pint bottle of Jack Daniels from his inside jacket pocket. After Harry provided the set-up, Dwayne paid the three dollar price which was triple the regular charge in other clubs. He then poured a generous shot of liquor into the mix. This was the way one imbibed under the restrictions of Kansas prohibition.

"I seen that story on you in the *Eagle*."

"That's all over and done with now," Dwayne said.

"Yeah," Harry agreed. "Fame don't last, does it? By the way, I hear tell that there's a big movement to make Kansas wet. It might happen next year."

"That's gonna be bad news for bootleggers like Elmer," Dwayne commented.

Harry shook his head. "He'll still have the Roadhouse, and it'll prob'ly make more money if we can serve cocktails."

Dwayne grinned. "Then you'll be a real bartender."

"Yeah," Harry agreed with a chuckle. "I better learn how to mix drinks, huh?" He moved down to take care of another customer.

Dwayne settled in by himself, not wanting to talk to anyone, but also not wanting to be completely alone. Being in a crowd seemed better than solitude. He ordered a couple more set-ups, and began to feel a mellow sort of intoxication putting a glow on his mood. The music also soothed his troubled disposition. He began to think that perhaps he had been reading too much into Donna Sue's behavior. After all, she had set some difficult goals for herself.

"Dwayne!"

He turned to see the lawyer Carl Banter standing behind him. "Hi."

"Hi," Banter said. "Say, I'm here with some friends from out of town. How about coming over to our table so I can introduce them to the hero of Wichita?"

Dwayne's first inclination was to refuse, but he thought it might make the evening a bit more interesting. "Sure."

Banter took him by the arm and steered him across the club. Dwayne could see two women and a man at the table. Banter presented Dwayne with a wave of his hand. "Folks, this is a famous private detective who very recently foiled a vicious gang's attempt to take over our fair city. I am pleased to introduce Dwayne Wheeler."

The man stood up. "Dwayne! You son of a bitch!"

Dwayne whipped his eyes to him, then he laughed aloud. "For Chrissake! Pete Van Dyke!"

"Hey," Banter said. "Do you two guys know each other?"

"We were in the Army together for about five years," Van Dyke said. He patted the shoulder of the attractive woman with him. She was a well-dressed, slim brunette with a patrician appearance. "This is my wife, Sybil."

"Hello," she said in a cordial tone of voice.

Banter laughed. "Well, now it's my turn to introduce my spouse. I don't believe she's met Dwayne either."

"Hello, Dwayne," Mrs. Banter said. "I'm Sally. I've heard a lot of good things about you."

"Sit down and join us," Banter said.

"Thanks," Dwayne replied. He glanced at Van Dyke, and memories of military service in Europe swept through his mind. Especially the postwar period.

———

THE DEFEATED NATION OF GERMANY HAD BEEN in disorganized chaos in the first months following the Allies' victory. The soldiers of the once proud German armed forces were behind barbed wire, waiting to be repatriated. Because of the fury and disgust about the concentration camps, these prisoners were held under barbaric conditions. Many lived in open fields without shelter, and were fed sparsely and irregularly.

Meanwhile, displaced persons from all over Europe were either wandering around loose in the cities and countryside, or living in camps set up for them. Many of these were former slave laborers who had been transported from their native soil under Nazi occupation to work in the war factories of the Third Reich. They had toiled under appalling conditions of long hours, short rations and brutal supervision. After being liberated by the arrival of the Allied armies, some wanted to go back home as quickly as possible. Unfortunately, others who came from areas in Eastern Europe now under Soviet control were not sure of their safety if they went back to their homelands. Rumors that the Russians were treating returned deportees as war criminals abounded, causing genuine fear and distress in the lives of those who had been forced to labor in Germany.

And there were the Jewish survivors of the death camps who also had no desire to live among people who had betrayed them. Most were attracted to the various movements dedicated to the desperate goal of establishing a permanent Jewish state in Palestine.

It was also a near lawless time in Germany in which both criminals and desperately impoverished citizens committed whatever acts necessary to sustain their lives. They lived in bombed out buildings, shanties and any other shelter they could find. Thievery was rampant and that included strong-armed robbery. A law of the jungle was in effect with the powerful feeding off the more vulnerable elements of the population in this vacuum between war and peace.

The German Reichmark was almost useless in those days and bartering was the norm in all transactions whether legal or illegal. Desperate women, many whose husbands had either been killed in the war or were captured and interned on the Eastern Front, sold their bodies for a few cigarettes or hunks of soap. Most of their customers were from the occupying Allied forces, and the trysts were held in places that offered only the barest of privacy. A prostitute with a client would seek out a suitable area within a ruined building or behind some rubble, then raise her skirt to provide the pleasure the soldier wanted.

Sergeant Dwayne Wheeler and Lieutenant Peter Van Dyke served in a U.S. Army military police battalion in those frenzied days. Van Dyke was the executive officer of the company in which Dwayne was assigned as an investigative noncommissioned officer. Like the MPs of the British, French and Soviet armies, the Americans knew almost unlimited power and authority over the suffering civilians.

Van Dyke was from a New York City banking family that had lost everything in the depression. He had been a fourteen-year-old boy attending an exclusive prep school in Rhode Island when the crash of 1929 occurred. All his short life he had known luxury and privilege, having been born into an old New York family that were direct descendants from a line of original Dutch settlers. Although the Van Dykes had eventually become more English as generations of intermarriage with Anglo-Saxon families occurred, they were proud of those old ancestors from Holland who had been so instrumental in the founding of their city. The loss of the family fortune turned Pete's existence around, wiping away the good life for him.

The lad was forced to go home from prep school, not to the mansion that had been his residence since infancy, but to a small apartment in Queens. His parents sold their jewelry and other possessions bit by bit to keep a roof over their heads and the plainest of food on the table. The boy completed his education in a public high school in 1933. Rather than head for Yale or Harvard as he was originally destined, he had to find a job to help support the family. He spent as much time unemployed as he did working, going from job to job as a shoe salesman, waiter, taxi driver, Western Union deliveryman and service station attendant. This life of uncertain employment and low wages came to an end when the peacetime draft of 1940 was instituted. At age twenty-five the young bachelor was conscripted into the Army.

This unexpected military service provided Peter Van Dyke with a chance to move up into a gentleman's status. He applied for and was accepted into Officer's Candidate School, going through an accelerated ninety-day program that provided officers for the rapidly expanding armed forces. When he was commissioned a second lieutenant of the Military Police Corps, he was assigned to Fort Benning, Georgia to the same battalion in which young Private First Class Dwayne Wheeler from Wichita, Kansas was serving.

The two did not get to know each other very well at first due to the gap between officers and enlisted men. However, once the fighting war started and they were sent to the European Theater of Operations, the lieutenant and now corporal worked together in their battalion's activities. This included traffic control, guarding military installations, and escorting German prisoners of war to POW camps. They also worked for Army Intelligence and were sent into areas of recent fighting to search the corpses of the enemy dead for documents and other items needed by the G-2 Staff. During this activity, Pete and Dwayne began to form a friendship based on mutual respect. Dwayne admired the aristocratic side of the officer who had known privilege and money that he could only imagine. Pete, for his part, took note of how intelligent and quick-witted Corporal Wheeler was. In fact, thanks to Pete's enthusiastic recommendation to their commanding officer, Dwayne was eventually promoted to the rank of staff sergeant.

This friendship deepened after the war during the occupation of Germany. Dwayne was among several noncommissioned officers chosen to go to a special investigative course conducted by the area provost marshal. When their company's duties turned to crime solving, Pete worked with Dwayne and other investigators as detectives in everything from simple theft to murders, assaults, and rapes. And Lieutenant Van Dyke took special note of Dwayne's growing skills in investigations and interrogations of suspects.

Then the black market appeared in their activities.

This was a shadowy world of illicit, self-sufficient commercial enterprises that dealt in unlawful sales of property that the seller had purchased at a cheap price or had stolen. These dealers came from all factions of those people living in the German nation, including the occupying governments.

Dwayne was made the lead investigator in this field, and wrote up detailed reports on his findings and arrests. All this paperwork went directly to Pete, who perused it carefully before passing it up to higher echelons. After several weeks of this activity, Pete's innate talent with finances inherited from his forebears kicked in. He quickly devised a way to infiltrate the black market and make a good deal of money. And he turned to Staff Sergeant Dwayne Wheeler as a partner. He was well aware of the sergeant's poverty-stricken boyhood and the struggles he had endured as an adolescent, and thought him a suitable candidate to participate in illegal activities that would pay off handsomely.

Pete approached the Wichitan subtly, explaining he had figured out exactly how the black market worked, and the methods used to get merchandise to sell to make big profits. He also explained how money made could be sent to bank accounts in Switzerland to be squirreled away for future use. As Pete noticed a growing interest in his younger friend, he gradually edged from theory to practical application. Dwayne agreed to work with him.

Dwayne's investigations revealed names of players, and after they were arrested, the bad guys were brought in for "interrogation" in Pete's office. But rather than seek convictions, the officer made proposals. This practice cast a net that brought in more and more contacts, until Dwayne and Pete were dealing in numerous areas of the racket. The money rolled in, but while Pete was hiding his away in Switzerland, Dwayne spent his profits crazily, renting him and his German girlfriend a large expensive apartment, purchasing a car, and going partying like there was no tomorrow.

It may have taken them six months, but the U.S. Army's Criminal Investigation Division eventually became aware of the sergeant's revelry and wild squandering. A clandestine investigation was launched and the arrest made, and Staff Sergeant Dwayne Wheeler was confined in the nearest military stockade with some very serious felony charges levied against him. It looked like he would soon be going back to Kansas, but not Wichita; it would be to the Federal Penitentiary at Leavenworth.

Then irony entered the picture when the battalion commanding officer appointed First Lieutenant Peter Van Dyke as Dwayne's defense counsel. Pete knew that if Dwayne went down, he would eventually be dragged into the depths of imprisonment with him. It was time for some clever strategy to be applied, and Pete was just the guy who knew what to do.

The lieutenant went to the commanding general of their area to discuss the case. He pointed out that he was sure that the accused was guilty as charged, and that the best he could do for him would be to beg for mercy. However, there was something else to be considered; and that was that the publicity of an American military policeman participating in the black market would look bad all around. Their French and British Allies would be infuriated. And if a court-martial was convened, Sergeant Wheeler would be naming names, and that would include some high-up members of the military government who would also be implicated in the crimes. The American public's reaction to the situation would be one of outrage.

The general was not impressed. "Well, they *should* be outraged! They *should* be calling for heads to roll!"

"Oh, I agree, sir," Pete told him. "But unfortunately that would include your own. You see, sir—as our colleagues in the Navy say—all this happened on your watch. You are the commander of this area. Thus you have a great deal of responsibility for what occurred."

"Shit!" exclaimed the general.

He dismissed Pete and called in his adjutant and judge-advocate. They spent several hours discussing the situation with all its implications before reaching a logical conclusion. The result was that Staff Sergeant Dwayne Wheeler was brought from the stockade to area headquarters in the company of his counsel Lieutenant Van Dyke. Pete presented the prisoner to the three ranking officers. The judge-advocate, a lawyer in civilian life, addressed Dwayne in a diplomatic, sensitive way.

"See here, Sergeant," he said. "You've served your country honorably except for this black market affair. We hate for you to pay a terrible price after all you've done for the cause of freedom. The commanding general cannot see how justice would be served if you spent decades in the penitentiary. So he has decided to provide you with an option. Are you interested?"

Dwayne sensed he was being offered a break, replied with an appreciative, "Yes, sir!"

"Instead of a court-martial and conviction, we're offering you what is called a Discharge for the Convenience of the Government. While not an honorable release, it simply states that the powers-that-be thought it best if you were released from the Army and sent back to civilian life. What do you say?"

Dwayne turned to Van Dyke, who nodded affirmatively to him. The prisoner looked back at the judge-advocate. "I accept, sir."

Dwayne was shipped back to Fort Dix, New Jersey, to a separation center, and there orders were cut giving him a "convenience discharge." He turned in his gear and was given a one-way train ticket to Wichita, Kansas, where he had enlisted in the Army in the first place.

Case closed.

———

Now Dwayne sat at the table in the Roadhouse, idly sipping his drink as Carl Banter told the story about the attempted takeover of Wichita by a gang of racketeers from Kansas City. Although his version was not exactly accurate due to certain facts having been kept from the public, Pete and Sybil Van Dyke were very impressed.

"And it was all wrapped up," Banter said, "when Dwayne solved the murder of a local bookmaker by one of the Wichitans who had joined in with the out-of-town criminals. The fellow rolled over on his confederates, giving the full information on the operations in exchange for a life sentence rather than being hanged."

Pete glanced over at his old army buddy. "Way to go, Dwayne! I see you put your investigative talents and experience to good use since leaving the Army."

"Some good had to come out of that," Dwayne remarked. He pulled out his bottle of whiskey and passed it around. "So what are you up to, Pete?"

"You probably recall that my family was in banking before the war," Pete answered. "During my final days in Europe before being released from the Army, I made some contacts in certain financial circles. After I returned home to New York City, I set up my own business in investments and combined that with export and import activities between the States and Europe. I'm expanding to various parts of the country, and Carl here has agreed to act as my legal representative here in the southern Midwest."

"Good for you," Dwayne said. "If you need a private investigator, give me a ring."

"As a matter of fact, I would like to talk to you about some employment in my organization," Pete said. "Could you meet with me in the coming week? Sybil and I are stopping at the Riverview Hotel. Perhaps you could join us for dinner some evening."

"Sure," Dwayne said. "I'd be happy to."

"Well!" Banter said. "It looks like some new business is starting up here in good ol' Wichita, Kansas." He raised his glass. "A toast to the enterprise."

Glasses were raised, and Pete looked over at Dwayne giving him a wink.

CHAPTER 6

Dwayne Wheeler walked into the lobby of the Riverview Hotel, going straight to the bank of three elevators. One was available and he stepped inside. "Fourth floor."

"Yes, sir," the operator said. He was a tall lanky kid appearing to be in his late teens. He pulled the lever to close the door, then moved the drive handle to the **UP** position. "Hey, you're Dwayne Wheeler, ain't you?"

"Yeah."

"You know Jimmy Thompson, huh?"

"Yeah." Jimmy was the lead bellboy at the Riverview, and his knowledge of Wichita's night life had proven helpful to Dwayne on many occasions.

"Jimmy says he worked with you on that case with them Kansas City pricks."

"That's true," Dwayne replied. "He was a big help."

"Say, if there's ever anything I can do for you, let me know. I'm always available."

"I'll keep that in mind," Dwayne sincerely promised.

A private investigator couldn't have too many informers and snitches.

"Okay, Mr. Wheeler," the kid said. He brought the conveyance to a halt. "Fourth floor."

"Thanks," Dwayne said, stepping out of the elevator.

Dwayne walked down the hallway toward Room 406. He reached it and knocked on the door with three raps. The summons was immediately answered by Pete Van Dyke's wife Sybil.

"Hello, Dwayne," she said. "It's nice to see you again." There was a hint of genuine friendliness in her voice, despite a tone and accent that bespoke of large municipalities back east.

Pete Van Dyke appeared behind his wife. "Right on time as usual, Dwayne. Welcome to our abode even though it is temporary."

"Thanks," Dwayne replied. They had a three-room suite with a view of the Big Arkansas River and West Douglas Avenue. "Pretty swanky!"

"Yeah, we got this room, a bedroom and a small dining area with a refrigerator," Pete said.

"It must be expensive," Dwayne remarked.

"I'm spending investors' money," Pete said with a chuckle. "By the way, I appreciate you giving me the name of that bellboy Jimmy. He's been real attentive and efficient."

"He's a good contact," Dwayne agreed. "He knows his way around, believe me."

"I'll fix us some drinks," Sybil offered. "Jimmy brought us some scotch and vodka. Which do you prefer, Dwayne?"

"A scotch and water for me."

"I'll take scotch on the rocks," Pete said. Sybil already had a vodka tonic that was sitting on the bar. She walked over to tend to the men's requests. Pete spoke to Dwayne. "I've decided to order room service instead of going down to the restaurant. We need a bit of privacy. I hope that's okay with you."

"Sure."

"Here's the menu, choose what looks good to you and I'll call it down," Pete said. "Let's make ourselves comfortable."

Dwayne took the menu and settled on the sofa. As he started to read it, Sybil handed him his drink. After giving Pete's to him, she walked over to an easy chair by the window to settle down with her vodka mix.

Pete joined Dwayne. "I invited you to visit us for more than bringing up recollections about our glorious past."

"You made that clear at the Roadhouse," Dwayne said. "I'm always open to any interesting discussions."

"I'm talking about business of course."

Dwayne laughed. "Now why ain't I surprised?" He noticed that Sybil had pretty much butted out of the picture.

"We participated in some rather unique enterprises there in Germany, didn't we?" Pete remarked. "Unique and illegal, I might add."

"And how would you describe these latest activities that are keeping you busy?"

"Let's just say that I'm taking advantage of certain loopholes that one finds in international finance and commercial laws."

"I got no problems with that," Dwayne said. "As long as reg'lar folks don't get scammed. Big business and government bureaus, on the other hand, are fair game as far as I'm concerned."

"Then you'll approve of this enterprise, believe me."

"I'm a little curious where I might fit in," Dwayne

said. "I don't have a lot of experience in complicated financial stuff."

Pete glanced over at Sybil. "Dwayne spent his money like a drunken soldier over in Germany."

Dwayne laughed out loud. "That's because most of the time I *was* a drunken soldier!"

Pete spoke to his wife with a chuckle. "Our friend Dwayne here was also the ladies' man in Germany. He changed girlfriends as often as most guys change their socks."

"Well, now," Dwayne said, "I did keep that last *fraulein* for six months. But I'll own up to squandering my scratch."

"You may be careless with money, old friend," Pete said, "but you're one of the smartest guys I've ever known. And there's always room for an intelligent associate in a business that requires quick wits and steady thinking."

"You're pretty slick yourself," Dwayne responded. "I'll never forget how you kept me out of Federal prison."

"Dwayne, I kept us *both* out of jail!"

"Well, that sounds like you knew how to handle things," Dwayne said.

Sybil interrupted. "I'm hungry!"

"Okay, darling," Pete said. "I'll call down for room service. Have you studied the menu, Dwayne?"

"Yeah," he said. "The chicken fried steak looks good, but I'd like to have them substitute French-fries for the mashed potatoes."

"What about dessert?" Pete asked.

"Apple pie a la mode."

"You got it," Pete said. "Sybil and I have already scanned the menu and made our choices." He picked up the phone and dialed zero.

A HALF HOUR AFTER THE CALL WENT IN, A bellboy with a rolling table appeared at the suite door. He wheeled the food over by the window, and Pete slipped him a couple of dollars. The guy expressed his gratitude for such an unexpected large tip, then left quickly, and the three settled around the table. Sybil had broiled chicken with a vegetable medley while Pete had ordered a large steak with a baked potato. There were rolls with butter, and ice tea to drink.

Sybil looked at her tea. "I can't believe there is no wine. Even Jimmy couldn't get any."

"Yeah," Dwayne said. "The local bootleggers handle only hard liquor."

"Why is Kansas still dry?" Pete asked. "I don't see the point in it. National prohibition pretty much proved people are going to drink themselves blind no matter what the law says."

"We've got a lot of religious fuddy-duddies here in Kansas who see that blue laws are kept on the books," Dwayne replied. "The righteous bastards give a lot of dough to politicians to keep the status quo. But there's a strong rumor that the state of Kansas is going wet by next year. The radio broadcasts and newspapers are filled with information about it."

"That's good news," Pete remarked.

"Not for my bootlegger buddies," Dwayne stated.

The three turned their attention to the food, and Dwayne's chicken fried steak, French fries and gravy were complimented with a serving of green beans which he ignored completely. After a few minutes of eating, Dwayne stopped chewing long enough to ask, "Just what did you have in mind for me to do, Pete?"

"Okay," Pete said. "Let me explain the set-up without going into a lot of details. In fact, I've found it necessary not to reveal much to *any* of my associates. And I'm afraid that will include you."

"It sounds like the cells in espionage organizations," Dwayne remarked.

"The situation is exactly like that."

"At the Roadhouse you said you were in imports, exports and investments," Dwayne said. "Is there anything you can add to that?"

"Let me say that it is all money and products," Pete said. "Which doesn't really clear the muddy waters for you, does it? But what I need is a smart guy who can act as a courier from time to time. I can promise the pay is good. And if you move up in the organization, it will be better."

"Where does Carl Banter come in?"

"He will be our legal counsel in the American side of the operations," Pete said. "He has only the vaguest idea of what we're doing. And he never asks questions."

"Carl is a smart lawyer."

"That he is," Pete agreed. "And it will be to our direct advantage if we stay away from New York City, Boston and other port cities on the east coast. So we are, in effect, lying low here in Wichita. And one reason I chose this small city instead of a bigger one, is that I remembered this was your hometown. I was planning on looking you up, then you popped up at that nightclub like a genie out of a bottle."

"How long have you been here?"

"Just since Friday," Pete answered. "I had come primarily to meet up with Carl Banter. He was recommended to me by a shipping agent I've used in New York City. The guy is from Wichita and he's related to Carl. We won't bother with his name right now, even though you might know him. And I've asked Carl not to discuss him with anyone."

"Then I won't bring up the subject," Dwayne promised. "So what will I be couriering for you?"

"Various things like documents and money," Pete said. "Your work will all be Stateside for the time being. I already have a European office for operations over there."

Dwayne wiped a French-fry around in the gravy then forked it into his mouth. "Okay, Pete. I'd like to work for you."

"You're hired," Pete said. "But I want to tell you something real serious right now. This situation is very similar to what we had in Germany. And you recall that you got into trouble from flashing your money around. You cannot—I say again—*cannot* do that now. And if you do, we'll end your association with us in the blink of an eye. Understood?"

"Perfectly," Dwayne assured him.

"And, as I've strongly indicated, I also have bigger plans for you than delivering things. You are going to end up making a hell of a lot of money."

Sybil, who was beginning to feel a bit sloshed, smiled and raised her glass. "A toast to the new employee!"

————

FRITZ HARRIGAN, DOWN IN HIS BASEMENT studio, had grown tired of working on the portrait of Adolf Hitler. Too much concentration on one subject in the art of meticulous engraving leads to fatigue, and that means a possible irreparable mistake. He now had taken a break from *der Fuhrer's* features, and turned his attention to the value numbers that were in the upper left and lower right of the bills. The relatively bare plates with only numerals were almost refreshing to the artist after the larger and more complicated portrait, scrolls and wreaths on the crowded front plate.

A dry feeling had built up in his eyes, and Fritz stopped work altogether. He went into the bathroom where a bottle of eye drops was available. He had gotten the medication after making a special request for it from Karlis. Fritz knew that within a few short years he would be needing spectacles, but right now the drops cleared his vision and brought comfort to his eyes enough to only need a jeweler's glass for the more complicated aspects of the work.

He stepped back into the main room and looked longingly at the door. By his reckoning, Lotte should be coming in for a sexual tryst. Without a watch, there was no way he could accurately judge the intervals between their carnal encounters. But he was horny now and his erection was almost constant with unfulfilled desire. She had been timing her visits with an excellent estimate of when he was really hot for her; that meant she should be appearing very soon. However, on this particular occasion there was more than just lust making him anxious to see her. He had a special present for her, and he couldn't wait to see her reaction to it.

Fritz went to the refrigerator and got a bottle of Dr. Pepper. After prying off the cap with an opener, he sat down at the dining table to slowly sip it. The drops in his eyes soothed them greatly and he blinked a few times to get some tears flowing to add to the relief. The soda pop also refreshed him, and he knew he would be ready to get back to the engraving work within a half hour or so.

His thoughts were interrupted by the sound of the outer door opening. He gazed eagerly at the inner one, and he broke into a big grin when Lotte stepped into the basement. Karlis was right behind her, but he closed the door and locked it without entering. Fritz and Lotte walked toward each other, embracing and kissing as they came together. She reached down and felt his erection. "You are ready, eh, Fritz?"

"I sure am," he said. "But there's something I want to do first."

"Before having sex?" she asked with a look of surprise. "Whatever it is, it must be very important to you."

"I have something for you. It's a gift."

"How did you get a gift for me?"

"I didn't get it, I drew it," Fritz said. He walked over to the draftsman table and retrieved a rolled up piece of paper. When he returned to her, he unrolled it revealing a twelve-by-eighteen inch pen-and-ink drawing. "Here. For you. I did it with the extra art materials on the shelf above the drafting table."

Lotte took the illustration and studied it. "What a nice drawing, Fritz. A nude woman...wait...*ach! Mein Gott* It's me! The face on this woman looks exactly like mine."

"Yeah," he said. "Do you like it?"

"Oh, I love it! And you have made me appear so beautiful!"

"You are beautiful, Lotte."

She hugged him hard and kissed him on the cheek. "This is the best gift anybody has ever given me in my whole life!" She carefully laid the picture down on the chess table. "I will get a frame for it, and hang it on the wall."

Now Fritz, with absolutely no timidity, reached out and took her hand. As he led Lotte to his bed, she glanced fondly back at her portrait and smiled.

PETE VAN DYKE WHEELED THE FOOD CART OUT of the suite and into the hall for the hotel staff to retrieve. Before he rejoined Dwayne and Sybil, he went to the bar and mixed fresh drinks for everybody. After passing them out, he sat down on the sofa beside Dwayne. "When can you go to work?"

"Anytime," Dwayne replied. "I'm on a case for a bail bondsman, but it seems to be a lost cause. I can take a break when I want."

"Good!" Pete said. "I'm going to have a packet I need you to take to Chicago in the next week or so. It'll be a train trip."

"That'll be nice," Dwayne said. "I haven't ridden the rails since I came back to Wichita from Fort Dix. So where am I going in Chicago?"

"Only to the train station," Pete explained. "You'll make your delivery to a man who'll be waiting for you. I'll give you the details later. And you'll be paid one hundred dollars for the job."

"Does that include the price of the ticket?"

Pete laughed. "Hell, no! And you won't have to pay for your food in the dining car either."

Dwayne was embarrassed. "I guess that shows how new I am to big business, huh?"

"You're going to fit in, don't worry," Pete said. He looked over at Sybil. "Don't you think so, darling?"

"There is no doubt in my mind," she replied with a wink, raising her glass in another toast.

Pete turned serious. "Just remember to lay low with the money, and don't act like a rollicking G.I. This is just the first of many missions, and you'll be pulling in several thousand dollars or so every year."

"What about getting myself a new office?" Dwayne said. "The one I have is a pigsty."

"It's better if you keep it," Pete advised him.

Dwayne raised his glass in agreement, then took a deep drink of the scotch and water.

CHAPTER 7

D wayne knew that Donna Sue must have been as horny as he was from the way she writhed beneath him as she experienced multiple orgasms. Her ecstasy ended with a shudder, and they were motionless for a couple of moments. Then, after she exhaled as a signal he could continue, Dwayne humped to his own release.

The couple slowly separated and lay quietly side-by-side without speaking. Finally, Donna Sue asked, "What time is it?"

Dwayne took a languid look at his watch. "Ten minutes after six."

"Still early," she remarked.

It was Saturday evening and they had returned from the business college a little more than half an hour before. Donna Sue wasn't quite so concerned about her studies after this second four-hour session, and when they got back to her apartment she had not only wanted to go out that night, but she was in the mood to hop into bed before beginning the evening's activities.

Dwayne chuckled. "Y'know, right now in almost every apartment in this building, people are having sex."

"Well, that's what happens when strict landlords don't let girls have their boyfriends in after ten p.m. They do it before instead of after they go out on a date."

"I think it's your landlady more than her husband who enforces that rule," Dwayne commented. "It's creepy as hell the way she sits up late keeping an eye on the comings and goings of the couples."

"Mr. and Mrs. Greeley are equally prudish, believe me," Donna Sue said, referring to the owners of the apartment house.

Dwayne nudged her. "Are you sure you don't want to go to Western Danceland?" This was a country-western nightclub that attracted a clientele of redneck lowlifes. There was almost as much fighting as dancing in the place. "We haven't been there for awhile."

"No," she said. "In fact, I don't care if I ever go out to that place again."

"I never thought I'd hear you say such a thing," Dwayne said. "You used to insist we go there almost ever' Saturday night."

"That club is something I want to leave behind me now," Donna Sue said. "I want it out of my life. Western Danceland is rowdy with loud hillbilly music and I'd like to go to quieter places from now on. That's why I want to start going regularly to the Roadhouse when we're in the mood to spend an evening dancing."

"It's got more class," Dwayne allowed. "And those colored musicians play jazz and swing."

"That's a lot better to dance to."

"I can't do that jitterbug shit," Dwayne said. "Never could."

"I prefer cheek-to-cheek anyhow. It makes me feel like we're Gene Kelly and Cyd Charisse."

"That couple tap dances, too," Dwayne pointed out.

"Cheek-to-cheek suits me just fine."

"Yeah, me, too," Dwayne said. "Maybe I'll take tap dancing lessons and surprise you one of these evenings. What would you think if I suddenly whirled around like Gene Kelly and tippy-tapped across the dance floor?"

Donna Sue answered with a laugh and a poke to his ribs. She sat up and stretched. "I think I'll get ready."

"Yeah, me, too."

"I see you wore that gray suit," she remarked, getting to her feet. "Don't you think it's time for a new one?"

He shook his head. "I still got the blue one."

"Good Lord, Dwayne! It's in worse shape than the gray."

Dwayne shrugged. "It's pretty dark in the Roadhouse anyhow."

"That's another problem your betting is causing you," Donna Sue said. "You've got to save up some money for new clothing. And to move out of that awful room you have and find a decent apartment."

He felt a flash of temper. "What's the matter with you? We've been going together for close to a year and all of a sudden you're complaining about things."

"It's all about moving up, Dwayne. People should always try to improve themselves. It's a necessary ongoing process. Didn't you just hear me say that I want to leave certain things behind and move on?"

"I told you about the deal I've made with my old army buddy," Dwayne said. "That means quite a bit of extra money."

"You'll just throw it away on the races!" she snapped. "Why don't you save yourself a lot of trouble, and simply go over to that barbershop and hand your money to those bookies all at once? That's what you're doing now, except they're getting everything in dribbles and drabs." She took a deep breath and let it out slowly as she fought down her irritation. "What sort of work are you doing for your old pal? You didn't elaborate much about it."

"It's financial and investment stuff that calls for secrecy," Dwayne said. "And that's all I can say about it. A private detective is like a lawyer; he can't tell nobody about arrangements with his clients."

"He can't tell *any*body!"

"You've sure been nagging me a hell of a lot lately," he complained. "Even about the way I talk."

She started to say something else, then changed her mind. "Do you need the bathroom? I'm going to be in there awhile."

"Yeah," he said, getting off the bed.

———

DWAYNE DROVE INTO THE ROADHOUSE PARKING lot with Donna Sue sitting beside him. She gazed out the window. "Look at all those snazzy cars. I bet most of them are brand new."

"Yeah they are," Dwayne agreed. "And here comes poor ol' Dwayne Wheeler in his beat up jalopy."

"You said that, not me."

"I thought I'd save you the trouble," Dwayne grumbled, as he pulled into a parking space. They got out of the car and he muttered, "There really ain't any sense in locking the doors. Nobody'll steal it."

Donna Sue didn't bother to make a comment as they strode across the macadam lot toward the building. Jack Wallace and Dennis Tarball were manning the front door, and they both gave the couple friendly smiles. Jack said, "Hi, Donna Sue, we ain't seen you for awhile."

"That's right," she remarked. "I thought it was time to drop by and enjoy the ambience of a nice place like the Roadhouse."

"But Dwayne came back fairly quick," Dennis remarked.

Donna Sue shot a look at Dwayne. "When were you here last?"

"A week ago when you wanted to stay home and study," Dwayne replied. "I didn't want to sit around all evening in my room."

"I see," she said, her eyes narrowed with suspicion.

"Anyhow, this is where I ran into Pete Van Dyke." He turned to the doormen. "We'll see you guys around." He took Donna Sue by the arm and guided her into the nightclub.

They went inside and stopped at the podium where George Baldwin the maître d' acted as the official greeter. If Dwayne had been alone he would have gone straight to the bar. "Hi, George."

"Hi, Dwayne," Baldwin replied. "How are you, Donna Sue? Nice to see you again. Most of the tables near the dance floor are taken, but we've got a few good ones off to the side."

"That sounds okay," Dwayne said. "We ain't particular."

Baldwin led them across the room to a table, and pulled out a chair for Donna Sue. "Your waitress shouldn't be too long."

Donna Sue glanced at Dwayne as she sat down. "Isn't this so much nicer than Western Danceland?"

"I never said it wasn't," Dwayne groused. He pulled a pint bottle of Jack Daniels from his jacket and set it on the table. There was a small lamp that offered weak illumination that was just right for a nightclub's atmosphere.

A waitress showed up within a couple of minutes. "What can I get you folks?"

"A couple of soda waters with ice on the side," Dwayne said.

"You got it," she said cheerfully. "And the grill is open if you get hungry."

"Thanks," Dwayne said. "We'll keep that in mind."

By the time they had gotten halfway through their first drinks, the black musicians had shown up for their performances, and walked across the dance floor up to the small bandstand. The crowd burst out in appreciative applause for the popular group. They smiled and waved back as they prepared to play. The piano man rippled his fingers over the keyboard while the bass violinist, saxophonist and guitarist tended to some preliminary tuning up. With everything ready, the pianist gave his signal and they began *In the Mood*, and the first dancers came out to begin the evening's activities.

Dwayne and Donna Sue sat out the first song, then got up to dance to *Tangerine*. As they swung by the combo, Dwayne grinned and nodded at the saxophonist. He had known the guy when they both attended Wichita High School East before the war. The musician wiggled his instrument at his old classmate and winked a greeting.

After a couple more dances, Dwayne led Donna Sue back to their table. The music turned a bit hot with *Basie Boogie* and *Blowin' Up a Storm*, and since Dwayne wasn't much for dancing to fast numbers, they stayed at the table. By the time their third drinks were done and they had begun the fourth, Dwayne had to go to the restroom.

The Roadhouse's facilities were clean and modern though they were hooked up to a septic tank rather than a sewage system. The lights were bright and stark, and when Dwayne compared his gray suit to the garb the other three guys in the place were wearing, he noticed it was a bit on the worn side like Donna Sue had pointed out.

He left the restroom and walked past the maître d's station when he noticed Judy Miller. She was lawyer Carl Banter's secretary, and was with a man Dwayne didn't recognize. They were speaking with George Baldwin, and as Dwayne approached them, he heard the maître d' apologize since they now had a full house and couldn't seat the couple. Dwayne turned and joined the group. "Hey, George, I got two extra chairs at our table."

Judy gave him a big smile. "Why hi, Dwayne. You're just popping up all over the place, aren't you? Are you sure we won't be an inconvenience?"

"Not a bit," Dwayne said.

"That's real nice of you." She nodded toward her date. "This is Brian Murchison. Brian, Dwayne Wheeler."

Dwayne shook hands with Murchison, recognizing the name as being one of Wichita's leading families. "You two come on with me," Dwayne said. "I'll introduce you to my girlfriend. We're enjoying a night on the town."

He led the way back to the table, and quickly presented Judy and Murchison to Donna Sue, explaining there had been no table for them. As they all sat down, Dwayne spoke to Donna Sue. "Judy is the secretary for Carl Banter the lawyer. I work for him from time to time." He glanced at Judy. "Donna Sue is in secretarial school."

"Well, welcome to the club," Judy said with a smile.

Murchison was a tall, handsome man with chiseled features that gave an impression of golf, tennis, and a high-powered line of business that paid plenty of money.

"That's a most important profession," he commented. "Secretaries are indispensable in the business world."

"I'm not quite a secretary yet," Donna Sue said. "I have twelve more hours of classes to go before I graduate."

Dwayne interjected, "Right now she's waitressing at the Jayhawker Restaurant on West Douglas."

Donna Sue's reddening face was not apparent in the dim light. "I hope to be out of there soon."

Murchison pulled out his wallet and retrieved a business card. He handed it to Donna Sue. "Give me a call when you're ready to begin your job search. I believe we'll be having an opening in my firm, or at least a position available where you could begin your new career."

"Oh, thank you!" she said, reading the card. "What sort of business is Murchison Enterprises?"

"It's a combination of all our family's interests," Murchison replied. "I'm in the oil production side of the operations."

Dwayne didn't like the way the conversation had turned. "I may hire her for my own business when she finishes her studies."

"That'll be my bad luck," Murchison said. "What is your line of work, Dwayne?"

"I'm a private detective."

Judy interjected, "Dwayne is the investigator who was instrumental in stopping those Kansas City mobsters from taking over Wichita."

"Oh, my God!" Murchison exclaimed. "So you're the hero, hey?"

"I was just doing what I had to do in the situation," Dwayne said. "I got a lot of investigative experience as a military policeman in Germany after the war. We went after racketeers and the black market mostly. So when the

K.C. gang showed up, I used what I knew to infiltrate their organization."

"I see," Murchison said. He pulled a pint of Canadian Club Whisky and another of Gilbert's Gin from his jacket. "Let me add these to our larder, hey?"

When the waitress came up, Murchison ordered more soda water for Dwayne and Donna Sue as well as tonic water and lime juice. "Bring the check to me," he added with a gracious smile. "These nice people provided us with a place to sit." He turned to Dwayne. "So you were in the ETO, were you?"

"Yeah," Dwayne said. "Did you serve in the war?"

"Yeah," Murchison replied. "I was in a parachute infantry regiment in the 82nd Airborne Division. We participated in the campaigns on Sicily and Anzio. I was wounded in the last operation, but recovered just in time for D-Day."

"Brian was awarded the Silver Star for bravery," Judy said. "And he was wounded twice more."

"Getting wounded isn't anything to brag about," Murchison said modestly, taking a sip of his gin and tonic.

Judy couldn't stop. "He was a captain."

"Everybody did their part in the war no matter their rank," Murchison said, assuming that Dwayne had been an enlisted man. The music started up, and he took Judy's hand. "Let's trip the light fantastic, shall we?"

From that point on, the evening evolved into one of drinking and dancing with intervals spent in conversation that did not improve Dwayne's dwindling mood. He grew even more uncomfortable when Murchison danced with Donna Sue several times. He also did some jitterbugging, teaching her a few steps and turns. Dwayne managed to get Judy out on the dance floor only twice when slow tunes were played.

After a couple of hours, the ladies excused themselves to retire to the restroom. Donna Sue had been envious of Judy's evening dress and as they freshened up their makeup, she was able to give the garment a close study in the light. "That is one of the most beautiful dresses I've ever seen."

"Why thank you," Judy said. "Believe me; I couldn't have afforded it on my salary. I got it from my boss as a bonus."

"Wow!" Donna Sue exclaimed. "You must have done some real special work."

"It wasn't work," Judy said. "I simply agreed to go out on dates with important clients now and then."

Donna Sue gave her a wary look.

Judy laughed. "Hey, I'm the type of gal they like to have on their arms at social events. Know what I mean? It doesn't go any further than that."

"Are you out with Brian on a date like that?"

"Oh, no," Judy answered. "I've been dating him off and on for about a year. We get along, but there's been no romance. He's a real charming guy with scads of money."

"He seems to be."

"And he's giving you the eye," Judy said. "Don't be surprised if he asks you out sometime."

"Doesn't he know Dwayne is my steady?"

"That doesn't make any difference to him," Judy said. "Dwayne could be your husband, and Brian would still be interested in you."

"He isn't married, is he?"

"No," Judy replied. "He's the quintessential eligible bachelor and quite rich, like I said. Most of the time we go to the Prairie Wind Golf and Tennis Club for dining and dancing, but he decided he wanted to go slumming tonight." She gave Donna Sue a close look. "You're an attractive woman, Donna Sue. When you get a secretarial position, you're going to be given a lot of attention by the top men of the company where you work. How you handle those situations is strictly up to you. You have to keep in mind that this is a man's world, and there are certain games we ladies must play to gain any advantage in that age-old sport."

Donna Sue thought, *The last person that said that to me was trying to recruit me to be a call girl.*

They finished their primping and went back to the table.

CHAPTER 8

When Dwayne drove over to Donna Sue's apartment house on the morning after the visit to the Roadhouse, he experienced more unsettling feelings, but these latest emotions were affected by thoughts of Brian Murchison and the attentions he had been giving Donna Sue.

During the evening as everyone got a little tipsy, Murchison's interest in her had increased to the point Dwayne was considering dragging him out to the parking lot and using his fists to impart a forceful lesson on male etiquette concerning another guys' girlfriend. Evidently in Wichita's high society, the men weren't particularly proprietary of their women. Even the basest honky-tonking redneck would look down on that attitude with utter contempt and derision, considering such an attitude stupid and cowardly.

But at closing time Murchison did a complete turn-around in his behavior. He politely thanked Dwayne for allowing him and Judy Miller to sit with them, even shaking his hand with a remark that he hoped to see him again sometime. Then he gave Donna Sue a cordial polite farewell, and escorted Judy out of the nightclub.

But Dwayne still worried about Donna Sue's attitude toward the wealthy businessman. No one like Murchison had ever intruded into their lives, and it particularly disturbed Dwayne because of Donna Sue's ambitions to move up in the world.

Dwayne ended up spending all day Sunday with Donna Sue, and in spite of his wariness, things seemed normal. They began the day by going out to breakfast, then decided to take a drive out of town. Dwayne headed south on U.S. 81 all the way to the U.S. 177 cut off. He continued down to Oklahoma going to the town of Blackwell. This community was a small place, and the two city people drove around the streets, taking in the few sights offered in the locale. Donna Sue insisted he pull over and park so they could get out of the car for a stroll and see what was displayed for sale in the shop windows. As they walked along, the few locals on the streets gazed at them with a polite inquisitiveness and nodded silent greetings to them as was customary in rural areas. Dwayne and Donna Sue, a little confused by the subtle friendliness, smiled back.

Unfortunately, there wasn't much to scope out, and everything was closed down since it was Sunday. Donna Sue found only one dress shop, and wasn't too impressed with what the bucolic establishment displayed in its window. When she remarked on it, Dwayne laughed. "Now you know why Sears Roebuck and Montgomery Ward catalogs are so popular in these little places."

They drove out of Blackwell for a look at the countryside. As the morning eased by, Dwayne kept glancing at Donna Sue, but she seemed her old self, and hadn't nagged him once about betting on horses. Of course that might be a bad sign if it meant she was losing interest in him. He just wished she'd keep the nagging down long enough for him to kick the continuing mood of uncertainty.

Around noon they were hungry again, and he took Oklahoma State Highway 11 East over to U.S. 77 North, and drove straight up over the Kansas line to Arkansas City. They found a café open just south of town, and stopped in for lunch. The community was a lot bigger than Blackwell, and nobody paid them any special atten- tion. After that, they headed back to U.S. 81, and took it straight to Wichita.

The couple arrived back at Donna Sue's apartment a little after six, and she fixed a small meal of fried eggs and ham with toast. All this time Dwayne had tried to see if some change in her demeanor would develop, but her mood and attitude seemed the same. He decided not to complain about the lack of French-fried potatoes so she would retain her good disposition.

Later, when he instigated some kissing and hugging, he had no problem getting her into the bedroom. The sex was great and Donna Sue had more of her usual rollicking multi-orgasms.

———

THE NEXT DAY, DWAYNE WENT STRAIGHT TO HIS office after breakfast at the Jayhawker. Because of his promise to A.J. Kessler, he figured he should forget his personal life for a bit, and take at least a few days to try to find out where the hell Fritz Harrigan had wandered off to. He had just sunk into his thinking process of putting his feet up on his desk, lighting a Lucky Strike cigarette, and staring out the window. His thoughts were interrupted when the phone rang. "Yeah?"

"Hi, Dwayne, this is Pete. Are you available for a job that'll take you out of town for a couple of days?"

"You bet," Dwayne replied, thinking that a quick payment of a hundred dollars would have to be given priority over A.J. Kessler and Fritz Harrigan. "Just give me the word."

"Great. Since you're at your office I'll meet you there. Where is it?"

"All you have to do is go out the front of your hotel on Douglas and head east," Dwayne said. "It's in the Snodgrass Building on the south side. You can't miss it, it's a five story rundown place of dirty brown bricks. I'm on the second floor; Room 205."

"I'll be there."

Dwayne hung up the phone, smiling to himself. Between his work for A.J. and this new set-up, he was going to really be in the dough for at least the next couple of months. Of course losing that hundred bucks on the horses put a dent in his financial well-being, but that was more than a week ago, so it didn't count anymore. Dwayne was a strong believer in not dwelling on bad luck; this meant he quickly forgot any losses that occurred in any previous three or four days.

Pete Van Dyke showed up at the Snodgrass Building in a very short twenty minutes carrying a rather new briefcase. Small but sturdy padlocks were on both hasps. He glanced around the office. "It's easy to see you weren't lying when you said that a lot of your money went for betting on the ponies."

"You sound like my girlfriend."

"If she's nagging you about wasting your shekels, she knows what she's talking about." He set the briefcase on the desk. "But at least you aren't as careless as you were in Germany."

"I've outgrown most of that craziness."

"Thank God for that," Pete said. "By the way, you'll be catching the train at Newton at eight p.m."

Dwayne's eyes opened wide in surprise. "Newton?"

"Yeah," Pete said. "We want to keep as low a profile as possible here in Wichita. I'll drive you up there."

"Understood."

"Okay. Here's your delivery. You'll be going up to the Chicago Union Station to meet your contact, arriving at seven a.m. The guy will be wearing a tweed jacket and a brimmed slouch hat of the same material. He'll be standing on the north side of the station. When you spot him, go near him, then stop and light a cigarette. Then approach the guy and say, 'Can you tell me the best way to get to Fulton Street?'"

"Good challenge," Dwayne remarked. "So what's the password?"

"He'll reply 'North on Jackson Street.' With that done, set the briefcase beside him, then wait for him to pick it up and go out into the street. At that point you look for a nearby bench and settle down for a half hour."

"I think I'll take a book with me."

"Good idea," Pete said. "After that half hour you can leave the station and go over to Adams Street. There's a hotel there where you can spend the rest of the day and night lying low. It's small but don't worry, the place is clean and even has a bar and grill. It's a handy spot for people with long waits. You'll catch the return train back to Newton at seven a.m. the next morning. You should arrive around eight in the evening. I'll be waiting for you."

———

DWAYNE STARED OUT THE PASSENGER CAR window at the dark countryside as the Atchison, Topeka, and Santa Fe passenger local swayed and clacked northward on the tracks, headed for Chicago's Union Station. He checked his watch and estimated he was about halfway through the trip. He could recall going through Kansas City, Missouri, and Des Moines, Iowa, but the other two short stops had slipped his mind. It would have been nice to have a map to keep track of his progress, but it hadn't occurred to him to bring one.

The briefcase, with the locks on it, was between his feet next to his valise. He had only dozed occasionally as he maintained a watch on the luggage. Pete hadn't said anything about the possibility or danger of an interception of the mission, but expecting the unexpected was an important maxim when it came to guarding material goods. Dwayne was armed; packing his .45 Colt semi-automatic in his shoulder holster. His permit to carry a concealed weapon was only good in Kansas, but he felt better having the pistol with him. If an incident occurred and local law enforcement found him illegally armed, his private investigator's license should get him through the difficulty.

Dwayne glanced around the semi-illuminated car, noting that most of the dozen or so other passengers were sleeping. A couple of insomniacs had the small lamps above their seats turned on, reading magazines; and one stalwart was making changes and additions with a fountain pen on some papers he had laid out on his briefcase.

All secure and quiet.

Dwayne patted the pistol and glanced up and down to take a look at both ends of the car, then settled back for another brief catnap, making sure that if anyone moved the briefcase it would alert him.

———

THE CONDUCTOR WALKED THROUGH THE CAR calling out, "Arriving at Chicago Union Station! Arriving at Chicago Union Station!"

Dwayne checked his watch, noting they had reached his destination at six-fifty-one a.m. He had been wide awake since they sped through Peoria, Illinois, and he sat his valise and briefcase on the empty seat beside him. The train slammed and bucked its way to a stop, and Dwayne picked up his luggage and moved toward the door. The conductor was ahead of him, and exited the car with a step stool as soon as they came to a complete stop. Dwayne immediately followed, descending to the platform and walking rapidly as he crossed the loading area and entered the station proper.

The terminal was crowded as would be expected in a large city like Chicago, and Dwayne was turned around in the bustling activity of travelers. A black porter pushing a dolly came by and Dwayne gestured to him. "Which way is north, buddy?"

"That way, sir," the man replied, pointing.

Dwayne took his time working through the crowd until he reached the doors leading out of the station. He glanced around and saw a man wearing a tweed jacket and a brimmed slouch hat who was standing just inside the building. Dwayne walked toward him, then stopped and sat the briefcase and valise on the floor. He lit a cigarette, and the guy looked over at him.

Dwayne nodded and said, "Say, pal, can you tell me the best way to get to Fulton Street?"

"Sure," the guy said. "Go out the door and walk north on Jackson."

"I appreciate that," Dwayne said.

The man picked up the briefcase and walked out the door to the street. Dwayne grabbed his valise and headed over to a nearby bench and settled down. After noting the time, he began the half hour wait.

———

THE HOTEL ON ADAMS STREET WAS EXACTLY AS Pete Van Dyke had described it. It was a small establishment of four stories, and when Dwayne walked in he noted the lobby was clean and well-arranged. He also spotted a lantern-jawed man in a slouch hat sitting on a sofa, reading a newspaper. The stranger looked at him and their eyes locked for an instant, then the man turned his attention to getting a cigarette from his jacket.

Dwayne went up to the front desk and spoke to the clerk. "I have a reservation. The name is Wheeler."

The clerk turned to a box of three-by-five cards, and pulled one out. "Yes, sir. Your room is ready." He rang the bell, pushing the registration book toward Dwayne. A bellboy appeared, and took the key handed to him by the clerk. "Room 320."

After Dwayne finished signing, the kid picked up the valise and led the way to the single elevator. The bellboy operated the conveyance. "Are you gonna be here long, sir?"

Dwayne shook his head. "Just overnight."

The elevator stopped on the third floor, and the bellboy led the way down the hall, stopping at the room. After ushering Dwayne inside, he put the valise on the luggage stand. "Is there anything else, sir?"

Dwayne handed the guy fifty cents. "What time does the bar and grill open?"

"Eleven o'clock, sir. The grill closes at ten p.m., but

the bar stays open 'til two a.m. If you want breakfast, there's a nice diner just down the street." The kid flipped the fifty-cent piece, then stuck it in his pocket. "And if you need anything special, just call down to the desk and ask for a bellboy."

"Okay," Dwayne replied, thinking of his friend Jimmy Thompson at the Riverview Hotel in Wichita. Jimmy made most of his money fetching call girls and bootleg liquor for guests who were in Wichita on business or to attend conventions.

The kid left, and Dwayne decided against breakfast. He hadn't gotten much sleep the night before on the train, and a couple of hours of snoozing would do him a world of good. When he woke up, he'd go down to the bar and grill and get a bite to eat.

———

IT WAS ALMOST NOON BY THE TIME DWAYNE awakened. He took a shower and shaved, then changed into the fresh clothing he'd brought with him in the valise. After leaving the room, he went to the elevator and pressed the button. A couple of minutes later, the bellboy showed up and opened the door for him. They exchanged greetings and Dwayne was taken down to the lobby.

The bar and grill was a small room. The bar was located on one side with booths directly opposite. A bartender was on duty along with a barmaid who tended to a half dozen customers in the booths. Dwayne, looking forward to having a real drink in a real bar, took a stool.

The bartender was a guy with a friendly grin, and he walked up laying a napkin down in front of Dwayne. "What can I get you?"

"A scotch and soda," Dwayne replied. "With a twist."

"You got it."

"What's on the grill?"

The bartender gave him a menu.

Dwayne scanned the listed offerings. It consisted mostly of hamburgers and sandwiches with side dishes. When he got his drink, he said, "I'll take a grilled cheese sandwich with French-fries." The bartender took the menu back, then wrote up the order. He took it down to the end of the bar where a fry cook had his workstation. Dwayne tasted the drink, glancing in the mirror behind the bar.

The lantern-jawed gent was in a booth, and quickly turned his attention back to his newspaper when he perceived Dwayne looking at him. Something about the guy fired up every nerve in Dwayne's detective psyche.

CHAPTER 9

The train from Chicago arrived at the Newton, Kansas depot fifteen minutes late. Now, at a little past eight-thirty p.m. Dwayne sat in the automobile as Pete Van Dyke drove south on U.S. 81 toward Wichita, a bit more than twenty miles away. They rode in a black 1940 Buick sedan with a well-tuned motor that purred like a cat.

Dwayne was impressed. "I meant to ask you where you got these wheels when you drove me up here yesterday."

"I bought it at a used car lot when I first got to Wichita," Pete replied. "You might inherit this after I leave."

"You ain't gonna keep it?"

Pete shook his head. "Nope. I got it because I didn't want to rent a car. An arrangement like that leaves a record such as the day it was rented, the day it was returned and all the mileage put on it in between. There's also a need to sign a bunch of papers. A quick cash deal in a used car lot is only a simple transaction."

"I take it your real name ain't on the title."

"Nope. I had a phony New York driver's license and used that as an I.D."

"If you pass this car on to me, I can put my real name and address on the papers," Dwayne said. "That way if someone does any tracing on the New York license, all I got to say is that I bought it from a guy I met downtown somewhere. If they want a description I can say you were about five foot six and weighed maybe two hunnerd and fifty pounds." He laughed. "I'll tell 'em your nickname was Lard Ass. Anyhow, as long as the title is signed over to me, there's no problem since it ain't a stolen vehicle. So it's a legal sale."

"You've got it covered," Pete commented. "And I'll be getting a different car for each of my frequent trips to Wichita."

"I'd be real happy with a Packard or a Cadillac."

Pete chuckled. "I'll see what I can do."

"So, anyhow, I delivered the briefcase as ordered," Dwayne said. "There was a man there in the Union Station just like you said he'd be. We passed the challenge and the password, and ever'thing went smoothly."

"Aren't you curious about what you were delivering?"

"Sure," Dwayne answered. "But I know better than to get nosy."

"Well, I'll tell you what you delivered from Wichita to Chicago. It was a ream of blank typing paper."

"You're shitting me!"

"Nope," Pete said. "This was a two-pronged test. One was to check out if the procedures we devised would work since we haven't sent anything up between Wichita and Chicago before. And the second was to show the organization you were a dependable guy. Of course I personally had no doubts about you, but you're a complete stranger to the others involved in these transactions."

"I take it that I passed the test."

"With flying colors," Pete assured him.

"By the way," Dwayne said. "There was a guy in the hotel that caught my attention."

"Oh, yeah? What'd he look like?"

"Big, husky bruiser type," Dwayne said. "Well dressed though, and he had one of them undershot jaws. He'd be a real load in a fight."

"That's one of our guys," Pete admitted. "He was supposed to see if you stayed at the hotel or went out wandering around."

"You should give him a lesson in being inconspicuous," Dwayne said. "O'course, it wasn't his fault. He kind of stands out in a crowd."

"Not to ordinary citizens," Pete countered. "If any run-of-the-mill people tried to give details about his appearance, they'd give varying descriptions of the guy. That's the way it always is. Everybody see people differently."

"When do I get paid?"

"There's an envelope in the glove compartment," Pete answered. "You'll find sixteen ten dollar bills. The extra is for your expenses."

Dwayne retrieved the money and stuck into his inside coat pocket. As they continued down the highway, he thought about how impressed Donna Sue would be with the amount he had earned so quickly. Maybe she'd back off nagging about his gambling.

———

ON WEDNESDAY MORNING, DETECTIVE SERGEANT Al Gallagher of the Wichita Police Department Homicide Squad pulled up his unmarked '41 Ford sedan at the entrance to the alley between Rock Island and Mosley. This location was just north of First Street in the Warehouse District. As the detective got out of the car, a cop standing near the curb walked over to him. "How's it going, Sergeant?"

"Nothing to write home about," Gallagher replied. "What do we have here?"

"A 'John Doe' laying in the alley," the cop answered. "Looks like a robbery. All his pockets are turned out."

"Okay."

Gallagher strode down the alleyway to where a couple more of Wichita's Finest stood with a seedy individual in dirty clothes. The detective glanced at him. "Who's this?"

The first cop replied, "He's the one that found the stiff."

Gallagher walked up to him. "I know you. I think I've run you in a dozen times if I did it once. Your name is Cockroach, right?"

The guy grinned. "That's perty funny. Ha! My name is Cochrane. Eddie Cochrane." Eddie was one of the local moonshine derelicts who bought half-pint jars of the homemade whiskey for fifty cents each.

"So what do you have to say about this?" Gallagher asked.

"Nothing," Eddie said. "I was walking down the alley and seen the dead guy and all that blood. So I went over to the cigar store and told the owner. And he called the cops."

"You're a good citizen, huh, Cockroach?"

"Sometimes."

Gallagher walked over to the corpse. The dead man, still uncovered, lay on his back in a slightly twisted position. Gallagher ignored the two cops and gazed down at the victim. When he spoke, it was obvious he was talking to himself. "Well dressed...clothes rumpled from what looks like being searched...well-nourished and clean... bullet hole in right eye...two chest wounds . . ." Now he looked at the cops. "Have you guys gone around the neighborhood to see if anybody heard or seen anything?"

"Yeah, we did, Sergeant," one of them replied. "They all said it was quiet out here, so it looks like this happened last night. This place is pretty much empty overnight."

Gallagher looked around at the warehouses. "There must've been a night watchman or two on duty in some of them buildings."

The second cop spoke up. "We went to ever'place on the block, Sergeant. The people in the offices said that there wasn't any reports of gunfire noted by their security guys on their reports from last night."

"Aw!" Gallagher said. "Them watchmen are all old farts. They'd sleep through a prairie tornado." He thought a moment. "Unless the killer used a silencer."

"I doubt that," the first policeman said.

Gallagher knelt down to take a closer look at the body. "This guy was prob'ly trolling for hookers. They use this alley to pick up johns and take 'em to one of them cheap hotels over on Douglas."

The second cop shook his head. "Naw. No hooker is gonna do something like this."

"That's right, Sarge," the first cop said. "You're forgetting the queers. They come down here sometimes because of the privacy and darkness. Maybe he picked up some guy in one of them arcades on Douglas and got hisself rolled."

"You're prob'ly right by the looks of things," Gallagher acknowledged. "Whoever done this to him could have stole his car, too."

"It's dangerous being a faggot," the second cop

commented. "There's too many guys who set 'em up for fast and easy assaults and robberies."

"The queers are asking for it," his buddy added. "If they stuck with pussy like men are supposed to do, they wouldn't get themselves into bad situations."

Gallagher stood up. He walked slowly around the area, looking for any signs of a struggle or something that might lead to the identification of the deceased. But there wasn't so much as an expended cartridge case. "Okay," he said. "Let's get the crime scene dudes down here for pitcher taking and all that shit. And put in a call for the coroner's wagon. Meanwhile get a statement from Cockroach here."

"Right, Sarge."

Gallagher walked back down the alley to his car.

———

FRITZ HARRIGAN HAD FINISHED THE MOST complicated plate he had been assigned. This was the one that included the portrait of Adolf Hitler. Now, with Karlis watching closely, the young artist ran a brayer through a spread of printer's ink, then rolled it over the plate. He laid a piece of paper over the ink, then used a roller to put pressure on the image. When he pulled it off, he held up the proof. After glancing at it, he handed it to Karlis.

"What do you think?"

Karlis studied it under the light, then got the original that Fritz had used as a model. He uttered a happy remark in a foreign language, then switched to English. "Is perfect! Look like original."

"Try it with this," Fritz said, handing him a powerful magnifying glass.

Karlis used the device, looking back and forth between the original and proof several times. "No difference! Is no difference! Every line is same."

"I'm glad you like it," Fritz said. "I have to finish the scroll work on the plate for the back side. The value plates for the numbered ones are finished. As soon as the back is done, I'll start on the fives, then go to the tens, twenty-fives and fifties."

"You do good past few days," Karlis said.

"That's the way it goes sometimes when you're involved in engraving," Fritz explained. "There's days when you can't seem to accomplish anything, then all of a sudden everything just flows along nice and easy." He grinned a bit sheepishly. "I suppose those visits from Lotte have a lot to do with it."

Karlis frowned, then nodded. "Yes." He took another look at the finished product. "You are ahead of schedule. Nice work you are doing."

"I'm feeling pretty good," Fritz said. "I'm sure I can finish the back one in ten to fourteen hours. That way a complete bill can be printed to add the value ones with the numbers." He looked down at the plate, and studied it. "What kind of money is this? Or are they coupons? Stock certificates, maybe?"

Karlis didn't answer. He turned and walked toward the door with the proof Fritz had printed for him.

———

SERGEANT AL GALLAGHER WENT THROUGH THE police station's front entrance, going straight to the dispatch room. He walked over to the telephone desk that was manned by a veteran patrolman who had grown too old for street duties. The guy was reading a copy of *Look* magazine, and glanced up. "What can I do for you, Sergeant?"

"Have you got any calls about missing persons?" Gallagher asked. "I'm talking about something that would have come in this morning prob'ly."

The patrolman nodded. "Yeah." He picked up a message sheet. "A lady with a weird name called in about her old man who hadn't come home last night. I told her to wait twenty-four hours then contact missing persons." He handed the piece of paper to Gallagher.

"Well, well," he said. "A Missus Emilija Kilitis seems to be missing her husband Mikelis." He laughed. "What kind of fucking Bohunk names are these?"

"I don't know," the patrolman said. "But she had a funny accent."

"Okay. Thanks."

He took the report with him and went upstairs to the homicide squad room. He walked inside, going past several detectives at their desks to the built-in office in the back where his boss Detective Lieutenant Ben Forester performed his administrative and command duties. When Gallagher rapped on the door, Ben motioned him to come in. "What's the latest, Al?"

"There was a homicide in the Warehouse District," Gallagher said. "The body was a 'John Doe'. One of the reprobates who float around the area found him."

"Anything special?"

"Yeah," Gallagher replied. "The guy was well-dressed, and obviously not the type to traipse around a neighborhood like that unless he's looking for a cheap hooker. On the other hand, he might have gone into the alley to either get or give a blow job from a queer." He handed the phone report to Ben. "This call came in this morning. It could be about our victim whose wife said he didn't come home last night. I thought I'd go see her and find out if she's got a pitcher of the guy. If it don't look like the body, I'll let it go and see what develops later. But if it does, I'll bring her down to the morgue to make an I.D."

"Do me a favor, Al," Ben said. "Use a little finesse and dignity if her old man is the stiff. Can you do that?"

"Don't I always do that?" Gallagher asked defensively.

———

THE KILITIS HOME WAS NEAR THE WICHITA University campus on Yale Avenue. Gallagher parked in front of the house, taking a couple of minutes to give it a good study. It was a modest well-kept place, just the sort of domicile someone like that particular victim would choose to live in. He got out of the squad car and walked up to the small front porch. He rang the doorbell, and it was quickly answered by a woman in her middle years. "Yes?"

"Hi," Gallagher said, flashing his badge. "I'm Sergeant Gallagher of the Wichita Police. Is this the residence of Missus Kilitis?"

"Yes," she answered in a worried tone. "I am Mrs. Kilitis."

"Did you phone in a report about your husband not coming home last night?"

"Yes, I did," she said. "Do you have information about him?"

"I don't know," Gallagher said, noting the foreign accent. "I need to ask a few questions."

"Please come in," she said.

Gallagher went in the house, and the woman led him into the living room. The policeman asked, "Where does your husband work?"

"He is a professor of European History here at the University."

Gallagher figured a well-to-do European intellectual would probably be a secret homosexual while married to a woman. "Where do you two come from?"

"We are from Latvia," she said. "When the Germans invaded and drove the Soviets out of the country, my husband and I managed to get ourselves smuggled aboard a ship to Sweden. From there we went to England for the rest of the war, and when it ended we immigrated to America. We did not wish to return to Latvia where we would have to live under Soviet rule like before the war."

"I'd like to see a pitcher of your husband."

"Of course." She went into the bedroom, and returned with a studio portrait of two people. He took it from her hand and gazed at it. The woman was her, and the man was the dead guy in the alley.

"I got bad news for you, lady."

Chapter 10

The crowd in the Jayhawker Restaurant was dense and hungry on the morning after Dwayne returned from his trip to Chicago. He couldn't find an empty stool as the customers rushed through their breakfasts prior to heading for work. They were mostly single people or had spouses who also worked, meaning that it was a lot of trouble and bother to fix their own morning meals. It was easier to breeze into the diner and order their food rather than have to put up with the extra time of preparing their breakfasts, then having to clean up after themselves. It also meant at least another half hour of sleep.

Dwayne went toward the back to the coffee machine. He poured himself a cup and lit a cigarette. Donna Sue winked at him, and he watched as she and Maisie worked quickly and efficiently taking orders and serving the meals in a routine born of experience and teamwork. They were good at it, having toiled together for close to two years. Their chores also included working the cash register, which was evidence of the amount of trust the owner Art Manger had in his waitresses. He only came in two or three times a week to pick up the cash from the safe and take it to the bank.

After Dwayne had been there fifteen minutes, a couple of guys paid for their food and hurried out to the street. Dwayne slipped onto a stool, settling down to smoke his cigarette and sip the coffee. He was never in a hurry to eat, and Donna Sue and Maisie kept the breakfast process rolling along without giving him any attention. Then, as quickly as it began, the rush tapered off until only a trio of slow eaters was left. They dawdled over newspapers, eating up the last of their eggs, toast, and sausage links or bacon.

Donna Sue went over to the kitchen window and said, "Dwayne's here."

The cook Arnie Dawkins knew that meant he was to prepare the private eye's favorite breakfast. He hollered out, "Hey there, Dwayne! I'll have your grub ready directly."

"Thanks, Arnie!" Dwayne yelled back. He nodded to Slim the dishwasher as the Texan came out to collect the dirty cups, plates and flatware.

Donna Sue, now able to enjoy a break, took a deep breath and let it out slowly as she reached into her apron pocket and pulled out her tips. She spread the coins out beside the pie rack. Maisie did the same. After counting the take, she announced, "Two bucks and fifteen cents. What'd you get, Donna Sue?"

"Two dollars and thirty-five cents."

Maisie was a realist. "The prettiest waitress always gets the most tips."

"I only got twenty more cents than you," Donna Sue pointed out.

Arnie interrupted the conversation, yelling, "Dwayne's grub!"

Donna Sue went to the window and got the breakfast, setting it down on the counter. "How was your trip?"

"I got the job done," Dwayne said, spreading butter on a piece of rye toast.

"Do you think it's a good idea to deliver something when you don't know what it is?"

Dwayne shrugged. "That ain't unusual for a private eye. It happens all the time." He pulled a roll of bills out of his shirt pocket, and handed it over to her.

Donna Sue made a quick count. Her voice dropped to a whisper. "You got five hundred and fifty dollars for an overnight train trip?"

"And that's just the beginning," he said.

"Good Lord, Dwayne, what have you gotten yourself into?"

"After you meet Pete, you won't be so suspicious," he said. "Pete's an old army buddy, and he's a rich guy. His family were New York City bankers who lost ever'thing in the Depression. But they still got connections in finance and big business, and Pete got introduced to the right people."

"But it still seems kind of shady to me," Donna Sue insisted, handing him back the money.

"Honey bunch, you just don't understand. Big business deals have got to be kept under the table. There's lots of competition and it's all cut-throat. Underhanded and sneaky sharpers try to find out what the other guy is doing so they can sell the information to the highest bidder." He stopped talking and turned all his attention to eating while the waitresses began wiping down the counter.

After he finished, instead of sticking around and chatting, Dwayne got to his feet. "I've still got some business with A.J. It's a chance to earn more scratch," he said, wanting to further impress her.

"Okay," Donna Sue said.

"I'll be back in time to give you a ride home."

———

DWAYNE PULLED UP IN THE REAR OF THE CEMENT block building A.J. Kessler used as his headquarters. He walked around to the front door and stepped inside. The young secretary Jill was on the phone, and she waved at him and pointed toward A.J.'s private office to show where he was. Dwayne nodded his thanks and walked over and rapped on the door.

"Come in," came a less than enthusiastic reply.

Dwayne walked in and found the little man smoking a cigar with his feet up on the desk, staring at the ceiling.

Dwayne grinned. "Busy day?"

"Oh, yeah," A.J. replied. "I just might work myself into an ulcer. What's up, ol' buddy?"

"I just got back in town from running an errand," Dwayne said, taking a chair. "I'm free right now, so I thought I'd drop by to see if you had anything on your agenda that I might help you with."

"Only Fritz Harrigan," A.J. said. "He still ain't showed up."

"Okay," Dwayne said. "I can give him some attention for the next couple of days if you want me to."

"That'd prob'ly be a good idea," A.J. said.

"The problem is that Fritz don't have any connection to the streets. All my usual contacts and snitches wouldn't know the guy if he walked up and kicked 'em in the balls."

A.J. laughed. "If he did they'd sure as hell remember him after getting a boot in the crotch, wouldn't they?"

"The trouble is Fritz ain't the type that draws much attention."

"By the way," A.J. said. "Do I owe you any money?"

"No. We're even-steven." Dwayne got to his feet. "I think I'll start with the pawn shop. Maybe he went back and pawned his toolset again."

"I doubt it," A.J. said. "I think I'm out a half a c-note."

"I'll be checking in later."

A.J. waved and turned his attention back to smoking and staring at the ceiling.

————

DWAYNE FOUND A PARKING PLACE IN FRONT OF Joe Wallek's pawn shop on East Douglas. He stepped up on the sidewalk and glanced up and down the street to see if any of his contacts were around. Seeing none, he went inside. Both Joe Wallek and his son Henry were behind the counter. Joe, a bald fat man of sixty-some years with rugged features, gave Dwayne a smile. "Hi, Dwayne. Henry told me you were prowling around looking for somebody a few days go."

"Yeah," Dwayne replied. "A little guy named Fritz Harrigan."

Henry stated, "If I remember, he's a bail jumper, right?"

"Yeah," Dwayne replied. "I was wondering if he came back and maybe pawned the toolset again. Or maybe something else."

"We ain't seen hide nor hair of him," Henry said.

"When Henry told me somebody else had picked up his property, I thought maybe he'd been robbed or something," Joe said. "But Henry said the guy was turned out pretty good and didn't look like the type that would want much to do with a pawn ticket. What kind of tools was it?"

"Engraving," Dwayne said. "Fritz is an artist."

Joe looked at Henry. "Check any art supplies we got. Maybe he came back and pawned some brushes or other supplies when you and me weren't here."

"Okay," Henry said. He walked back to the file box and began going through it. "This'll take a few minutes."

"I'm in no rush," Dwayne said. He thought about the money in his pocket; maybe he should buy something for Donna Sue to show her the financial advantages to his new arrangement with Pete. "I think I'll take a look around."

"Help yourself," Joe invited.

Dwayne walked along the glass counter peering at the watches, fountain pen sets, musical instruments and other things that people down on their luck had brought in to exchange for money. He wandered down to the end, and saw some pictures along one wall. Maybe Donna Sue would like a landscape or something to brighten up her apartment. He walked slowly past the display, eyeing each. Most of them could be had for a dollar or two.

Then he came to a pen-and-ink drawing of a nude.

His first interest in the work was the sexiness of the woman. She was curvy with full breasts, round sturdy thighs and she wore her hair in a contemporary long style, brushed back to reveal her shoulders. For some reason he was attracted to it for more than the erotic aspects of the work. He stared at it for several moments, then took notice of the pattern of shading. All was done with straight lines of various thicknesses spaced to produce an illusion of differing tones of gray.

This was the exact style of the sketches by Fritz that Mrs. Harrigan had showed him. And it was also like the art hanging on the wall in Attorney Carl Banter's private office. Now Dwayne's eyes went down to the right lower corner and he saw the careful block printing that read **FRITZ HARRIGAN**.

Dwayne rushed back to the counter. "Where'd you get that drawing over on the wall?"

"Which one?" Joe asked. "There's dozens over there."

"Come here," Dwayne said, going back.

Both Joe and Henry followed after him. When Dwayne reached the sketch, he pointed at it. "This one."

Joe looked at it. "That just came in yesterday. Eddie the Cockroach pawned it." He laughed. "I gave him four bits for it."

"Did he say where he got it?"

Joe shook his head. "Naw. He prob'ly found it in the trash or something. It was all rolled up, but it looked pretty nice. So I got an old frame to give it some class."

Dwayne pulled out his wallet. "If I give you back the frame, how much do you want for it?"

"I can't sell it yet," Joe said. "Cockroach might want to redeem it."

"Are you kidding?" Dwayne asked. "You know damn well that half buck you gave him has already been spent on moonshine whiskey."

"Okay," Joe said. "Give me a dollar."

Dwayne pulled a bill from his wallet. "Here you go." He hurriedly pulled the picture off the wall, and pried out the back of the frame. He removed the sketch and carefully rolled it up.

"Christ!" Henry said. "You must really like that drawing." He chuckled. "Or at least drawings of nekked women."

———

DWAYNE SPENT THE REST OF THE AFTERNOON driving slowly around the Warehouse District trying to find Eddie Cochrane. He saw a couple of the drunk's colleagues but inquiries about their associate's location were answered with shrugs of negativity and requests for small change.

Dwayne parked the coupe and prowled up and down alleys, looking behind trash cans and heaps of rubbish to see if Eddie had drunk himself into a stupor with the money he'd gotten pawning the sketch. Only feral cats were prowling the area, looking for rats that had dug deep into the refuse piles. It was close to five when Dwayne remembered he was supposed to drive Donna Sue home from work.

When he arrived at the Jayhawker, Donna Sue and Maisie had to unlock the front door for him. He came in and got a bottle of Orange Crush from the pop cooler and waited while the two emptied the till and added up the take. Then they put the money into a bank bag with the day's order tickets, and Donna Sue took it back and put it in the safe.

———

DONNA SUE NOTICED THAT DWAYNE WAS unusually quiet as they drove over to her apartment house. After they'd gone a couple of blocks, she said, "You seem to have something on your mind."

"I do," he replied. "Y'know, right now I got two capers going on at the same time. The one I'm doing for A.J. Kessler seemed like a lot of nothing, and I was going to give it a couple of more days before calling it off. Hell, I wasn't even going to charge him for it, but now there's something really weird going on."

"What's that all about?"

"There's a rolled up paper back of the seat," Dwayne said. "Get it and take a gander."

Donna Sue reached back and found it and unrolled the sketch. "What's this? A pin-up girl?"

"That is art, my dear," Dwayne said. "And from the looks of it, I'd say it's pretty new."

"Yeah," she agreed. "I'd say it was done recently."

"Well, the artist put his name on it, and it's the bail jumper I'm looking for," Dwayne said. "So I'd say he's still in Wichita someplace."

"I'm a bit confused."

"The thing was pawned by Eddie Cochrane, a rummy who hangs around in the Warehouse District," Dwayne explained. "The pawn broker thinks he prob'ly found it in the trash somewhere. Now I got to find Eddie and get him to tell me where and how he got his hands on it."

"Ah! Another case to be solved by the master detective Dwayne Wheeler!" Donna Sue exclaimed with a laugh.

He grinned at her. "Look out, Dick Tracy, I'm taking over!"

They pulled up in front of the apartment house, and walked up to the front porch. The landlady Mrs. Greeley was sitting on the glider, reading a copy of the *Ladies' Home Journal*. Both she and her husband had developed a grudging admiration for Dwayne since the publicity about him in the *Wichita Eagle*.

"Hello, Donna Sue," she said. "How are you today, Mr. Wheeler?"

"Fine, thanks," Dwayne replied. "I hope all's well with you and Mr. Greeley."

"Oh, yes," she replied. "I'll tell him you said hello."

The couple went through the front door and upstairs to the second floor where Donna Sue's apartment was located. They went inside and Dwayne hurried past her to get an Orange Crush out of the refrigerator.

"Do you want me to fix something to eat?" she asked.

"Let's go out somewhere," Dwayne said. "We ain't been down to the El Charro. I could do a job on one of their combination dinners."

"Sure," she said. "I'm in the mood for Mexican food. Wait until I slip into something appropriate."

"That reminds me," Dwayne said. He fetched out the money he'd been paid by Pete, and peeled off some ten dollar bills. "This is for you."

Donna Sue had no qualms about taking it. Either she would get it or Longshot Jackson the bookie would. "Thanks, sweetie! That's really nice of you."

"I thought you might want to get a fancy outfit," Dwayne said. "A dress, hat, shoes, purse and anything else your little heart desires."

"I'm going to do exactly that," she said, thinking she could use the attire for job interviews. She walked toward the bedroom with the bills, humming happily.

Dwayne, taking a drink of the pop, appreciatively watched the pleasing view she provided.

CHAPTER 11

L otte Gutmanis (*née* Sippel) was in the bedroom above the basement where Fritz Harrigan did his engraving. She had just returned from a shopping trip in which she had purchased a frame for the portrait the boy had made of her.

The woman was excited as she took off her coat prior to preparing the piece of art to be hung on the wall. She went to the dresser and pulled out the top drawer, but the illustration was missing. Lotte frowned in puzzlement and went to the second drawer. The sketch was not there nor was it in the bottom one.

A search in the closet produced nothing nor did she find anything in the unlikely chance that it was in the bathroom. She walked out to the living room where Karlis sat in an easy chair, reading one of the books he had brought with him to Wichita. It was a novel written by his favorite Latvian author Janis Akuraters.

"*Wo ist mein Porträt?*" Lotte demanded to know.

Karlis looked up languidly from his book, answering, "I threw it out."

Her face reddened with anger. "Why did you do that?"

"I told you when we first set up this house that the only things that come up from the basement are plates and proofs."

"This had nothing to do with the business. It was a present from Fritz to me. That portrait was my personal property!"

"It had Fritz's name quite noticeable down in the corner. What if someone had come in the house and noticed it? We already know that he is being sought by a bail bondsman."

"Who is going to come in here?"

"Suppose something went wrong and we were compromised?" Karlis asked. "Such a situation could result in an unexpected event such as a surprise visit by the police who might be searching for the lad."

"The whole idea is preposterous," Lotte protested. "You just did not want me to get a nice gift from the boy." She paused, then said, "You are jealous!"

He laughed aloud. "You have been selling yourself to other men since nineteen forty-five. Why should I be the jealous husband now?"

"You *are* jealous. If it was not for my body we would have starved during those last months of the war. I noticed you did not object when they wanted me to keep the boy amused. You said we could use the extra money when we got back to Europe."

"It was a logical decision," Karlis argued. "And you went along with it."

"It was the decision of a bitter man."

Karlis raised his voice in irritation. "Of course I am bitter!"

"I am the one who should be bitter," Lotte insisted. "I

caught gonorrhea; and from an American officer! Now I am barren. I can never be a mother."

"Bah!" Karlis retorted. "And I served the Third Reich faithfully and bravely as a member of the Latvian SS Legion on the Eastern Front. When you were *Fräulein* Sippel, you were happy enough to marry me when I held the rank of *SS-sturmbannführer*. That was the same as a major in the regular army. You may have been German, but you would never have done that well with your own countrymen. The best you could have hoped for was a sergeant. You were only a cook in a small hotel owned by your parents."

"I attended a chef's school in Berlin," Lotte protested. "I was more than a cook. If it had not been for the war I might have been one of a few female chefs working in four or maybe five star restaurants."

"You were overjoyed to marry an officer and get away from being trapped in that miserable little hotel kitchen."

"You would not have been an officer if not for your service in the Latvian SS," Lotte said. "And you were honored to serve the Nazi cause."

"And what were the rewards for my accomplishments and sacrifices?" Karlis asked. "I ended up on the losing side in the war and had to retreat from the Soviets back into Germany. There I was forced to endure having other men fucking my wife while we tried to survive in a defeated and devastated nation. This will be the last time here in America that you are a prostitute, and I have no desire that you have any romance. You are becoming too fond of that young artist."

"He is a kind-hearted boy," Lotte protested. "And frankly he is wearing me out. I thought of the nice drawing he made of me as a bonus of sorts."

Karlis shrugged. "*Das macht nichts.* The trash truck

has come and gone. Your portrait is now rotting under garbage in a refuse dump."

"It was cruel of you to throw out my nice gift."

"I have already explained why it was necessary," Karl said. He gave his attention to his book for a few more moments, then turned his gaze back to Lotte. "And I did not join the SS to serve the Nazi cause. I did it because I am a Russian-hating anti-communist patriot of Latvia!"

Lotte wiped at the tears in her eyes, then turned and went back to the bedroom to enjoy a good cry.

———

DWAYNE WAS BACK AT HIS HUNT FOR EDDIE "Cockroach" Cochrane. He slowly prowled the Warehouse District in his coupe, getting honks from impatient motorists who had to drive around him. Now and then he would see one of the homeless drunks who wandered the area, but none turned out to be Eddie or knew where he was.

After scouting the main streets, Dwayne turned off to go down the alleys and past the loading docks of the warehouses. Eventually, as he crossed Rock Island Avenue, he spotted the familiar hunched figure of the rummy looking into trash cans.

Dwayne pulled up beside him, and gave the horn a tap. Eddie turned with a look of irritation, then smiled. "Hey, Dwayne."

"Hi, Eddie," Dwayne said. "Need a ride?"

"Naw."

"Well, get in anyway. I need to talk to you."

"I'm looking for bottles to cash in," Eddie said. "I really need a drink right now."

"C'mon," Dwayne urged him. "I'll give you a buck."

Eddie opened the door and slid into the seat. He waited silently until Dwayne handed him a dollar bill. That guaranteed a full pint of moonshine. "What do you want?"

Dwayne noticed the yellowish tinge to Eddie's skin. It was a sure sign of approaching liver failure. "Well, I was over at Wallek's Pawn Shop. I seen a pitcher that you pawned."

"I didn't steal it," Eddie said. "I found it. Okay?"

"Sure, Eddie. I don't care one way or the other so I ain't trying to make trouble for you. But I'd like to know where you found it."

"I found it in a trash can north of Central."

"Do you remember where?"

Eddie shook his head. "No. But it was a place with a big tall fence. It was the tallest in the alley."

"D'you suppose you'd recognize it if we went looking?"

"Prob'ly," Eddie said. "I was sober at the time."

"It'd mean a lot to me if we could find the spot."

"I'd be real happy to help you out, Dwayne. You're the onliest guy that don't call me 'Cockroach'."

"Okay," Dwayne said. "Then let's see if we can find the place."

Dwayne turned the car around and headed north toward Central. "Do you remember how many blocks you went up?"

"It wouldn't have been more'n six since I never go farther'n that," Eddie said. "How's come you want to know where I found it?"

"It'll lead me to a guy I'm looking for," Dwayne said. He turned west on Central going to Saint Francis Avenue, then went a half block to the first alley. He rolled down the narrow lane, heading north. After going six blocks up to Tenth Street, he turned left, going down the next alley between Saint Francis and Topeka. Finally, after they crossed Murdock Avenue, Eddie pointed to a high fence. "That's it."

Dwayne noted the location was on the east side of the alley, meaning the house was on Emporia. He pulled up to the place and stopped where a couple of trash cans stood. "This is it, huh?"

"Yeah," Eddie said. "It was in the first can. I remember the handle on one side was missing."

Dwayne got out of the car and gave the immediate area a quick inspection. There was nothing remarkable to be noted. Then he stepped back and determined that the target residence was the third down from Murdock. He slid back into the driver's seat, and gave Eddie another dollar.

"This is something extra because you been a lot of help, Eddie."

"Glad to do you a favor. You was always a swell guy, Dwayne."

"Do you want me to drop you off where I picked you up?"

"Naw," Eddie said, getting out. "I'm going to get me a couple of pints of moonshine. See you later."

Dwayne drove off, already planning his approach to get inside the house. With the discovery of where the sketch had come from, it was a certainty that he was a step closer to finding Fritz Harrigan. But there were some big doings that night, and he had to pick up Donna Sue for a visit to Buck's Department Store.

———

DONNA SUE HAD ARRANGED TO GET OFF AT three o'clock and she was waiting in the Jayhawker when Dwayne drove up and honked. She hurried out and quickly got into the old coupe. She was excited about going shopping, and laughed delightedly, saying, "To Bucks on the double, chauffeur!"

"Yes, ma'am!" Dwayne replied with a wink. "Buck's Department Store at your command."

He had been in the men's department a couple of days before to get a new suit after Donna Sue's constant nagging. He bought a wool double-breasted chalk stripe off the rack for twenty-five dollars. They had called up that morning to tell him that the sleeves and trousers were now sewn to the right lengths and ready for him to pick up. Donna Sue, on the other hand, was going to take the money Dwayne had given her and buy a couple of dresses, shoes and a matching purse.

When they went inside, Donna Sue hurried off to the women's department while Dwayne went to try on the new suit. He planned to simply grab it and go, but Donna Sue insisted he slip into it to make sure the fit was correct.

"Never walk out of a store until you're completely satisfied with the purchase," she had counseled him.

It took twenty minutes to check out the new purchase and everything was fine just as he had expected it would be. The salesman slipped a paper garment bag over the suit, and Dwayne walked through the store to find Donna Sue. He knew he was in for a long wait, and he was right.

It was close to closing time before Donna Sue had made her final purchases after taking dozens of items of apparel into the changing rooms to try them on. In the end, she chose a sort of somber outfit consisting of a jacket, skirt, and blouse for twenty-five dollars that she planned to wear to the first job interview. It would also be good as a secretary or stenographer's working garment. But for the special occasion she would be attending with Dwayne that same evening, she chose a dress-up frock of rayon crape romaine for thirty dollars.

Her final purchases were a pair of cordovan platform shoes for twelve dollars and a matching saddle leather purse for ten dollars. These would go well with either dress. All total she had spent seventy-seven dollars. And she was wickedly happy about the splurging. She still had money enough to go shopping later to purchase one more dress suitable for work.

As Dwayne and Donna Sue left the department store for the car, she clung to his arm while he wrestled with all the packages. She cooed, "I can't wait to get home and try all this stuff on!"

Dwayne frowned. "Chrissake! You've already done that!"

"Dwayne, you are so silly. That didn't count."

———

THE AFFAIR THEY WERE GOING TO THAT EVENING was at no less a place than the Prairie Wind Golf and Tennis Club where Wichita's *crème-de-la-crème* played, danced and dined. Their hosts were Mr. and Mrs. Carl Banter; and in addition to them, Mr. and Mrs. Peter Van Dyke would be part of the dinner that was going to be held in a private dining room.

Normally Dwayne wouldn't have been particularly interested in the function, but going to the prestigious club had made Donna Sue deliriously happy, especially with the prospect of being able to wear the new cocktail dress. As for Dwayne, he was sure that when she met the Banters and the Van Dykes, she would be extremely impressed with this new commercial enterprise he was associated with.

When they reached the gate of the prominent establishment, the guard on duty gave the old coupe a suspicious glare. But when Dwayne recited their names, and the guy found them on the list for an evening with the Banters, he suddenly broke out in a positive show of respect and cordiality.

"Please go in, Mr. Wheeler," the guard said. "And enjoy your evening."

"Thank you, my good man," Dwayne said, then he turned and winked at Donna Sue as he drove through the gate.

The automobiles in the parking lot were even classier than those at the Roadhouse. Donna Sue had heard of the Prairie Wind Golf and Tennis Club, but she had never imagined she would ever go there. When they parked, she didn't get out of the car until she checked her makeup in the mirror on the sun visor.

"You look great," Dwayne assured her. "C'mon! Let's go."

As they walked toward the clubhouse, Dwayne saw Pete drive his Buick in and park. He steered Donna Sue toward it, and waved when Pete and Sybil Van Dyke got out. After a quick introduction to Donna Sue, the two couples went inside the club. The maître d' at his station gave them the directions to the private dining room.

The interior of the place reminded Dwayne of the time he tailed a suspect in the Kansas City caper to that same building where the mobster had an appointment to meet a member. The latter guy turned out to be a fraud who had convinced the select few of the membership committee he was a real estate tycoon. He was later found out to be involved in narcotics distribution in the Midwest.

As for Donna Sue, she was mesmerized by the sight of the elegant diners—all dressed to the nines—who occupied the swank surroundings. The dress she'd bought for the evening now looked almost tawdry in comparison to those the women wore. And that included Sybil Van Dyke's.

When they entered the small dining room, Carl Banter got up from his chair to greet them. "Sit down," he said. "We've plenty of time for cocktails."

Dwayne once more went through an introduction process with Donna Sue. Now she noted that Sally Banter's dress was also quite superior to her garment, and she was glad to sit down to hide most of it.

Donna Sue was surprised when the waiter showed up and they actually ordered drinks instead of set-ups. When high-ranking members of business, the law, and politics belong to a social organization, such trivial matters as obeying the state liquor regulations are casually ignored. When everyone gave their orders, Donna Sue couldn't think of a libation, but Dwayne stepped in and ordered her a gin and tonic.

Carl Banter gave Donna Sue a smile. "Do you remember me? I've eaten at the Jayhawker a few times after visits to the OK Barbershop."

Donna Sue had no idea who he was before Dwayne introduced her, but she diplomatically replied in the affirmative.

"Donna Sue is finishing up secretary school," Dwayne said. "I hope to have her working for me pretty soon."

Donna Sue could have kissed Sybil when she said, "Pete met me when I was a secretary at an import and export business in New York City."

"I've been thinking of taking up shorthand later," Donna Sue said. "Do you know how to do it?"

"Yes," Sybil said. "And if you can possibly find the time, I heartily recommend that you enroll in a course. It will pay off in many ways."

"Thank you," Donna Sue said. "I believe I will." She felt much better and took a sip of her drink, thinking, *Maybe this dress isn't so bad after all.*

At about the time the cocktails were consumed, a waiter appeared with menus. As Donna Sue studied the entrees, she was shocked at the prices. Some of them went as high as ten and fifteen dollars. There were also the names of a few items she didn't understand, and thought it best to ignore them. When she noticed that Sybil and Sally whispered their preferences to their husbands, she leaned close to Dwayne's ear. "What should I get? Everything is so expensive."

Dwayne spoke softly, saying, "Didn't I tell you I was moving into an upscale organization? Anyhow, don't worry about the prices. Carl is picking up the tab. I'll order something for you."

When the waiter returned, Pete put in his and Sybil's order, and then it was Dwayne's turn. "My lady wants the baked chicken with the vegetable medley and rice. I'll take the New York strip steak medium-well. Hold the vegetables. And could I substitute French-fries for the baked potato?"

"Of course, sir," the waiter said. "And your salads?"

"We'll both take the house salad with ranch dressing."

Carl took over picking out the selections for him and Sally. "And bring two bottles each of the DuBose cabernet sauvignon nineteen-thirty-five and Roma chardonnay nineteen-thirty-eight."

Immediately after the waiter's exit, a bus boy came in

with baskets of various types of hot rolls, and two butter plates. Before leaving, he took up the drink glasses. When the wine was presented, the steward accompanied the waiter.

Donna Sue stared mesmerized as the steward poured a small portion of wine into two glasses. Carl tasted each after breathing in the aromas. "Excellent," he announced, and the waiter took the wine around to pour the preferences of the diners.

Dwayne whispered to Donna Sue. "You want the chardonnay."

"I do?" she whispered back. "Why?"

"I learned in Europe that white goes with chicken and fish."

When the waiter appeared at her shoulder, Donna Sue spoke with cheerful confidence. "I believe I prefer the chardonnay."

Carl raised his wine glass. "May I propose a toast to our joint international enterprise headed up by the very competent Peter Van Dyke? I also wish to include our investigator Dwayne Wheeler in this tribute, and—if I may—myself as the genial attorney."

Everyone raised their glasses, and Pete said, "And may I propose a toast to the lovely ladies who add charm and beauty to this auspicious occasion?"

Donna Sue was beginning to have the time of her life.

The waiter came in again with the bus boy trailing him with a food cart. The salads were served, and Donna Sue carefully observed which fork the others took. She picked up the correct one with self-assurance, nudging Dwayne when he didn't.

It was a very short time after the salads were finished that the dishes were cleared, and the waiter and bus boy once more appeared with the food cart. This time the main courses were passed out, and when everyone was served, the meal began.

Pete spoke to Dwayne. "We'll probably have another trip for you sometime next week." Then he looked at the others. "Sorry to bring up business at a time like this."

"Why not?" Carl asked. "I think of work and leisure as things that go well together. Why do you think I play golf?" He laughed. "Because I like the silly game? Hell, no! We always conduct business out on the links."

When Pete mentioned the work ahead for Dwayne, Donna Sue remembered Dwayne telling her about Germany and the trouble he got into. Pete was part of that black market affair, and she wondered if the New Yorker was now working in a truly legitimate enterprise. Dwayne had a decidedly reckless side to him, and if he saw an advantage in something, he would not hesitate to bend rules or break any inconvenient laws that stood in his way.

"You might be interested to know that I'm laying out our organization here in Wichita in such a way that we won't be required to form a Kansas corporation," Carl announced. "The less publicity, the better."

"Good," Pete said. "We don't want our enterprise to become common knowledge. Business competition in this post war world is cutthroat at best. Especially when Europe is involved."

"I agree a hundred percent," Carl declared, taking a sip of wine. "The decline of currency values in France and Great Britain creates special problems."

"By that you mean the implementation of legal procedures that cut down on the ability to make certain types of investments," Pete said. "We must work out ways to get around all that bother."

"Well, yes," Carl replied. "But that also will include a

constant scrutiny of the rates of exchanges that are completely unpredictable."

"I suggest we change the subject," Pete said with a grin. "We're starting to talk business too much."

Donna Sue cut a slice of chicken, and chewed it slowly and thoughtfully. She definitely didn't like the way the conversation had been slanted.

The perfect evening drifted on pleasantly through the main course and desert. After-dinner liqueurs were ordered, and Carl presented cigars to the other two male diners. At that point, Sally, Donna Sue and Sybil left the table to visit the ladies' powder room.

———

THE DINNER PARTY BROKE UP AROUND midnight, and the group left together. They split up at the parking lot, each couple going to their own car. When Dwayne and Donna Sue got to the old Pontiac, he unlocked the doors. "I hope the next time we come here, we'll be in one of the new '48 models."

Donna Sue got into the coupe. "Yeah. Me, too."

CHAPTER 12

During the eighteen months that Dwayne had been a working private investigator, he had picked up some miscellaneous items to help him in his work. Some were purchased at various times for specific cases as needed, while others were things he ran across that looked as if they had a potential usefulness sometime in the future. Among the latter type, he had acquired a pair of faded green overalls and a billed cap somewhat like an army service type except it had a smaller crown and was pale blue. The headgear was obviously a model to be used in certain civilian jobs by taxi drivers, filling station attendants, milkmen and other workers wearing military-like attire in their occupations. Dwayne was also the proud owner of a stethoscope he had lifted out of a U.S. Army ambulance at the scene of a jeep accident he had been assigned to investigate one dark, rainy evening while on MP duty in Munich, Germany.

Dwayne returned to the Fritz Harrigan caper that Monday, dressed in the cap and overalls with the stethoscope in his back pocket. He also had a clipboard with him that contained some loose leaf notebook paper. He had placed the front cover of a Bell telephone book on top, to give the appearance of it being some sort of work document for the phone company. He had taken it from the one hanging by the phone in the hall of his rooming house.

Dwayne's destination was the residence on the east side of Emporia Avenue down from Murdock. That was where the trash can that had contained the print of the nude was located. Using his access to the locater files in city hall by dint of his investigator's license, he had discovered the name of the present resident was Watkins.

Now, at mid-morning, he parked his coupe around the corner out of sight of the house. He got out and strode down the street with the clipboard, slowing enough to study the place as he approached. It was a one-story frame home that appeared to have been built sometime before the turn of the century. He walked purposely up onto the front porch and rang the bell. There was no answer, and he had to press the button three more times before he perceived someone stirring inside.

The door opened and a tall, husky man with close-cropped balding hair appeared. He gave Dwayne a decidedly unfriendly glare. "Yes?"

"How do you do, sir," Dwayne said cheerfully, making sure the phone book cover on the clipboard was plainly visible. "I'm Morris of the Bell Telephone Company. Would you be Mr. Watkins?"

"Uh...yes," replied Karlis Gutmanis.

"We have a report of a break in the telephone line in this area, Mr. Watkins," Dwayne said. "We're trying to locate it. I'm here to check your telephone."

"Is necessary?"

Dwayne noted the foreign accent that did not fit the

name Watkins. "Oh, yes indeed, sir. This is very important." He had learned in Germany, that it was easy to
confuse foreigners if English was spoken rapidly in a
confusing manner, using redundant words. "Even if your
phone is working properly, it can indicate a possible even
probable location of a breakdown known as a communications space which is a void that must be filled or there
won't be communications such as the equipment is
designed to do really fast." He paused and smiled. "I must
look at your telephone."

Karlis hesitated, but figured if he refused there might
be unwanted consequences. "Coming in, if you must."

"Thank you, sir," Dwayne said, stepping through the
door. "Your cooperation is most appreciated by Pa and
Ma Bell and all the little Bells. Yes, sir!"

Karlis led him over to the phone. Dwayne gazed at it
for a moment. "Ah, yes. That's a Type Four." He gave
Karlis a serious look. "Type Fours are notorious for failing
during tornados and thunderclaps. This may be the
source of all the trouble here in the neighborhood. If it
fizzes out, the flow of power breaks on all the circuits to
which it is attached along with the other phones
connected forthwith." He paused and ominously added,
"A *big* problem."

Karlis had no idea what the babbling telephone
repairman was going on about, but he nodded as if he
understood the situation.

Dwayne took out his stethoscope and slipped it into
his ears. He went to the phone and dialed it several
times with the receiver still on the instrument. He
listened with the device. "Wow! I don't like that noise
this thing is making. It sounds like a couple of studs are
missing on the widget inside. I'm afraid I'll have to
report it."

He dialed zero and waited. A feminine voice came over the line. "Operator."

"Hello, Operator. This is Repairman Morris."

"Sir?"

"We're testing for that line break on Emporia Avenue."

The operator was perplexed. "I don't understand what you're talking about, sir. What number do you want?"

"I'm afraid the chief inspector was right," Dwayne said in an extremely serious tone of voice. "I'm on a Type Four phone that may be the problem."

"Sir," the operator said. "Do you wish long distance?"

"Oh, I'm certain of that."

"Perhaps you wish me to connect you with information," the operator said, now more confused. "Or my supervisor?"

"Of course I'll do that," Dwayne said. "Tell the chief inspector I'll get back to him right away." He hung up. "Do you have any more phones in the house?"

Karlis was getting worried. He hoped the situation wouldn't end up attracting a lot of attention. "No more phones do we have."

"Okay then," Dwayne said. He went back to the telephone and traced the line by hand from the instrument to the wall connection. He pointed to it. "Was this the hook up when you moved into this house?"

"I am not sure of what you say," Karlis said. "Is same phone. We don't get new one."

"Then why'd you change this?"

"We don't change nothing."

"Who is 'we', sir?" Dwayne asked with a heavy hint off accusation in his voice.

"Is my wife and is me."

"How many children do you have?"

"No children."

"Are there any more adults living here?" Dwayne demanded to know.

"No," Karlis said. "Only two here. My wife. Me."

"How about pets? Do you have a dog?"

"No. A dog we are not having."

"What about a monkey?" Dwayne asked. "Do you have a monkey?" He chuckled. "Those little dickenses! A lot of 'em learn how to dial a telephone, did you know that?"

"I know nothing for monkeys," Karlis replied. "Why do you ask me this?"

"Because pets sometimes chew on wires, sir," Dwayne said in a tone of voice indicating he was surprised by the man's ignorance.

"No animals," Karlis said. "Living here are only my wife and I."

"I want to believe you, sir," Dwayne said. "But something is out of whack. I'll have to trace the phone wiring through the house."

He put the stethoscope to the wall and began to feign listening for some kind of tone, then moving down the wall, listening again, then going to the doorway to the next room. This was the dining room and Dwayne surveyed the house carefully as he simulated following the path of wires in the wall. From there he went into two bedrooms, then came out and worked his way to the kitchen. It was there that he discovered the stairs leading to the basement.

"Do you have a telephone down there?"

"Down is no phone!"

Dwayne instantly sensed a sudden increase of uneasiness in the man. His face was reddening and his breathing short and brisk. Now was the time to back off, and put the guy at ease. "All right. I think things are just fine here then." He replaced the stethoscope in his back pocket. "Thank you very much for your cooperation, Mr. Watkins. I have eliminated your house as part of the trouble. On behalf of the Bell Telephone Company I am pleased to inform you that there is no communications problem in your house. Sorry to have bothered you."

Karlis was obviously relieved; he even smiled. "Is no trouble."

"Say," Dwayne said. "Where are you from?"

"I am coming from Latvia."

"Ah," Dwayne said. "Interesting!"

He walked to the front door whistling cheerfully. He opened it, and looked back with a grin and a wave, then left the house.

Karlis heard a knocking at the basement door downstairs. It was a good thing that hadn't happened when the telephone repairman was on the premises. He descended the stairs and unlocked the first door, then the second. Lotte stepped out, and went up to the kitchen while he relocked the portals. He hurried to join her.

"*Was ist los*?" Lotte asked. "Was there somebody here? I thought I heard talking so I did not knock right away."

"It was a telephone repairman," Karlis said. "There is some problem on the lines in this neighborhood. Our telephone seems to be fine, so the man left."

"I was afraid there was trouble."

"I handled everything fine," Karlis assured her.

She walked toward the interior of the house, glancing back at him. "Do not tell Fritz you have thrown away the sketch. It will hurt his feelings."

———

DONNA SUE CONNORS WIPED DOWN THE counter where a couple of customers had just finished eating. The door to the restaurant opened and she looked up. Brian Murchison stood there smiling at her. "Hi! Remember me?"

"Sure, Brian," she replied, a trifle ashamed at him seeing her disheveled from six hours of work.

He sat down at a stool. "What's the special today?"

Donna Sue laughed. "There're never any specials at the Jayhawker. But everything is served on clean plates."

"Well, then," Brian said. "I'd like a hamburger and a Coke."

"Do you want French-fries or potato chips with that order?"

"The potato chips sound just fine."

Maisie, at the other end of the counter, gave Brian a look of genuine admiration. Then she turned her attention to studying Donna Sue's attitude toward the handsome man. They seemed to know each other, but she had never heard Donna Sue mention him before.

Donna Sue turned the order in, then fetched a bottle of Coca-Cola from the pop cooler and opened it. "Do you want a glass and ice with this?"

"No," Brian said. "It'll be fine just as it is."

Donna Sue set the bottle of pop in front of him. "What brings you to the Jayhawker?" she asked, smiling. "Is it because of its similarity to *Duffy's Tavern* on the radio where Archie the Bartender describes it as the place where the 'elite meet to eat'?"

"Of course," Brian said, laughing. "By the way, I saw you at the Prairie Wind Saturday night. I wanted to say hello, but you disappeared into one of the private dining rooms. Was that Dwayne with you?"

"Yes," Donna Sue answered. "He's working for some

sort of group headed up by a gentleman from New York and a local lawyer."

"That would be Carl Banter," Brian said. "I know him well."

Arnie the cook hollered out the order was ready, and Donna Sue picked up the plate along with a bag of potato chips and served it to Brian. He took a bite of the hamburger. "So what sort of business are Dwayne and Carl conducting, if I may ask?"

"It has something to do with investing or finance," Donna Sue explained. "They're pretty secretive, but part of their enterprise has connections with Europe."

"Interesting," Brian remarked. "I would imagine that Dwayne is involved in thwarting industrial espionage or some such thing." He lowered his voice. "I have some information that might interest you. I thought you might want to keep it confidential here where you work."

Donna Sue sensed something special, and she leaned down toward him. Maisie at the end of the counter began cleaning the coffee urn, keeping a close eye on the two. She was expecting a quick and furtive kiss to be exchanged between them.

Brian said, "There is an opening for a secretary in our company. It's just popped up, so no want ads have been ordered yet."

"I finish my course this Saturday," Donna Sue said. "Is that too late?"

Brian shook his head. "I can set up an interview next Monday for you. That's a week from today. What time is best for you?"

Donna Sue was hesitant because of Dwayne. She felt she should tell him what was going on, but she had sensed he was not overly fond of Brian that night at the Road-house. Then she saw no good reason to put things off.

Dwayne certainly couldn't hire her to work for him even if the arrangements with Pete Van Dyke and Carl Banter did pay big money. He would waste it all gambling.

"I can make it in the afternoon," she said. "Would four o'clock be too late?"

"Not at all," Brian assured her. "Our offices are out east on Maple Street. Turn north on Hoover and you'll find a new business complex after you go about a mile. We've just moved into the place. You'll spot a sign reading 'Murchison Commercial Park'." He paused. "As a matter of fact I'd be glad to give you a ride. I could drive in and pick you up."

Donna Sue almost accepted the offer, but doing so would create an awkward situation with Dwayne. She figured it would be better to get him to take her. That would also keep everything out in the open. There had been times lately that she perceived a certain uneasiness in him that seemed to come and go, and she didn't want anything to upset him.

"I can get Dwayne to take me to the appointment."

If Brian was disappointed, he didn't show it. "Great! I'll set it up." He pulled a business card out of his jacket pocket and wrote on it. "When you get there, stop at the gate and ask for directions to the administration building. You'll be looking for Miss Ralston's office."

Donna Sue took the card. "I should have my diploma and grades from Keystone Business College by then. They told us all the documentation on our course results would be ready after the last class Saturday."

"Be sure and bring them along," Brian said. "And I have no doubt that you're an honor student."

She smiled. "As a matter of fact I'm first in the class ratings."

Maisie moved down the counter to the kitchen door

where Arnie stood smoking a cigarette. He, too, found Donna Sue and the handsome fellow something to wonder about. Maisie smiled and whispered, "I think Dwayne has got a rival."

"If that's the case," Arnie said, "I sure as hell feel sorry for *that* guy."

———

WHEN DWAYNE WALKED INTO A.J. KESSLER'S building, the young secretary Jill gave him a look of inquisitiveness. The cap and overalls he wore pretty much boggled her mind. He sensed her curiosity. "I'm moon-lighting as a mechanic at a Bay Petroleum gas station."

Jill decided to ignore him since it was obvious he was trying to fool her. "A.J. is in his office."

Dwayne walked to the door and rapped on it. "Mr. Kessler! Your car is ready!"

A.J. appeared with a puzzled frown. "What the hell?"

"We got to talk," Dwayne said.

They went inside the office and Dwayne settled down in a chair while A.J. positioned himself on the other side of the desk. "Just what's going on?"

"I think I've found Fritz Harrigan," Dwayne announced. "I'm pretty sure he's in a house on Emporia near Murdock."

"Who would he hole up with over there?"

"He may not be holing up," Dwayne said. "I got a strong hunch that our artist is being held against his will. It could be a kidnapping."

"Mmm," A.J. said. "That would explain a lot. Got any ideas?"

"Not a thing right now," Dwayne admitted. "But it's a for sure thing that I gotta get inside that house."

"Let's back up a bit," A.J. said. "How'd all this come about?"

Dwayne gave a quick narrative on the sketch in the pawnshop, how he went to where Eddie Cochrane found it, and the telephone ruse. "There was a foreign guy there," Dwayne said, wrapping it all up. "Big tough son of a bitch. As far as I could determine, he lives in the house with his wife. But I didn't see her."

"My obvious question is; what's your next step?"

"I'm gonna put the place under surveillance," Dwayne said. "If I can establish a routine of coming and going with the residents, I can pick out a time to break in."

"That's against the law," A.J. pointed out.

"Oh, dear!" Dwayne said with a grin.

A.J, chuckled. "So how are you gonna organize this little foray?"

"That's gonna take some time."

"Well, you got a little while more now," A.J. said. "I went with tears in my eyes to Carl Banter's office and he managed to get a stay from the judge. Fritz's court date has been moved forward two weeks. Will that help?"

"At this point, I can't say for certain."

A.J. was silent for several moments, then said, "This whole thing confuses the shit out of me."

"Well, I think I can clear it up eventually," Dwayne promised.

"I ain't talking about the case," A.J. said. "I'm talking about that stupid outfit you got on."

CHAPTER 13

Dwayne didn't have time to change clothes after he left A.J.'s place of business, and his arrival at the Jayhawker aroused as much curiosity as did his appearance at the bail bond office. When he walked in, Donna Sue caught sight of him and stood in silence for several moments with both hands on her hips.

"Well?"

"Well, what?" Dwayne asked, enjoying himself. He walked down the empty counter to the pop cooler.

"Why are you dressed like that?"

"It's the latest thing for us suave men-about-town," Dwayne said. "The designers in Paris are turning out these outfits by the thousands. I understand Clark Gable and Van Johnson are fighting over 'em out in Hollywood. It seems Robert Taylor and Tyrone Power already have several of their own." He had been expecting a wisecrack or two out of Maisie Burnett, but instead of saying anything, she was giving him a sort of look that silently implied, *I know something you don't know.*

Dwayne looked at her for a moment, then turned to drinking his Orange Crush while she and Donna Sue finished cleaning up the restaurant. A couple of times Maisie walked past him and snorted a little laugh with an expression of derision on her face. They had never gotten along since he'd made a crack about her being unfaithful to her husband who was stationed overseas with the Air Force. He couldn't quite figure out this haughtiness toward him. Donna Sue had made him promise to be nicer toward the woman, and he hadn't said a derogatory thing to her in weeks.

Then Arnie Dawkins the cook and Slim the dishwasher came out of the kitchen to go home after cleaning up their work areas. Both nodded to Dwayne with peculiar looks in their eyes that bordered on uneasiness. Dwayne finally chalked it up to the outfit he was wearing. By that time Donna Sue and Maisie had finished with the cleanup and clearing the cash register.

Dwayne and Donna Sue walked hand-in-hand toward the Pontiac coupe, as the downtown rush hour moved slowly both ways on Douglas. Dwayne figured they would be better off taking side streets on the way to her apartment house to avoid the jams that always occurred around the uncoordinated traffic signals. When they reached the car, he held the door open for her. She seemed to be avoiding his eyes, and once again he experienced that sense of uneasiness.

After they turned off Douglas and headed up Water Street, she finally spoke. "Do you want to go out to eat, or should I fix something at my place?"

"I think it would be better if we ate in your apartment," Dwayne replied. "I'm not exactly dressed for going to a restaurant." Then he added, "Unless you want to go to a truck stop."

"Suppose I whip up a pancake supper?" she offered, either missing or ignoring the humor.

"That sounds fine to me."

Dwayne purposely avoided continuing any more conversation to see what sort of a mood Donna Sue was in. She remained silent and gazed out her side of the car, but didn't seem to be pouting or sullen. Evidently he hadn't done anything wrong. At least not lately.

When they arrived at the apartment house, they greeted Mrs. Greeley who was occupying her usual early evening station on the porch glider. The couple went upstairs to the apartment, and Dwayne waited for Donna Sue to unlock the door, noting her hands were slightly unsteady. She went to her bedroom to change, and Dwayne settled on the sofa. He picked up a copy of *Argosy* magazine he'd left there before, and began to idly page through the publication.

It took Donna Sue fifteen minutes to get into a regular dress and redo her makeup. She came out, giving him a smile as she walked past the counter that divided the living room and the kitchen area. She got what she needed from the pantry and refrigerator, then began mixing the pancake batter.

"You never did explain about the outfit you're wearing," Donna Sue said, breaking an egg into the bowl.

"I had to get into a house on this caper I'm doing for A.J.," Dwayne explained. "I told the guy living there that I was a telephone repairman checking the line."

"You're a sneaky private eye."

"That's how I earn my money."

"What were you looking for?"

"I needed to find out if our bail jumper was in there," Dwayne said. "But I couldn't find anything, so I'll have to put the place under surveillance." Then he added, "Or break in and look around when there's nobody at home."

"That could get you into trouble, Dwayne."

"A lot of things I do could get me into trouble."

Donna Sue began heating up the griddle over a gas burner. She wanted to bring up the subject of a ride to the job interview, but every time she started to say something, she hesitated. After a couple of false starts, she decided it would be best to wait until after they ate. She turned her attention back to the preparation of the meal.

They sat side-by-side at the counter after Donna Sue put out a couple of plates of pancakes. Dwayne, as usual, used plenty of oleo and syrup on his, and ate hungrily. He continued to avoid instigating any *tête-à-tête*, and Donna Sue slowly consumed her food in silence. When the meal was over, she cleared the counter and washed the dishes while he dried. She put everything away since Dwayne could never remember what went where in her kitchen organization.

After the clean-up chore was done, they went to the sofa. Donna Sue turned on the radio to *The Bob Crosby Show*, a musical program that featured Bob Crosby and his orchestra the Bobcats. Dwayne and Donna Sue listened to the swing tunes and a couple of songs that were sung by the evening's guest star Dinah Shore.

Donna Sue cleared her throat. "Are you picking me up after school on Saturday?"

"Well, sure," Dwayne said. "Don't I always?"

"That's the last day of the course. I get my diploma."

"Then you're ready to find a secretary job, right?" he said. "Too bad I can't afford to hire you."

"Actually, I have a job interview on Monday afternoon at four o'clock."

"Wow!" Dwayne said. "You didn't waste any time."

"Could you give me a ride?"

"I don't know why not," Dwayne remarked. "Where's it at?"

"It's on Hoover north of Maple."

"That's really far out there in the boondocks," Dwayne said. "It must be a new company."

"Actually it's an old established one that recently moved to the area."

"What company is it?"

Donna Sue cleared her throat again. "It's Murchison Enterprises."

Dwayne didn't say anything for a moment. "That's Brian Murchison's family business, ain't it?"

"Yes."

Dwayne began to feel a trifle upset. "How'd you hear about the job?"

"Brian came into the restaurant and told me about it," she said a little quicker than she wanted to, knowing it made her sound nervous.

"What if something comes up and I can't give you a ride. How will you get clear out there?"

Donna Sue steeled herself. "Brian said he could give me a ride if I needed one."

"When did that shit happen?"

"Well...when Brian came into the restaurant."

Dwayne was silent for a few moments, then stood up. "I'll tell you what. Why don't you let him take you out there then?"

"Well...I guess if you can't, I'll have to."

"Yeah," Dwayne said. "You'll have to." He got to his feet and walked directly to the door.

"Where are you going?"

He abruptly left the apartment, and Donna Sue followed him out into the hall. "Dwayne!" He continued down the stairs, and she looked over the banister. "Come back! Dwayne!"

He ignored Mrs. Greeley as he strode across the porch. When Dwayne drove away, he shifted the gears methodically, and rolled down to Douglas, to head east for his rooming house.

———

IT WAS DARK AS DWAYNE SAT UP ON HIS BED IN his room, leaning on the pillow propped against the headboard. The only illumination came from a streetlight in front of the house shining through the one window, and it made the place look even gloomier than usual.

As he sipped Jack Daniels from a glass, Dwayne's thoughts turned sour. The revelation of Donna Sue going to work for Brian Murchison galled him; not into a rage but with a nagging irritation that set him on edge. He let the liquor soak into both his brain and mood.

His mind rambled at him, *Well, it's happened again, Self, ol' buddy. A dame has decided you ain't what she's looking for. How many is this? It never mattered much to you before, did it? If some cunt wanted to break up, you couldn't care less. Well, it's differ'nt this time, ain't it? Really differ'nt.*

He threw back a deep slug of the whiskey.

Self, you know now why you was getting all them uneasy creepy feelings. You knew damn well you and her was heading for the end of this thing. Why the hell couldn't she have just left well enough alone? You had a really nice situation, keeping each other comp'ny, damn good sex, and going out on the town to have fun Saturday nights. The trouble started when you had to stash her away after the Kansas City mob threatened to kidnap her because you and

Benny Gordon beat up them two pimps. That was when Donna Sue got exposed to that goddamn typewriter and took to it like a duck to water. That's what made her decide she didn't want to be a waitress no more. First there was the typing test, then the high school exam and finally the business college. Everything that's going on now is the end result of all that shit.

Dwayne took another swallow of the whiskey.

Life was pretty good before all that, and she didn't complain about nothing. Sure, you make a lot of bets on the ponies and lose plenty of scratch. And you fall behind in your office rent and get locked out now and then with the phone shut off. But things always work out in the end. Life is simple and good, and you manage to pull in a few bucks as a shamus. Maybe you ain't got reg'lar weekly paychecks like a working stiff, but you don't need 'em. A.J. comes through with enough work to take the pressure off. Things was under control; there wasn't nothing to worry or stew about.

He drained the glass and poured in a generous shot.

And let me tell you something else, Self. The biggest fucking mistake you ever made in your whole fucking life was asking Judy Miller and that fucking Murchison to join you guys at your fucking table at the Roadhouse. Way to go, you dumb bastard. You could sense that oily son of a bitch wanted to make a play for Donna Sue, couldn't you? That would be the guy to give her enough encouragement to want to change her lifestyle. A lifestyle that ain't gonna include you, you knucklehead.

Dwayne took a couple of more swallows of the liquor.

It's over between you and Donna Sue. Don't even try to think it ain't. As the Krauts say, Auf Wiedersehen. *Ah, well, it's prob'ly better all-around like with them other broads when things didn't work out between you and them.*

Hell, you don't want to get married or nothing like that. You are who you are, and she's changing into somebody else. You ain't going along with that shit. It just ain't you. But it is kind of sad, ain't it? And that's why that punchboard Maisie was giving you them uppity looks at the Jayhawker. She must have figgered that something was up when that bastard Murchison walked in the place. Nothing would please the little bitch more than to have Donna Sue give you your walking papers.

The bottle was empty and he got off the bed a bit unsteadily, going to the closet to get another.

———

WHEN DWAYNE WALKED INTO HIS OFFICE THAT next morning, he was hung over bad. The only reason he had come downtown was that his small room had begun to close in on him. He had no plans to do anything that day, other than sit around and let the hours drift by.

The phone rang, and Dwayne let it go on three more times, then thought it might be Pete Van Dyke. He picked up the receiver. "Yeah?"

"Christ!" came the voice of Detective Lieutenant Ben Forester. "You sound like warmed over death."

"Well," Dwayne conceded, "with any luck I'll be dead before noon."

"Okay. But before you die, come over and see me. I think I got what might be a pretty good job for you."

Dwayne's spirits picked up and the pounding in his head quickly eased back to throbbing. A different caper would get his mind off things. "Sure. I'll be there in about twenty minutes."

He struggled out of his chair and left the office. The coupe was parked nearby, and he got it started with the usual pushing and pulling on the choke. The drive to the police station on William Street took less than ten minutes, and he scored a parking place in front of the Eagle Building around the corner.

The Homicide Squad room was empty except for one lone detective who labored on a report with the hunt-and-peck style of typing that required only two fingers. The guy didn't bother to look up as Dwayne went back to Ben's office.

The lieutenant saw him approaching through the glass in the door, and he gestured for him to come straight in. Dwayne entered and slumped down on the chair in front of the desk. "What's up?"

Ben looked at him with a wry grin. "What was the special occasion for the drunk?"

"Oh, just a little shit that slipped into my life," Dwayne said. "Nothing that liquor can't handle."

"Maybe I can brighten your day," Ben said. "Are you aware of the murder in the Warehouse District?"

"I saw something about it in a newspaper at the OK Barbershop," Dwayne replied. "It was a 'John Doe', right?"

"Not for long. Al Gallagher made—"

"Fuck Gallagher," Dwayne snarled. He and the detective sergeant shared a strong personal animosity toward each other.

"As I was saying," Ben continued, "Al Gallagher made an I.D. on the victim. He was a professor of European History at W.U. His name was Mikelis Kilitis."

"What kind of a name is that?"

"Latvian," Ben answered. "Take a look at this."

Dwayne was handed some photos and a written report. There were half a dozen pictures of the body taken from different angles. "What was a guy like that doing in a Warehouse District alley?"

"We ain't figured that out," Ben said. "Prob'ly looking for a hooker or a queer; if that's what *he* is."

Dwayne turned his attention to the written report that had been typed by a stenographer from notes containing Detective Sergeant Al Gallagher's scrawl. Gallagher's handwriting looked like a combination of Egyptian hieroglyphics and Chinese block characters, and most of the police stenos hated to wade through the mess. After Dwayne finished reading the simple statements, he looked up at Ben.

"You ain't solved this yet, huh?"

"No," Ben said. "It's still open, but we can't proceed any further. We're at a dead end with no leads whatsoever. When I told this to the widow—name of Emilija Kilitis, by the way—she was pretty upset. By that I mean sad and disappointed not pissed off. She begged me to continue on. Then I told her about you."

"I take it she wants to hire me to see what I can do with it."

"Exactly," Ben said. "I told her you charge twenty-five bucks a day and expenses, and it didn't faze her a bit."

"That's unusual for a professor, ain't it? I didn't think they earned much."

"He doesn't, er, didn't," Ben said. "But they had escaped from Latvia when the Germans took over and got to England via Sweden. Both man and wife worked with Allied intelligence on the Balkan Desk, and earned some pretty hefty paychecks from several sources. They saved most of it, and came to America after the war."

"Okay," Dwayne said. "I'll take the caper. The only thing is that I'm helping A.J. Kessler out with a bail jumper right now. It might be a few days before I get over to see her. Is she still at the address in the report?"

"Right," Ben answered. "You can take it and the photos with you. Meantime, I'll give her a call and tell her you'll be in contact with her within a week or so. Does that sound about right with you?"

"Sure," Dwayne answered. He gathered up the documents and pictures. "Thanks, Ben. I'll try not to make the Wichita Police Department look too bad when I solve this thing."

"Oh, thank you so very much!" the detective lieutenant replied with a wry grin.

CHAPTER 14

I t was two a.m. and Dwayne sat in his coupe on Emporia Avenue almost directly across from the house he had entered using the telephone repairman ruse. His mood was still bad, and he found it troublesome to concentrate. Each time his attention slipped to the breakup with Donna Sue, he angrily brought himself back to the job at hand.

Dwayne had been at the spot for a couple of hours wanting to discover what sort of activity was going on in the target house. He was especially interested in seeing residents or visitors coming and going. He was hoping to see an appearance by Fritz Harrigan no matter how brief or furtive.

So far the surveillance had been a complete waste of time. Not a single person stirred around the residence, though there had been lights showing from the windows except for the basement. The house eventually went completely dark not long after he arrived on the scene.

Dwayne stepped from his car and walked quietly across the street, keeping an eye on other houses to make sure he wasn't seen. He stopped by an elm tree to look and listen, and the entire street was quiet. The last thing he wanted was some casual late night stroller walking his dog to blunder onto the scene. After a couple of minutes he continued toward his destination, and crossed the yard, easing up to one corner of the house. Another period of silent observation followed before he stepped behind a hedge to move closer to the residence.

The basement was his main concern since he hadn't been able to descend the stairs during his visit. He knelt down at one of the small windows near the ground, and shined his flashlight on it to see if he could get a glimpse into the interior. He was surprised to see that the opening was sealed shut with plywood painted black that had some sort of heavy caulking around the edges. If there was any kind of activity in those confines, it would take a physical investigation to check it out.

After going to a couple of more windows and finding the same arrangement, he withdrew from the yard and returned to his car. Dwayne settled down behind the wheel, deciding to spend no more than another hour before abandoning the surveillance. Then he would go back to his room and get drunk again. A few minutes passed, then a bright light suddenly blazed into his car.

A police patrol vehicle had pulled up alongside. "What's going on here?"

"Kill the light," Dwayne said. "I'm on a stake-out here."

The spotlight went off and a young cop got out of his vehicle and walked around to Dwayne's window. "What's this stake-out shit, buddy?"

Dwayne reached in his jacket pocket and produced his Kansas private investigator I.D. "I'm trying to locate a bail jumper."

The cop took the identification card. "Oh! You're the guy that worked with Lieutenant Forester and Sergeant Gallagher on that Kansas City case, ain't you? I remember seeing you in the *Eagle*."

"That's me," Dwayne said. "How're you doing?"

"Fine, thanks," the cop said. He was a young husky guy appearing to be in his early twenties. "I'm Patrolman Tommy Joe McNeil. I hope I didn't fuck up your assignment."

"Naw," Dwayne said. "It's been a bust so far."

"Which bail bondsman are you working for?"

"A.J. Kessler."

"The midget, huh?" McNeil remarked. "I hear he's a tough little son of a bitch."

"Yeah."

"Which house are you interested in?"

Dwayne pointed directly across the street. "That one. The guy I'm trying to make is a little skinny shrimp. His name is Fritz Harrigan."

"I tell you what," McNeil said. "I'll be on duty here 'til eight in the morning. I'll keep an eye out for you."

"Thanks," Dwayne said sincerely. He pulled out a business card, and handed it to the young policeman. "I can be reached here if you see anything. There's three numbers on the back, too. Whoops! Wait a minute." He took the card back and scratched out the Jayhawker Restaurant. "There's actually only two numbers. That's the OK Barbershop and my rooming house."

McNeil took the card. "I'll let you know if anything interesting happens." He paused. "As a matter of fact, if you ever need an extra hand in any of your cases, give me a call. I'm always looking for part-time work."

Now Dwayne reached into his jacket one more time, pulling out his notebook and a pencil. "Write your name and number here. Ever' once in a while I can use a temporary partner."

McNeil scribbled the information and handed the notebook back. "This is great. I'll tell the guys working the morning watch to keep an eye out for anything special going on around that house. Especially if some skinny little guy shows up. I can ask them to pass the word on to the afternoon watch. We can do that for a few days. Maybe something'll pop up. You never know."

"That's great," Dwayne said. "Well, I think I might as well knock off work for tonight. I don't think anything's gonna be happening around here. And thanks again, Tommy Joe. I'll be seeing you around."

"Sure thing, Dwayne. Be seeing you around."

DWAYNE WAS AWAKENED BY A LOUD KNOCKING on his room door. Mrs. Busch's voice, with more than just a little irritation in it, could be heard. "Dwayne! You got a call on the phone out here in the hall."

"Coming," Dwayne said. He got out of bed and slipped into his pants through the haze of his hangover before padding barefooted across the floor to the door. The landlady was waiting with the earpiece in her hand. "Somebody tore the front page of the directory off. Do you know anything about it?"

"No, ma'am."

She handed the earpiece to him. "A bunch of hoodlums! That's who I'm renting rooms to."

Mrs. Busch walked off and Dwayne spoke into the mouthpiece. "This is Wheeler."

"Hello, Dwayne," said Pete Van Dyke. "I've got another job for you. Can you come by the hotel sometime today? You don't have to be in Chicago until tomorrow night."

Dwayne checked his watch, noting it was nine a.m. "Yeah, I can make it. Any particular time?"

"Nope," Pete answered. "I'll be here in the suite all day on the telephone taking care of some business back east."

"Okay," Dwayne said. "Let's make it this afternoon. I was out on a stake-out 'til early this morning."

"Hey, sorry to wake you up, guy."

"Perfectly all right," Dwayne said. "Especially when there's a chance to make some money."

"This trip is going to be a bit different than the first one," Pete said. "I'll fill you in when you get here. Bye."

Dwayne hung up and returned to his room. After flopping into bed, he tried to get back to sleep, but was too restless. He finally got up and filled his percolator with water and put some coffee in the basket. After setting it atop the hot plate on the dresser, he got into a shirt and shoes. A glance outside showed a nice sunshiny Kansas day. The hangover wasn't too bad, so he figured he would be clearheaded within an hour or so.

By the time he finished his morning toilet, the coffee was ready and he poured himself a cup. His stomach rumbled a bit with hunger, and he felt the need for breakfast. Eating at the Jayhawker was out of the question now, and he pondered where he might find a suitable replacement café for meals. He recalled a small diner on First Street just east of the Warehouse District. He had eaten there a couple of times when he was in the neighborhood. The place was clean, and they served decent food. They also sold meal tickets and he thought it might be a good idea to buy a few to use on those rainy days when he was broke. There would be no more free chow to be had from Donna Sue.

Dwayne drank the coffee and smoked a cigarette, deciding that morning would be a good time to call on the widow of the murdered Latvian. He had the phone number given him by Ben Forester in his jacket pocket.

He drained the cup, then went out to the hall to give the lady a call.

———

DWAYNE HAD BREAKFAST AT THE TIP TOP DINER, and decided to make it his permanent eating place after he had no trouble getting them to substitute French-fried potatoes for the hash browns on the breakfast menu. That had been the most important criteria for choosing the place as far as he was concerned. After eating and purchasing five dollars' worth of meal tickets, he went out to his first appointment of the day.

He drove north on Hillside to Seventeenth Street, turning right and going down to Yale. A left took him to the middle of the block to the Kilitis residence. When he stopped in front of the house, he recalled visiting the widow of another murder victim not long before. That had been a bookie's wife, Mrs. Stubb Durham. He hoped this wasn't going to become a regular occurrence in his life as he walked up to the porch and rang the bell. There were more pleasant ways to begin a day's work.

A lady with graying blond hair answered the door. "Yes?"

"Good morning, ma'am," Dwayne said. He flashed a badge that read **PRIVATE INVESTIGATOR** that he'd bought at Wallek's Pawnshop. It was more impressive than an

I.D. card to people outside of law enforcement. "I'm Dwayne Wheeler. Detective Lieutenant Forester of the Wichita Police Department said he told you about me. I believe you'd like the case involving your late husband investigated."

"Oh, yes," the woman said. "Please come in. I am Mrs. Kilitis."

He followed her into the living room, waiting for her to sit down before he took a padded straight-backed chair. "I want to be honest with you from the start, Missus Kilitis. Since the police are stymied, I can't guarantee I can do much better than them. And my fee is twenty-five bucks a day and expenses, but I think Lieutenant Forester has already told you that."

"He did," Mrs. Kilitis said. "Lieutenant Forester recommended you most highly, and I am desperate to have the killer of my husband brought to justice. So I wish to hire your services." Her foreign accent, while not heavy, was noticeable.

"That's fine, ma'am," Dwayne said. "And I accept the case. Before we get into the nitty-gritty of the crime, could you give me a brief rundown on you and your husband? It prob'ly sounds like useless snooping to you, but it helps to learn as much as possible about a client. Sometimes surprising information pops up that can shed a light in the darkness, if you know what I mean."

"I understand," Mrs. Kilitis said. "We are from Latvia. My husband was a professor at the University of Riga before the war. It was not a happy time for us since we were under the domination of the Soviet Government. The Latvian people suffered mistreatment and mass arrests under Stalin, and we hated the Russian occupiers very much."

"I was stationed in Germany after the war," Dwayne

said. "We had a few run-ins with Ruskies, too. They ain't nice people."

"So when the Germans invaded, we welcomed them as liberators," Mrs. Kilitis continued. "But it did not take long before we realized we had traded one set of tyrants for another. Of course, that was the attitude of the intelligentsia for the most part. The common citizens were not so bothered. Even when the Germans began arresting our Jewish countrymen and deporting them, no outcry or protests came from the masses. A few members of university faculties and students voiced objections, and as a result of their protestations, they quickly disappeared as had dissidents under Soviet rule."

Dwayne's note taking was sparse at this point.

"The Germans were completely taking over our country. They even formed an SS unit made up of Latvian volunteers. Are you familiar with the German SS, Mr. Wheeler?"

"Yes, ma'am. During the war I helped interrogate German prisoners of war, and a lot of them guys were *SS*. They was pretty dedicated to the Nazi way of doing things as I recall. And they were tough fighters, too. At least that's what I heard from guys that was at the front in combat. I was a military policeman and did my duties mostly in the rear areas."

"Many of our young men joined the SS as a chance to fight against the Soviets," Mrs. Kilitis said. "This created much dissention between those who wanted to serve the Germans, and those who recognized that the Nazis were as evil as the Soviets. My husband and I were among the latter. We were lucky in that an organization of anti-Nazis arranged to have us and other intellectuals smuggled out of Latvia to Sweden. After arriving there, my husband and I went to the British Embassy and were able to be taken to

Great Britain. This was facilitated by the fact we had spent some time in exchange programs at Cambridge University. Several professors with whom we formed friendships there sponsored us."

Dwayne nodded. "Lieutenant Forester said you and your husband worked for Allied intelligence."

"Yes," the lady said. "After the war, because of our participation, we were given the choice of either immigrating to Canada or America. Naturally we would have lost our freedom and eventually our lives if we returned to Latvia, and we chose the United States. My husband was fortunate enough to find a position as a professor of European history at Wichita University."

"Okay," Dwayne said, having learned more than he wanted to. "Did your husband have any enemies here?"

"No. Not a one, I am sure."

"Did anybody from Europe show up here in Wichita that might have had it in for your husband?"

"Do you mean an enemy from Latvia? I admit there were confrontations between my husband and certain members of the Latvian SS and other German sympathizers before we fled the country. But we have never seen any of them since leaving our home. We presume most of them are dead. Because of the danger of captivity and being sent back to face certain execution by the Soviets, many fought to the death in the last battles of the war."

"Uh huh," Dwayne said. "Now your husband was found dead in the Warehouse District. Did he drive there?"

"No, Mr. Wheeler. Our car is still in the garage. I thought he was at the university grading papers at the time."

"He prob'ly took a cab," Dwayne remarked, thinking the guy had undoubtedly snuck out to get whatever kind of sex he was looking for. He put his notebook away. "Like I said, I want to be honest with you, Missus Kilitis, I ain't got a lot to go on here."

"Lieutenant Forester said you had ways of obtaining information from contacts you have on the streets," Mrs. Kilitis said. "All I ask is that you do your best."

"I can promise you that, Missus Kilitis," Dwayne said, standing up. "I'll be on my way now."

She walked with him to the door and let him out. "Thank you, Mr. Wheeler."

Dwayne stopped on the porch, suddenly remembering the man in the house on Emporia Avenue. He turned toward her. "Are there people from Latvia who would have the name 'Watkins'?"

Mrs. Kilitis shook her head. "That is most definitely not a Latvian name, Mr. Wheeler."

"I see," he remarked, then went down the porch toward his coupe.

———

DWAYNE'S NEXT STOP WAS THE RIVERVIEW Hotel to check in with Pete Van Dyke. He got out of the elevator on the fourth floor and walked down to room 406. Sybil opened the door and invited him in. "Hello, Dwayne. Nice to see you again."

"It's good to see you, Sybil," he replied. He looked over her shoulder and saw Pete talking on the telephone. "I'll sit down and wait."

"Can I get you a cup of coffee?" she asked.

"Do you have something a little stronger?"

Sybil laughed. "Sure. How about a scotch on the rocks as an eye-opener."

"A couple of shots of scotch without the rocks would fill the bill."

"You got it," she said. "A little hair of the dog?"

"Yeah," Dwayne said. "It looks like Donna Sue and I have split up, so I'm oiling my way through the next few weeks with hard liquor."

"Oh, Dwayne! I am so sorry to hear that." She went to the bar and fixed his drink, then brought it over to him. "You two seemed a perfect couple."

Dwayne took a deep sip of the libation. "I guess we been drifting apart for awhile. Like the old song says, 'It was just one of those things'." He didn't say anything else for a moment, then added, "'Just one of those crazy things'." He chuckled, "I better shut up or I'll start singing."

Pete hung up the phone and came over. "Hello, Dwayne."

"Hi, Pete."

Sybil said, "He and Donna Sue have broken up."

"Gee, guy, that's too bad," Pete said, sitting down beside him. "How're you doing?"

"Adapting," Dwayne replied. "Whatcha got for me?"

"Same as the last time, but no briefcase is involved," Pete said. "You're going to pick up a small package—a manila envelope, actually—and there's no big deal about it. You don't have to be armed."

"That sounds positively boring," Dwayne joked. "Packing heat always adds spice to any job."

"Spoken like a true shamus," Pete said with a laugh. "I'll try to send you into harm's way next time. I promise."

"Okay," Dwayne said. "What's the arrangements?"

"I'll take you up to Newton to catch the morning train

tomorrow," Pete said. "Once you're in Chicago, you'll be met by the guy you noticed at the hotel bar and grill on the first trip. He'll give the envelope to you. There may be some people who wish to meet with you. At any rate, you return Thursday night to Newton. I'll be waiting for you there."

"Sounds fine to me," Dwayne said.

Sybil gave him a sympathetic look. "Would you like another drink before you leave?"

Dwayne handed her the glass. "Yeah, please."

CHAPTER 15

It was the morning slow period at the Jayhawker Restaurant, and Donna Sue and Maisie were leaning against the counter by the coffee urn. Donna Sue slowly and pensively sipped from a bottle of Royal Crown Cola while Maisie smoked a cigarette; inhaling, then languidly exhaling, letting the smoke drift upward toward the ceiling. They watched dully as Slim the dishwasher picked up the last of the breakfast dishes to take into the kitchen.

"Dwayne hasn't come in for a day or two," Maisie commented.

"I wasn't expecting him," Donna Sue replied, slightly irritated.

"Are you guys on the outs?"

Donna Sue only shrugged.

"That was a good looking guy who came in here to see you the other day."

"Uh uh."

"What's his name?"

"Brian," Donna Sue told her.

"Is there something going on between you?" Maisie asked, smothering her eagerness.

Donna Sue remained silent.

"I mean, you two was acting like you had a secret between you. You was putting your heads together."

"We were just talking," Donna Sue said, not wanting to reveal her plans of interviewing for another job.

"Are you seeing him?"

"Not in a way you might think."

"Does Dwayne know about him?"

"He knows him," Donna Sue said.

"Did you give Dwayne the brush-off?"

"Not exactly."

Maisie was feeling stymied. "What do you mean by that?"

Donna Sue glared at her. "What do you think I mean by that? I mean *not exactly*!"

Maisie snuffed out her cigarette in a nearby ashtray. "Dwayne was always mean to me 'cause I go out with other guys while Harry's overseas."

"Do you think that's the right thing to do?"

"Oh, come on!" Maisie protested. "What the hell do you think he's doing over there in Korea? I'll bet he ain't even going to a whorehouse to get his ashes hauled. It's for sure that horny bastard's got a little slant-eyed hottie on the side all to hisself. So why shouldn't I get me some loving, too?"

"Suit yourself."

"That's exactly what I'm gonna do," Maisie said. "I'm gonna damn well suit myself just as much as I want." She lit another cigarette. "I know what's going on with you and Dwayne. Maybe I ain't got much education or nothing, and I ain't real smart, but I can tell that you're changing and he ain't. That guy Brian is a slick type and I bet he's got plenty of money. You're good looking enough to get a guy like that to fall for you, Donna Sue. If you married this Brian, you could end up living in a big house and wearing expensive clothes." She took a deep pull of the extra-long Pall Mall she was smoking. "I been thinking that you ain't long for the Jayhawker, what with all that schooling you been getting lately."

Donna Sue walked down the counter away from the other waitress, and went into the kitchen.

"Where you going?" Maisie hollered after her.

Donna Sue walked past the grill and the sinks without speaking to Arnie or Slim. Both men gazed at her as she stepped out into the alley. She stood in the shade of the restaurant, looking down the narrow thoroughfare to Douglas Avenue without really seeing anything.

Donna Sue wasn't sure if Dwayne was out of her life for good or not, but it was beginning to seem it was almost a certainty that they wouldn't be a couple again. He was a man set in his ways, and he liked the way he lived, and he liked betting on the horses, and he was perfect for the work he was doing since the uncertainty and risks seemed to stimulate him. There was no way in hell he would be changing to match what she now wanted in a man. There would be no job for her in his office; he couldn't pay rent on a regular basis much less provide a living wage for a secretary. He'd keep driving that jalopy Pontiac coupe until it fell apart, and all he would be able to afford would be another piece of similar junk to drive around in. And that would be just fine with Dwayne Wheeler.

Donna Sue felt a strong sense of loss and began to weep silently with tears welling in her eyes to trickle down her cheeks. She reached in her apron pocket and fetched a handkerchief to wipe her face.

Maisie appeared at her side. "Aw, kid!" The two wait-resses embraced, and Maisie held Donna Sue close to her.

In spite of all the negativity about Dwayne, Donna Sue still had a deep and hurting affection for him, even though their affair was apparently all over and done with. And nothing could salvage what they once had for each other. It was all past tense.

Donna Sue regained her composure, and she and Maisie went back into the restaurant.

———

IT WAS THURSDAY AT AROUND HALF PAST EIGHT p.m. when the Santa Fe local pulled into Chicago's Union Station. Dwayne wasn't as anxious to get off the train as he had been on his first trip, and he stayed in his seat until it came to a complete stop. Then he picked up his battered valise and made his way to the door, step-ping down onto the platform. He walked into the termi-nal, knowing the direction to go to meet the man with the undershot jaw. He moved slowly through the crowd, giving way anytime someone happened to cross his path as he headed for the rendezvous. He almost felt like he was on a brief vacation, because of the work waiting for him when he got back to Wichita. He would have the capers for A.J. Kessler and Mrs. Kilitis to take care of, and there were perplexing, even irritating aspects in each.

Dwayne spotted his greeter, and walked toward him, still taking his time. The big husky guy watched him dispassionately almost without interest as he approached. When Dwayne reached the guy, he nodded. "I'm Wheeler."

"Yeah," the guy responded. "I've seen you before. I'm

Jabaran. C'mon, there's a car waiting for us outside at the curb."

They went through the station exit, and Dwayne was led to a gray 1940 Desoto. Jabaran opened the door and motioned Dwayne to enter. The shamus got into the backseat with Jabaran following. Jabaran spoke to the man at the wheel. "All right."

Dwayne recognized the driver as the guy who had met him on the first trip to pick up the briefcase. The car eased into the evening traffic, and after a few turns it was driven onto some sort of parkway. Since Dwayne had never been in Chicago except once before, he had no way of knowing where they were headed, and after twenty minutes he lost his sense of direction. Since Jabaran didn't seem to be in a talkative mood, Dwayne settled back to enjoy the ride and gaze out at the sights of the metropolis that was unknown to him.

They left downtown and moved through residential neighborhoods. A half hour passed and these areas thinned out until they were in an open space of extremely large homes with a good deal of distance between them. Eventually, the driver wheeled off the road and continued up a driveway that led to a gate. It reminded Dwayne of Mrs. Davies' property in north Wichita. The driver dimmed the lights and a couple of men appeared from somewhere off to the side. One kept a close eye on the car while his buddy opened the wrought iron barrier. With that done, the trip continued up a tree-lined drive that suddenly curved off to the left. A one-story over-sized bungalow came into sight, and the driver pulled up in front of a large veranda on the side of the structure.

Jabaran opened the door and stepped out. "Leave your valise," he ordered. "You ain't gonna be here long."

Dwayne left the piece of ancient luggage and scooted

across the seat to the door. He followed after his companion who led the way to a side entrance. They entered a well-furnished parlor that boasted a piano.

"Take a seat," Jabaran instructed curtly. He went through another door and disappeared.

Dwayne settled down on a settee, looking around the room. Heavy curtains framed the windows and large paintings were hung around the walls. A couple of ornate lamps, sitting on tables, were turned on and provided a shadowy illumination. Ten minutes passed before Jabaran appeared with another man. The new guy was dressed in a wool worsted suit and tie with short golfing trousers and long stockings. There were leather patches on the elbows of the jacket.

"I say, you must be Wheeler, what?" he said in an upper-class English accent.

"Right," Dwayne replied.

"I'm Hawthorne," he said, offering in his hand. "Peter speaks quite highly of you. Sit down and make yourself comfortable." He turned to Jabaran. "I say, Paul. There's some damn fine Irish whiskey on the sideboard next to the wall. Do pour a couple of stiff ones for Wheeler and me. There's a good fellow."

If Jabaran felt any resentment about being treated as a servant, he gave no indication of it. He fetched a couple of glasses of the amber liquor and handed each man one.

"Now, Wheeler, old boy," Hawthorne said. "I wanted to meet you so that we might get to know each other. This is absolutely necessary, you see, since Peter has made it perfectly clear that you are on your way to becoming an important member of this organization."

"He hasn't said nothing specific about it."

"Evidently it is something he has firmly decided. Actually, you are much more than a courier, you see, old chap. When things are set up firmly in our cozy little undertaking, you will be given a great deal of responsibility. Jolly good, what?"

"Yeah," Dwayne replied, appreciating the likelihood of making a great deal of money. "But I got to tell you something, Hawthorne; I got no idea what we're doing."

"Now's not the time for you to learn, old chap," Hawthorne said. "But I'm sure you're going to be jolly well happy with what you're into." He turned to Jabaran who was standing by the door. "I say, Paul, there's a manila envelope on my desk. Be a good chap and bring it here."

Jabaran went out the door, returning almost immediately with the requested object.

"Give it to Wheeler, if you please," Hawthorne said. "You may open it, old boy."

Dwayne set his drink down on a table, and undid the flap. He pulled out several sheets of paper about eight-by-ten inches in size. They were basically the same color of gray, but seemed to be of different ages. The more faded had small wrinkles. Dwayne ran his fingers around the sheets. "These are a little thicker'n reg'lar paper."

"That they are, old chap," Hawthorne said. "There is a great deal of cloth and fiber in their make-up. Rather expensive, if you know what I mean. It would be something King George might use to write out a proclamation. Haw!"

"What are they for?" Dwayne asked.

"As of the moment, they are for you to take back to Peter Van Dyke in Wichita," Hawthorne said. He finished off his drink and stood up. "So that's that then. Awfully to nice to have met you, old chap. Ta! Ta!"

Jabaran nodded toward the door. "We'll take you to

the hotel near the Union Station for the night. You'll catch your train back in the morning like the last time."

Dwayne drained his glass and followed Jabaran out of the bungalow, carrying the manila envelope containing the sheets of paper with him.

———

PETE VAN DYKE STOOD BY THE BUICK ON A SIDE street bordering the Newton railroad depot. The Santa Fe local from Chicago had just pulled in and, as could be expected in a small town, not too many people got off. Within a couple of minutes, Dwayne Wheeler appeared walking toward him, carrying the beat-up valise he seemed to be so fond of.

Pete walked around the car and got in on the driver's side, while Dwayne slid in to ride shotgun. Pete started up the big automobile. "How was the trip?"

"Nothing exciting," Dwayne replied, as they rolled away toward U.S. Highway 81. "They gave me some pieces of weird looking paper for you."

"They're quite important," Pete said. "As you'll find out later."

"And I met Hawthorne."

"He's quite a guy."

"He seemed pleasant enough, I guess. What's the story on him?"

Pete lit a cigarette off the car's lighter. "I met Nigel Hawthorne in Germany not long after you left. He was in one of those fancy British Army guards outfits—grenadier guards or fusilier guards, or whatever they call them—and he was a captain, and a liaison officer between the Limeys and Americans. I ended up being assigned to act as a sort of escort for the guy when he was billeted at our garrison.

By then I'd put a hell of a lot of distance between myself and the black market."

Dwayne laughed. "I can't blame you for that."

"Well, the job with Hawthorne went along pretty much as a boring routine, then the guy ended up in a very bad situation."

"Really?" Dwayne remarked, surprised. "He struck me as being pretty straight laced."

"Gambling was his undoing," Pete said. "He got himself pretty deep into hock to an illegal German casino in Frankfurt, and fell into that classic trap where Communist agents set out to blackmail him into spying for them. He either cooperated, or they would reveal his heavy gaming debts to British intelligence."

"That's some real bad shit," Dwayne remarked.

"You bet," Pete agreed, steering the Buick down the highway. "It would have ended his career. Anyhow we had become pretty close friends, and he revealed all his troubles to me at our officers' club one evening while we sat over in a corner alone. I told him that he should own up to it and take his licks. That'd be a hell of a lot better than being on the hook to the Soviet NKVD for the rest of his life."

"He took your advice, right?"

"Not at first," Pete said. "He started babbling about the disgrace to his family if he were cashiered for conduct unbecoming an officer and gentleman. They weren't royalty or anything like that, but they were upper class and he had several male relatives holding responsible positions in the King's government. One of the Hawthornes had even been assigned to their embassy in Washington throughout the war. Hawthorne scared the hell out of me by saying he'd take the only honorable way out a gentleman would have. He had to write a note revealing his misdeeds along with an apology. There was nothing to do after that, but fire a bullet into his head."

"God!" Dwayne exclaimed with a grimace.

"But," Pete said, "in the end he didn't want to die."

"So he did come out in the open about it, huh?"

"Yeah," Dwayne said. "And he was cashiered in disgrace from his regiment. He couldn't bear to go back to England, so he stayed in Germany. The guy was cut off without a dime by his father, and he ended up getting a job in the branch of a British bank there in Frankfort. We stayed in touch, and as he became more acquainted with the financial dealings in postwar Europe, he came up with a scheme. I was offered a piece of the action. Things developed and here we are."

"I learned something more about this operation anyhow," Dwayne said. "But I still can't figger out what the hell all this is about."

"Not to worry," Pete said with a smile. "You're getting closer to the inner circle. You got some good things going for you, Dwayne."

Dwayne nodded and fished a Lucky Strike cigarette out of his shirt pocket as they continued the ride to Wichita.

CHAPTER 16

L otte Gutmanis, wearing her favorite blouse given as a Christmas gift by her mother before the war, sat quietly on the chair in the basement. She faced Fritz Harrigan where he had positioned himself on the bed. Her head was turned slightly to the left as per the young artist's instructions. The bright lamp from the drafting table had been set up to illuminate her features to the maximum.

The day before, Lotte had gone out to purchase some water color equipment for Fritz. This had been approved by Karlis after the artist asked for a special favor. The young man explained that working in another art medium would give him a break from the meticulous chore of engraving, and would refresh him. Karlis agreed to the request, and Lotte went by cab to an art store downtown to buy the items on Fritz's shopping list.

Lotte came back with a packet of cold-pressed papers; various round and flat brushes; some pencils; a knife with a retractable blade; a studio palette; fiberboard and tacks; and eleven tubes of paint as specified. Fritz chose colors that would allow him to mix a maximum quantity by having the primaries of blues, reds and yellows; secondary's of orange and green; and neutrals of gray along with two shades of brown. The brown were auxiliaries of a sort with which the young artist could mix a large variety of different colors as he had learned to do in his art classes at Wichita High School East.

This whole thing had come out of a ruse thought up by Lotte. She had not told Fritz that Karlis had thrown out the nude sketch he had made of her, but she requested a more modest portrait. She explained that she wanted a likeness that could be framed and displayed in her living room.

"I would be so proud of something dignified and demure to show my friends," Lotte explained.

"I understand," Fritz said. "Some people who don't really appreciate art would be offended by a nude. I'll be real happy to make a new one for you."

Lotte planned to sneak the final product out of the basement and hide it until she and Karlis left Wichita and returned to Europe. By then there would be no reason for him to throw it away.

When the woman mentioned she did not want Karlis to know of this latest portrait, the artist was confused. When he asked the reason, Lotte was vague, saying only that she preferred it to be their secret. That didn't really answer his question, but he figured if it meant so much to Lotte, he would do as she asked.

There had been times when he sensed some resentment on the woman's part toward Karlis, so he promised to keep the work hidden among the other papers on the shelf above the drafting table where Karlis wouldn't stumble across it. Lotte said that Karlis would think they were having sex while she was posing, and not disturb them. When she asked him the favor of making their couplings as rapidly as possible to allow more time for the watercolor, he agreed to it. Lotte said she would make up for it later with some special techniques of sex she had not shown him.

Now Fritz worked on an eleven by fourteen inch piece of cold-pressed paper pinned to the fiberboard. He had been treated to a quick but satisfying session of fellatio by Lotte before they began the session. One thing he had discovered during the trysts in the basement, was that when he was sexually satiated, his creativity increased markedly. Because of that, he had decided that after he finished his work for Karlis and was paid off, he was going to make an effort to find a cooperative girl who would meet with him before he began any projects. With his passion satisfied, he would be able to create great works of art.

Fritz had even considered talking Lotte into becoming his mistress on a permanent basis. It was a well-known fact that most famous artists lived with paramours; Picasso was a good example. Of course if Fritz did that, he would have to leave Wichita because of his mother. She would never stand for such an arrangement. Perhaps if he earned enough money from the present engraving job, he could take Lotte to New York City, and they could live together in a Greenwich Village loft.

Fritz sketched Lotte's face carefully, making mental notes on the light shadows he would put across her features when he applied the water colors. She had wanted a smile, and in his artist's mind he didn't feel it should be a broad one. Her face was a trifle wide as it was, and a toothy grin would make her look heavier. Fritz had drawn her mouth somewhat like that of the Mona Lisa, although a bit more good natured. Lotte also had hard eyes, and he decided to soften them in subtle gray shades to make her appear more cheerful. As he worked and gave her likeness a closer study than he had done before, the young artist began to realize that there must have been a lot of unhappiness in her life; perhaps even mistreatment and humiliation.

"Would you like me to include the broach?" Fritz asked, referring to the pin at the collar of the blouse.

"Yes," Lotte said. "It will make me look more modest."

"Sure," Fritz said. "I promise you will find the end result quite dignified and flattering."

"I have no doubt of that," Lotte said, pleased that he was following her requests. She glanced at her watch. "I think I must go now."

"All right," Fritz said. "All I need is one more sitting for the sketch, then I can work on the water coloring alone."

Lotte removed the broach and unbuttoned the top two buttons of her blouse to allow the collar to open far enough to reveal her cleavage. That way Karlis would think she'd been engaged in hot sex with Fritz. With that done, she walked to the door and knocked. A minute later it opened and she stepped out. Karlis locked the door, then stood back while she ascended the stairs. He followed her up to the kitchen. "You took longer than usual."

Lotte shrugged. "Not too much longer. Perhaps he's getting used to it now so he doesn't ejaculate so quickly. He is becoming more sophisticated in his lovemaking."

"Was he satisfied with the purchases you made for him?"

"*Ja*," Lotte replied. "I suppose one must pamper the artist's temperament, *nicht wahr*?"

"I was told that was particularly important where

engravers are concerned," Karlis said. He changed the subject. "I could use a cup of coffee."

"I will make a pot. Would you like to drink it in the living room?"

"Yes. It is more comfortable than the kitchen."

Fifteen minutes later the couple sat together on the sofa, sipping the brew. Karlis took a slurp. "This is delicious. I wonder how long it will be before we have decent coffee in Europe again."

Lotte shrugged. "It is a matter of time before all the wartime shortages come to an end. But Germany will be the last to return to normal. The French, Belgians and Dutch will see to that. They are not going to do us any favors."

"I have been thinking," Karlis said. "Perhaps when we return to Europe and are paid off, we should go to Switzerland to live. It has occurred to me that we would have a much better life there unless we stay in the organization."

"It makes no difference to me," Lotte said. "My old home is in the Soviet Zone, and I can never return there." She poured herself another cup of coffee, and put in two generous spoonfuls of sugar. "What will happen to the boy in the basement?"

"A bullet in the head," Karlis said. "What else?"

She tried to hide her emotions. "Will that really be necessary?"

"Of course," Karlis snapped. "He may not be aware of the real purpose behind this work, but he knows enough to give a great deal of help to any investigation that might occur."

"Will we never be free from violence?" Lotte wondered.

"Someday," Karlis replied. "The war is not over for us

yet, Lotte, and it will not be until we are comfortably established somewhere. And I will sacrifice anyone to finally escape from all the misery I've endured."

She gave him a cold glare. "I have not exactly been leading a blissful existence."

"You know I meant you, too."

"Sometimes I am not so sure of that, *Liebling* Karlis."

———

IT WAS EARLY ON SATURDAY MORNING WHEN Dwayne walked into the small restaurant across from the post office. He was responding to a phone call he'd received earlier at his rooming house. Patrolman Tommy Joe McNeil notified him that he had some information regarding the home on Emporia.

Dwayne glanced around the eatery and spotted Tommy Joe in a back booth. Dwayne knew the policeman would be writing up his report on the night watch before returning to the station.

He walked back to the rear of the eatery to join the young man, sliding into the booth opposite him. "How's it going?"

"Okay," Tommy Joe replied. "Like I said on the phone, I got some news for you. The guys on the evening watch got it from the day watch and passed it on to me. I got the info a little late, so it may not mean much anyhow."

"You never know."

"Thursday morning a cab came up to the subject house and a woman came out and got into it," Tommy Joe informed him. "She was a blond, maybe thirty to forty years of age with big tits. She was pretty good looking, but she had the look of a broad that'd known some tough times."

"I'm familiar with the type," Dwayne remarked, writing down some notes. "I don't suppose those guys were able to follow her, huh?"

"Nope," Tommy Joe replied. "They tailed her down to Douglas where the taxi turned west and headed for downtown off our beat. But there wasn't much going on, so the guys spent some extra time on Emporia Avenue to see if they could catch her coming back. It worked out, 'cause another cab showed up at the house about an hour later. She got out of it carrying a blue sack, then went inside." He paused. "That's it."

"Okay," Dwayne said. "Now I know what the guy's wife looks like; if she's really his wife. I may be showing up on your watch in a few days. I'm gonna do something illegal. Do you have a problem being a lookout?"

Tommy Joe shook his head. "I ain't riding with a partner so who's to know? I'll keep an eye out for you."

Dwayne slid out of the booth. "I'll be in touch, Tommy Joe, thanks a lot."

He went back to his car and immediately headed north to Murdock, going to the alley between Topeka and Emporia. He turned south and drove slowly down to the tall fence. After coming to a stop, he quickly got out and perused the trash. A blue sack like the one Tommy Joe described was in the can. Dwayne grabbed it and got back into his car, then drove down to the opposite end of the alley and stopped.

The sack had the imprint of the Downtown Art Supply Store on one side along with the address and phone number. He looked inside and saw a sales slip that indicated a purchase of art supplies, including watercolors. It appeared to have been a major buy totaling close to twenty-five dollars.

Dwayne stuck the receipt in his pocket and headed toward the address indicated on the sack. He found the store on Broadway just north of the Orpheum Theater. It was a small establishment, but its display window was filled with an extraordinary amount of art supplies. Dwayne entered the front door, giving the place a quick scrutiny as he walked up to the cash register at the counter. A slim man working an inventory sheet looked up.

"Can I help you, sir?"

"Yeah," Dwayne said. He pulled out his badge and flashed it. "I need a little information."

"Certainly," the man replied.

Dwayne laid the receipt on the counter. "Do you recall the lady who made this purchase?"

The man picked up the slip of paper. "That wasn't my sale. My clerk handled the transaction." He leaned slightly over the counter with his head turned toward a curtained door at the rear of the display room. "Ilse! Will you come out here please?"

The curtain was opened and a slim blonde woman wearing a shop apron came out. "What is it, George?"

"This policeman has a question regarding a sale."

Dwayne didn't bother to correct the man's assumption that he was on the police department. "It's just a routine matter."

Ilse walked up, seemingly a bit nervous. She took the receipt. "Oh, yes! I remember it quite well."

Dwayne noticed her accent, thinking that speaking with foreigners was getting to be a regular occurrence lately. "Can you describe the woman to me?"

"Of course," Ilse said. "She had blond hair, blue eyes

and was about my height. A bit heavier, however, and perhaps five years older."

"Was she an American?"

"No," Ilse said. "She was German."

Dwayne was confused. "Are you sure? Would it be possible that she was Latvian?"

"I am positive," the woman said. "You see, I am German and we spoke to each other in our native language. There is no doubt she was born and raised there. The lady said her home was now in the Soviet Zone."

George, the store's owner, interjected, "Ilse is a war bride."

"I see," Dwayne said. Now he knew the reason behind the woman's uneasiness. After years of living under the control of the Gestapo, most Germans had developed feelings of apprehension when it came to dealing with law enforcement. "You evidently chatted with her a bit."

"Yes," Ilse acknowledged.

"Did she mention why she was in Wichita?"

"She does not live here," Ilse said. "Her husband is in the city for the company he works for in Germany. They will not be here much more than three or four months at the most."

"What business is he in?"

"The lady said he was in investments or some other financial activity. She was not too clear on the subject, so I declined to ask further questions."

"Did she happen to tell you that her husband was Latvian?"

Ilse shrugged. "She did not mention his nationality, so I assumed he, too, was German."

"Did she give you an address?" Dwayne asked, hoping to get a confirmation she lived on Emporia Avenue.

"We did not discuss it," Ilse replied. "This was a cash sale, so knowing her address was not necessary."

"All right," Dwayne said. "Thank you very much." He took his business card out and handed it to her. "If she comes back in, please give me a call at one of these numbers."

Ilse took the card and gave it a quick glance then put it in her apron pocket. "I will do that."

"And please do not tell her about my visit," he added with a hint of firmness in his voice.

"Of course not, sir."

Dwayne left the store to ponder this new development. When he got to his car, he sat in it without driving off. Now there was another nationality involved in the activities at the Emporia Avenue address. The fact he found a fresh drawing obviously done by Fritz Harrigan was absolute proof he was staying in the place. If Fritz ventured outside he would eventually be spotted. He obviously wanted some art materials, so the woman was able to go out and make the purchases for him. There must be some advantage to the little artist to hide at the location in lieu of easily wrapping up the minor charge against him. One quick court appearance and the payment of twenty bucks would have done the job.

Dwayne started the coupe and pulled out into traffic. He wasn't going to be able to accomplish much without getting inside that house.

CHAPTER 17

Donna Sue agonized over what reason to give her boss Art Manger why she needed Monday off. She had seriously considered calling in sick, but she knew the truth would come out if she got the new job and gave notice. Art had been too good a boss to be treated in such an underhanded manner. In the end she reached the only decision her conscience would permit, and when Art came in on Saturday morning to pick up the receipts, she told him the truth.

"Art, I'm going to need Monday off," she said.

"Do you mean the whole day?" the boss asked.

"Yes," Donna Sue replied. She steeled herself and continued, "I have an appointment for a job interview. I'm trying for a position as secretary with Murchison Enterprises."

Art was disappointed but philosophical about it. "I figgered since you attended all them secretarial classes and got a high school diploma that you'd be leaving us before long. And I appreciate you telling me the truth, Donna Sue. You've always been a real lady."

"If I get the job I'll give you two weeks' notice," Donna Sue promised. "I really don't want to leave you in the lurch."

"I tell you what, Donna Sue. I'll get a replacement as quick as I can. I don't want to hold you up."

Donna Sue was relieved by his understanding attitude, but Maisie was more emotional about the situation. After the morning rush, she and Donna Sue had their usual get-together at the coffee urn. Maisie hugged her. "I'm sure gonna miss you, kid. We been working together for a long time."

Donna Sue squeezed her back. "I'll miss you, too, Maisie. You were a joy to work with."

"Have you heard anything from Dwayne?"

Donna Sue shook her head. "No. It looks like he and I have gone off in different directions."

"Are you in love with him?"

"I was never quite sure about my feelings for Dwayne," Donna Sue replied. "We never talked about marriage or anything like that, and it's just as well. It's like you said yourself; I want something different in life than he does."

"You'll find a man that can do a hell of a lot better for you than him," Maisie declared. "What I'm doing now I'll be doing for the rest of my life. Harry's sergeant's pay don't bring in much, so when he comes back stateside, I'll end up working at a snack bar on the base where he gets stationed. That's the same as working here at the Jayhawker."

"Maybe you should try secretarial school."

Maisie laughed. "Are you kidding? I'm not the smart type. I'd flunk out of there like I did reg'lar school. I'm a hash slinger, Donna Sue, born and bred."

"Let's clean up and wipe down the counter. The sooner we finish, the sooner we're out of here."

"Thank God Saturday's are half days most times," Maisie said.

"Yeah," Donna Sue agreed. "I have an appointment at the beauty parlor at one thirty."

———

ON MONDAY MORNING, DONNA SUE SLEPT IN. Brian Murchison had set up her interview at the Murchison Commercial Park for two p.m., promising to pick her up at the apartment house at one thirty. After getting out of bed and drinking a cup of Nestlé's instant coffee, she laid out the new outfit of the jacket, skirt and blouse she had chosen as a secretarial work garment. It was also business-like enough to suffice for the interview. The new purse and shoes would add to a no-nonsense appearance, and she had made a trip to Buck's Department Store Saturday afternoon after the visit to the hair salon to pick up an appropriate hat. It was a small beige tam with a feather that she felt imparted a smart look.

During that same shopping trip, she had also managed to get a pair of scarce nylons that had just arrived at the store. Now she wouldn't have to apply the leg make-up to simulate she was wearing stockings. If she landed the position she was after, a good part of her pay would have to go to expanding her wardrobe. Secretaries dress more expensively than waitresses.

Donna Sue took a bath and carefully arranged and combed her new hairdo. She'd had it cut a little shorter to give her a more serious look. With that done, she went to the toaster on the counter and inserted a couple of pieces of bread to eat before continuing her toilet.

This experience of an interview that would bring about the big changes she sought in her life was almost surreal. A couple of times she felt she was sleepwalking as she continued the task of getting ready.

Lunch was out of the question since her nerves were jumping big time as the hour of truth drew closer. This would be the ultimate test of all her hard work and preparation. She applied her makeup, then began carefully dressing in the new outfit. By the time she finished it was one fifteen, and she settled on the sofa to wait for Brian's appearance.

———

AT ALMOST THE SAME INSTANT THE MINUTE hand on the wall clock edged over six, a knock sounded on the door. Donna Sue wasn't surprised by Brian's punctuality. Since meeting him, she realized how efficiently and competently he conducted his life. She went to the door, and opened it.

He gave her a big smile. "You look fantastic!"

"Thank you," Donna Sue said. "Just a minute. I'll get my purse and school records."

They walked downstairs, past Mrs. Greeley who was sitting on the porch. The landlady gazed at Donna Sue. "Don't you look nice?" She gave Brian a smile of approval. "How do you do?"

"Good afternoon," Brian said.

He escorted Donna Sue to the curb where his new Packard sedan was parked. After opening the door for her, he went around and got in behind the wheel. The modern auto had a starter on the dash rather than the usual pedal on the floor. He turned the key, pushed the button and the motor purred to life. Brian made a U-turn in the street, going back to Douglas to head westward toward Hoover.

He glanced over at Donna Sue. "How is Dwayne?"

"I haven't seen him for a few days," she replied. "Actually it'll be a week today."

"Oh? Is his detective business keeping him busy?"

"I suppose it is."

"What does he think about you going for this new job?"

Donna Sue didn't answer right away. When she did, she spoke deliberately. "Dwayne and I seem to have reached a point where we don't want the same things out of life."

"Mmm. Sometimes that happens."

"Yes," Donna Sue said softly. "Sometimes that happens."

"Well, I think you'll find more than just a job with Murchison Enterprises," Brian assured her. "You're heading for a career—a *meaningful* career—if you get my drift."

Donna Sue didn't understand exactly what he meant, but she replied, "That's what I'm looking for."

They both remained silent until reaching Hoover Street. As Brian turned north, he said, "I don't know if I made it clear or not, but you won't be working at the same place you're going for the interview. The Commercial Park is a new set-up that is mainly for administrative and logistical purposes. The principal operations of the company will continue to be conducted downtown at the Murchison Building."

"I see," Donna Sue said. "That will actually be more convenient for me since that's closer to my apartment house."

"Your domicile will be another change in your life,"

Brian said. "But that's a later consideration."

He turned into the short drive to the gate of the commercial park. A young guard stepped out from the gatehouse. "Yes, sir?"

"Good afternoon," Brian said. "I'm taking this lady in for an interview with Miss Ralston."

"Do you have an appointment letter, sir?" the guard asked.

Before Brian could answer an older man joined the younger. "That's Mr. Brian Murchison, Tim! You don't hold him or any other executive up for anything, understand?"

"I'm only following—"

"Stop talking and open the gate, Tim!"

Brian interrupted. "Wait a minute, Fred. The young guy is only doing his job. I know for a fact he's never laid eyes on me before. And there is no appointment letter because I made all the arrangements personally over the phone. This guard doesn't deserve any chastisement, understood?" Then he added diplomatically, "His attention to his duties reflects very well on you as an excellent supervisor."

"Yes, sir," the older guard said, happy with the compliment. "Excuse me, Mr. Murchison." He went back into the gatehouse.

Brian looked at the kid with a smile. "You're performing your job assignment correctly, Tim. If you continue that practice, you'll do just fine around here and any other work you get into."

"Gee, thanks, Mr. Murchison," Tim said. "Let me get that gate for you."

With the barrier open, Brian drove into the park. Donna Sue now saw him in a new light. He had obviously just created a loyal employee for his family's business through friendly encouragement to a new worker. All this while praising the conduct of the young man's supervisor.

They continued past the parking lot up to the executive area, and pulled into a space. Donna Sue knew enough to wait for him to open the door for her, then they both went into the building.

"There's the reception area," Brian said, pointing. "Tell the girl there that you have an appointment with Miss Ralston. I have some business to attend to, and I'll meet you back here."

Donna Sue went to the open kiosk in the lobby. The receptionist showed a friendly smile. "May I help you?"

"I have an appointment with Miss Ralston. My name is Donna Sue Connors."

The receptionist picked up the phone on the intercom and pressed a button. "Miss Ralston, there is a Miss Connors here...all right." She hung up. "Miss Ralston will be here to fetch you directly."

Within a minute a very prim middle-aged lady in a severe dark brown dress appeared. She wore pince-nez glasses that gave her the appearance of a stern schoolteacher. "Miss Connors? Come with me, please." They walked down to an office door, and Miss Ralston led the way in. She indicated a chair in front of the desk. "Please sit down."

Donna Sue felt cold fear as she settled on the hard, straight back chair. She tried to show a friendly smile, but she knew it wasn't working.

Miss Ralston picked up a paper and read it. "Yes. You are going to be a special administrative assistant in the oil production department. That's in the Murchison Building downtown."

Donna Sue was confused. "Excuse me, ma'am, I think I'm here for an interview."

"Oh?"

Donna Sue took the manila folder and put it on the desk. "These are my records from the Keystone Business College secretarial course. I have no experience. This will be my first job as a secretary."

Miss Ralston took the folder and opened it. "Well! I see you earned a very impressive grade point average." She pulled out another sheet of paper from the folder. "And you have a letter of recommendation here from the president of the college."

"Yes, ma'am."

Miss Ralston relaxed, and she smiled. "I seem to have misunderstood who you were, Miss Connors. And, believe me, you already have the job I described. You are going to work for Mr. Brian Murchison as one of his personal assistants."

Now Donna Sue knew that the lady must have thought she was some empty-headed floozy that Brian had hired for sexual favors. "I am a fully qualified secretary, ma'am," she said defensively. "The only thing I lack, as I stated, is experience. Oh, and I've yet to take a course in shorthand."

"You are indeed qualified for the position, Miss Connors," Miss Ralston said. "And as far as shorthand goes, Murchison Enterprises will send you to school for a course in the Gregg shorthand system. It's a forty-hour program. That should be enough to get you up to forty words a minute. Advanced instruction will also be provided."

"Where will I go?"

"To your alma mater Keystone Business College. And your tuition will be fully paid by Murchison Enterprises."

"Oh! I certainly never expected that."

"And you will be provided with a company automobile. Do you have a driver's license?"

"Yes, ma'am," Donna Sue said. "This is all quite a surprise."

"Murchison Enterprise policy allows you personal as well as business use of the car," Miss Ralston said. "Let me see..." She turned her attention back to the paper that gave Donna Sue's job description and perks. "...it is a nineteen-forty-one Chevrolet, two-door sedan. And your salary will be seventy dollars a week...two weeks annual vacation...of course since you're salaried you will be required from time to time to work in excess of the regular forty-four hours per week without overtime compensation."

"That's fine," Donna Sue stated. She hesitated, then said, "I promised my present employer that I would give him at least two weeks' notice. But he said if he could let me go sooner he would."

"Those arrangements are between you and Mr. Brian Murchison," Miss Ralston said. She handed Donna Sue's manila folder back to her. "If you have any further questions, please refer them to him."

"Yes, ma'am."

"We have some forms for you to sign," Miss Ralston said. She retrieved a small packet of papers from her desk drawer. "These are for your income tax particulars, and a pledge of confidentiality agreement regarding proprietary matters between you and Murchison Enterprises. Please sign these. There is also a card for listing your address, phone number and other pertinent information. You can fill that out later and present it at your first day of work."

Donna Sue quickly signed the two forms.

Miss Ralston handed Donna Sue an envelope. "This is a hundred dollars cash. It is not an advance, but a bonus for incidental expenses of taking the position."

"Thank you!" Donna Sue said, surprised and pleased.

"Welcome to Murchison Enterprises, Miss Connors."

"Thank you for your help," Donna Sue said. She stood up and nodded a good day, then left the office going back to the reception area. There were chairs along the wall, and Donna Sue took a seat on one. She was so dazzled by what she'd learned of her new job that she didn't notice Brian as he walked up to her.

"How did it go?" he asked.

"I am flabbergasted. You didn't tell me I was already hired; or that I would have a car; or my salary and other conditions."

"I thought it best if Miss Ralston gave you all that information in her usual businesslike manner," Brian said. "Shall we go?"

They went to the car, and Brian was amused by her continued astonishment. She remained quiet as he pulled away from the parking space and headed for the gate. When he got there, he came to a stop. Tim stepped out of the gatehouse and nodded to Brian. Brian rolled down his window and held his hand out. "It was nice meeting you, Tim."

"I was pleased to make your acquaintance, Mr. Murchison," Tim said, shaking hands.

"Keep up the good work."

"Yes, sir!" Tim promised as he raised the barrier.

Brian drove out to Hoover Street, turning south. "There're two things I need to discuss with you."

"All right."

"I think it best for you to move," Brian said. "There is an apartment house up on North Market a couple of blocks past the post office."

"That's close to the Keystone Business College," Donna Sue said. "Miss Ralston said I'd be taking a short-hand course there."

"Right," Brian said. "You'll go two afternoons a week until you finish. Since you're the only one in the class it will be private tutoring. You should do quite well under those circumstances."

"Yes," Donna Sue agreed, reeling once more from the unexpected events of the afternoon.

"As for the apartment house, you'll be able to afford any of the flats there on your income. It's more suitable and proper for a lady in your new station in life. You'll receive an advancement in salary for the first and last month's rent. You can pay it back with five dollar a week deductions from your paychecks."

"Do I get to pick the apartment?"

"Of course," Brian said with a laugh. "We can take care of that at your convenience." He turned east on Douglas. "And there's one more thing. I hope it won't offend you."

"What's that?"

"I hesitate to get into this," Brian said.

"I promise you no resentment on my part. Especially after being given such a great job!"

"I think you should be called 'Donna' rather than 'Donna Sue'," Brian said. "It sounds better in a business environment. Donna Sue is rather countrified, if you don't mind me saying so. I hope you aren't offended."

"No," she replied. "Of course not."

"How long will it take you to get unengaged from your present job?"

"I'm not sure at this point," Donna Sue said. "I'll make it as quickly as I possibly can."

"Great."

The Packard continued on its way to the apartment house.

CHAPTER 18

Dwayne stepped into the building that housed A.J. Kessler's bail bond business, and stopped at Jill Stuart's desk. He glanced down at her. "What kind of mood is A.J. in?"

"Not good, not bad," the girl replied, secretly glad to see him. "At least for right now the only client on the lam is Fritz Harrigan."

"Okay," Dwayne said. "I may have some news to brighten his day."

"Good luck."

He walked over to the private office and banged on the door. "Anybody home?"

"C'mon in, Dwayne."

Dwayne entered and went directly to the chair in front of the desk. A.J. was cleaning his Beretta semi-automatic pistol slowly and methodically. The parts were laid out neatly on an oily rag in front of him. The little man peered down the barrel, then turned it so he was looking at Dwayne as if he were using a telescope. "Hey, shamus, what's up?"

"I know where Fritz Harrigan is."

"I believe we've discussed that situation before," A.J. said. "Maybe it was in another lifetime. Or perhaps was foretold me by a fortune teller."

"A lot less spectacular than that."

"Great!" A.J. said. "So when do we go get the peckerhead?"

"There's the rub," Dwayne said. "We got to break into a house to get him."

"No problem, bucko," A.J. said. "It's legal for a bail bondsman to do that."

"Well, there's a slight problem. It appears to me that Fritz is being kept down in the basement. We're gonna have to 'break and enter' like burglars. We gotta do that to keep the other folks in the place from knowing we're there. Especially since I've come to the conclusion they're the type that will shoot any unexpected visitors."

"What makes 'em so mean?"

"Because there's something fishy about the set up," Dwayne said. "I'm starting to think that Fritz is a prisoner."

"You mean kidnapped?"

"Exactly," Dwayne said.

"You also mentioned that the last time you was here," A.J. said. "And you also said we was gonna have to break into the place. So when do we get over this *déjà vu* shit? And what's happened to cause these updates to circumstances that've already got me good'n pissed off?"

"I'm getting ready to tell you," Dwayne said. "There's been a slight change to that situation." He cleared his throat. "As a matter of fact, A.J., *you* are gonna have to break in."

A.J. forgot about his pistol. "Now just what's this shit all about?"

"The best way into the place is through a basement window," Dwayne explained. "I'm too big, but you'll fit. Since Fritz is so skinny, he won't have any trouble climbing out."

"I don't like using basement windows, cellar doors or attics," A.J. said. "I really prefer breaking down the front door like a gentleman."

"It can't be done," Dwayne said. "I'm pretty sure the guy staying there is a light sleeper. And I ain't kidding when I say I've got him pegged as one son of a bitch who'll shoot first and inquire after your health later. I've also discovered there's a woman living there with him. She's got big tits."

"What's her tits got to do with anything?"

"Nothing really," Dwayne allowed. "I thought it was an inter'sting sidelight, that's all."

"Maybe," A.J. said. "Tits do brighten a story, but they ain't gonna make me want to break in the house through a basement window." He took a deep breath. "But I guess I can accept the hard fact it's gotta be that-a-way."

"Right."

"Okay," A.J. said. "So I go through the window. Is there something for me to step on down there, or do you just expect me to fall on my ass on a hard cement floor?"

"We'll use a rope," Dwayne said. "I'll hold on to it, and you lower yourself down. I can haul you and Fritz up the same way."

A.J. wasn't convinced. "And what if somebody spots you outside the basement window?"

"We're gonna have a lookout," Dwayne said. "Are you ready for this? It's gonna be a cop on the Emporia Avenue beat. He's a young patrolman by the name of Tommy Joe McNeil."

"I never heard of him."

"He's new on the force, and he's already been a lot of help to me. He's even got the cops on the other watches keeping an eye on the place. That's how I learned there's a woman living there and that she's got big tits. They spotted her coming and going. She came back with a blue sack of something or other, so I drove down to their trash cans in the alley and found it. It was from an art supply store and she'd bought a bunch of watercolors and stuff. A receipt showed ever'thing. That's another bit of proof that our artistic pal Fritz is currently residing there."

A.J. waved a small hand as a signal that he didn't want to hear anymore talking; he wanted to think. He lit a cigar and took a couple of drags.

"Let's do it to it!"

————

THE PORTRAIT OF LOTTE GUTMANIS WAS finished. Fritz Harrigan had sat up late several nights applying the watercolors to his sketch. After he finished, he wished he'd thought to do it in oils because of the life-like qualities he'd achieved. During the time he wasn't working on it, he'd kept it hidden among other sketches he'd made. Karlis had shown no interest in them during his trips to the basement, so the subterfuge had been unnecessary. The only thing the Latvian ever checked out was the progress made on the engravings.

The knock on the door kicked up Fritz's excitement; which was as much from wanting to find out what Lotte would think of the portrait as the unfettered sex he would enjoy. She came in and closed the door. This was followed by the sounds of it being locked, then the same thing happening to the outer portal as Karlis secured the exit. Lotte was wearing a low cut dress with a slit up the side.

She had put some curls in her hair, and her face was taste-fully but somewhat heavily made up. Fritz's erection didn't come up slowly; it sprung hard instantly.

"Hello, Fritz," she said, walking up and kissing him. As he embraced her, she put her hand on his crotch, massaging his throbbing member. "You are glad to see me, are you not?"

"Yeah," Fritz said.

He forgot all about the portrait and allowed her to take charge as she always did. Within a couple of quick minutes they were both naked, and the kid was between her legs, locked in tight by her solid thighs. He humped away, building up speed until he ejaculated; then he went limp and collapsed on top of her.

"Whew!" Lotte said. "Roll off me, Fritz."

He did as she asked, crumpling by her side.

"Now wasn't that nice?" Lotte inquired.

"Yeah." He didn't move for a moment or two, then he struggled up to his elbows. "Wait a minute." It took Fritz a good deal of physical exertion to get off the bed and stand up. After letting his breathing settle a bit, he walked over to the shelf by the drafting table. He rumbled through the mess, retrieving a rolled up piece of paper. He returned to the bed, and handed it to Lotte.

Lotte unrolled the eleven-by-fourteen sheet and looked at it, instantly sitting up. "*Ach*! Fritz, this is more beautiful than I expected."

"D'you like it?"

"It is wonderful," Lotte said. "Am I so beautiful as this? You have given me the appearance of an angel, yet it is still my face." She looked at it, smiling with tears welling in her eyes. "And the broach looks exactly as it did when my grandmother gave it to me." She leaned over and kissed him. "I shall treasure this to the end of my days.

How proud I will be when I have a home and can put it on the wall."

"I made the colors subtle, and concentrated on highlighting your features with delicate shadows," Fritz explained. "You have a spiritual side that makes you a beautiful woman to an artist."

"This portrait is who I really am, Fritz. And I am so grateful to you. Your skill has captured who I would have been had my life not turned out so horrid." She rolled it back up. "You must never, never speak of this to Karlis. Do you promise?"

"Sure, Lotte."

"I will sneak it upstairs and hide it among my clothes," she said, laying the portrait on the floor by the bed. "Are you ready for us to go again, or must you wait a few minutes?"

"I think I'd better wait a few minutes."

———

DONNA SUE DID NOT HAVE TO RETURN TO WORK at the Jayhawker. Art Manger had known he'd already lost her as an employee and the first chance he got, he went down to the employment agency to hire another waitress. Luckily there were three women available, and after interviewing them, he chose a heavyset redhead with a wide friendly face. She would fit in well with the downtown working customers who patronized the joint.

With Donna Sue's connection to the restaurant now permanently severed, she turned her attention to the new career. The first thing she tended to was building up a wardrobe that was suited to her new position in life. That was the real fun part of moving into a new career as far as she was concerned. Donna Sue took the hundred dollar cash bonus, and spent three hours in Buck's Department Store trying on and choosing new outfits. In the end, she had two more pairs of shoes, three dresses, three jackets, four blouses and a couple of extra skirts. The bus ride to and from the department store had been a slight inconvenience, but didn't spoil the fun.

When she got back to the apartment, she added to the enjoyment of the shopping experience by observing the various combinations of jackets, blouses and skirts, parading back and forth in front of the dresser mirror in the bedroom. The activity was interrupted by a phone call, and she hurried to answer it, hoping it would be Dwayne.

"Miss Connors?" a strange male voice said. "I'm Henley from Murchison Enterprises' company facilities. I called to let you know that I'll be handling the arrangements for your move to your new apartment. A lady from our department by the name of Mrs. Thompson is available tomorrow morning to take you to the building so you can choose a place that suits you."

"Oh!" Donna Sue said, pleasantly surprised at how fast things were moving. "That will be just fine."

"She'll also deliver your car," Henley said. "What time would be convenient for her to show up?"

"Well, I'm anxious to get settled in," Donna Sue said. "Would eight o'clock be all right? Do you know where I live?"

"Eight o'clock it is," Henley said. "We were given your address by Miss Ralston. And Mrs. Thompson will be there by eight o'clock. Goodbye."

She hung up, once more overwhelmed emotionally by all these latest happenings in that piled up one on top of the other. She was steadily moving farther and farther

away from the life of a waitress with each hour that
passed.

————

DONNA SUE SPENT THAT EVENING IN A RESTLESS
glow of anticipation. Even listening to the radio was done
in an impatient manner as she switched from program to
program, unable to find one with enough diversion for
her to concentrate on it. She finally settled for *Kay Kyser's
Kollege of Musical Knowledge*, a musical quiz show that
featured the popular bandleader Kay Kyser. The combination of jokes and music included a segment in which true
or false questions were asked of contestants picked from
the audience. The rub was that Kyser required the answers
to be given in reverse, i.e. if it were true the contestant
answered false and vice versa. When they chose the proper
answer, the band leader would holler out, "That's right,
you're wrong!"

The program amused Donna Sue to the point she
almost forgot the excitement of the new job for a short
time. But when she went to bed that night, the good
mood from the entertainment slipped completely away
from her consciousness. She hardly slept a single prover-
bial wink throughout the restless night.

————

WHEN THE KNOCK ON THE DOOR SOUNDED THE
next morning, Donna Sue eagerly answered it, dressed in
one of the combinations she had come up with the day
before. She found a rather young woman with a workman
standing behind her.

"Hello, Miss Connors, I'm Mrs. Thompson."

"Hi," Donna Sue said. "Please come in."

"Jerry here has brought some boxes for you to use for packing," Mrs. Thompson said. "It'll take him and his helper three or four trips to bring them up. Where would you like them placed?"

Donna Sue indicated the living room with a sweep of her hand. "Anywhere is fine."

"As soon as they finish with the boxes, we'll run over to the Royal Arms Apartments building. The manager will be waiting for us."

Jerry the worker and his assistant were able to complete bringing up the boxes within twenty minutes. They had brought packing tape with them, and Jerry gave Donna Sue a demonstration on how to put the containers together.

"Thank you," Donna Sue said. "I don't think I'll need them all."

"That's all right," Mrs. Thompson said. "Just use those you require and leave the others flattened as they are. The facilities department will pick up the leftovers." She reached in her purse and pulled out two double sets of keys. "These are for your car. It's downstairs."

"Oh! I'd forgotten about that."

"I would appreciate it if you could give me a lift back to the Murchison Building after we finish your apartment hunt," Mrs. Thompson said. "If it's inconvenient, I can call for a ride from facilities."

"I'd be very happy to take you back," Donna Sue said. "It's really not that far."

Donna Sue and Mrs. Thompson went downstairs. The new employee gasped when she saw the cherry-red sedan at the curb. "It's beautiful!"

"It drives nicely," Mrs. Thompson said. "I assume you wish to be behind the wheel."

"Yes, please!" Donna Sue exclaimed. "I believe they told me that the apartment house was on North Market."

The drive to the Royal Arms Apartments was pure joy for Donna Sue. The only other car she'd owned was a 1934 Plymouth she'd bought during the war when she worked for Boeing. The snazzy 1941 model Chevy with the gearshift on the steering shaft fairly hummed along. When Donna Sue pulled up to the curb in front of the Royal Arms, she was tempted to ask Mrs. Thompson if she could go around the block a couple of times, but she resisted the urge.

Mrs. Thompson led the way to the building, and Donna Sue noticed a coat-of-arms motif on each side of the lobby door. It was a shield surmounted by a plumed knight's helmet, making it appear as if it belonged on a castle. The letters **R** and **A** in large bold script letters were on each of the shields.

The two women went inside, going straight to the manager's office. It was obvious Mrs. Thompson had been there several times before. As they walked down the hallway, she asked, "I believe you require a furnished apartment?"

"Yes," Donna Sue replied. "I don't own a single stick of furniture."

The manager, a pleasant, balding man by the name of Sam Turner, was waiting for them when Mrs. Thompson knocked on the door. He answered the summons almost immediately, joining them out in the hall. "So nice to see you again, Mrs. Thompson. This must be Miss Connors, our new tenant."

"Yes, and we'd like to get her settled in as quickly as possible." She introduced Donna Sue to the manager, saying, "Miss Connors is a new employee of Murchison Enterprises."

"I have three to show her," Turner said. "All are suitable for a single lady. They are sixty-five dollars a month."

That was thirty dollars more than Donna Sue had ever paid for rent in her entire life. And she wondered if there were any rules about overnight male visitors, but she decided not to inquire.

They took a self-service elevator up to the third floor. Turner escorted the two women to an apartment on the west side. The door opened directly on the living room that had a window on one wall that offered a view of the street. It was furnished with a sofa, coffee table and two overstuffed chairs. The kitchen was a room by itself through another door, rather than like her old apartment where a counter in the living room sat in front of sinks, stove and refrigerator. A short hallway, where the bathroom and a closet were located led down to the bedroom. The boudoir had a double bed and a bedside table along with a closet that was larger than the one in the hallway.

Donna Sue walked through the place slowly, liking the layout. There was enough room for her to purchase a couple of items like a floor model radio and shelves to hold knickknacks. A breakfast nook was on one side of the kitchen with a small table that sat four. The bathroom also boasted a combination tub and shower.

"This is lovely," she said.

"I'll show you the other two," Turner said. "The layouts are practically the same, but they are on different sides of the building."

After the tour of the other flats, Donna Sue chose a vacancy on the fifth floor. It was on the east side, guaranteeing a bright morning sun. The first two apartments on the west would mean hot summer afternoons with the sun blasting through the large living room windows.

They went down to the manager's office to sign the

papers. Murchison Enterprises would send the first and last month's rent directly to Turner. He handed Donna Sue the keys, and she and Mrs. Thompson went outside to the car.

"It looks like I'll be busy packing for the next day or so," Donna Sue said, starting up the Chevy.

"Call me when you're ready for the movers," Mrs. Thompson said. "I'll need at least twenty-four hours."

"I'm giving you notice now then," Donna Sue said with a happy smile.

CHAPTER 19

I t was two a.m. as Dwayne turned his coupe off Murdock onto Emporia Avenue. A.J. Kessler sat beside him on the sofa cushions he usually kept in his specially-built Packard. They rolled along slowly before spotting Patrolman Tommy Joe McNeil's squad car parked at the curb a few yards past the corner street lamp. Dwayne pulled up beside the police vehicle, and stopped. He leaned toward the passenger window, speaking across A.J.

"How does it look, Tommy Joe?"

"Nobody's stirring in the house," Tommy Joe replied. He nodded to A.J. "How're you doing? I'm Officer McNeil."

"Hi, ya," A.J. said. "The name's Kessler."

"We're ready to move in," Dwayne said. "How're you gonna work this?"

"I'll position myself directly across the street," Tommy Joe said. "If something goes wrong I'll be able to move in quickly. With any luck I can cover your withdrawal by spending a good deal of time questioning anybody who saw you. You should be able to make a clean getaway if you act fast enough."

"Great," Dwayne said. "I'm gonna park down at the end of the block. If we got to haul ass, we can go back to the alley and head in that direction. All we need is time to get away and hop into the car. I'll drive away with the lights off."

"We're set then," Tommy Joe said.

Dwayne went down to the darker end of the street, and pulled up to the curb. After cutting the motor, he glanced at A.J. "Okay. We got the rope, flashlights, a chisel and a thin strip of steel."

"I got my Beretta fully loaded," A.J. said, patting his jacket. "And a couple of extra magazines."

"Man! You're loaded for bear, ain't you?"

"If I got to shoot my way out of that goddamn place, I'm gonna want firepower," A.J. declared defensively.

"Sure," Dwayne agreed. "I ain't trying to pick an argument. And I got my forty-five. Did you bring that baton of yours?"

"Hell, no!" A.J. said. "I ain't gonna let nobody get close enough to me to have to use it."

Dwayne took a deep breath. "Let's do what we gotta do." He had unscrewed the bulb in the ceiling of the coupe so that light wouldn't come on when they opened the door.

The two got out of the car as quietly as possible. Dwayne had the rope looped around one shoulder and had put the chisel and steel strip in his side jacket pockets. Each carried one of the flashlights in his hand. They could see Tommy Joe's police cruiser across the street as they moved closer to the target area.

When they reached the house, Dwayne waved over at Tommy Joe, then slipped into the side yard, going to the rearmost basement window. A.J. followed stealthily, keeping a wary eye on the residence. When they reached the corner of the house, they dropped to their knees.

Dwayne pulled the steel strip from his pocket, and slipped it into the bottom crack of the window until it made contact with the lock and hasp. He pushed gently at first, then increased the pressure. The bolt suddenly gave way and the window was unlatched. He pulled it up and out of the way. Next he got out the chisel and began pecking away at the caulking around the plywood barrier.

"Be as quiet as you can," A.J. warned him in a whisper.

"Gee! I'm glad you told me that," Dwayne said under his breath. "I was just about to kick this fucking thing as hard as I could to send it flying down into the basement to clatter around like Fibber McGee's hall closet."

"Sarcasm shows a lack of good manners."

"So does pestering a busy man."

They both quieted down as Dwayne continued working. He cleared the goop around both sides of the plywood and gave it a shake. It gave way a little, so he worked his way across the top and bottom. With that done, he firmly grasped the ends and pulled. It popped out, leaving the window open and empty. Dwayne stuck his head in and looked around as best he could, noting that a faint glow of light showed over on one side of the basement.

"Have you spotted anything?" A.J. asked.

"It's hard to see around the furnace, but there seems to be a table of some kind," Dwayne reported. "Prob'ly some other stuff, too. There's some kind of low illumination." He chuckled. "I bet Fritz is using a nightlight."

"It'll be handy when I get down there," A.J. pointed out.

Dwayne got the rope and uncoiled it. "Are you ready?"

"Yeah," A.J. warily replied. "I'm gonna put a loop under my arms so you can lower me slowly. When I get down I'll unloosen myself. Just hold onto the rope. When you feel a jerk, it'll be the signal to haul. It'll either be me or Fritz."

"It'll have to be Fritz the first time."

"Agreed."

The little man adjusted the rope, then slipped into it. He lay down and scooted through the window. The sudden jerk made Dwayne's hands almost slip but he managed to hold on. He slowly let the rope down until it grew slack. It wiggled a bit as A.J. freed himself.

Now on the basement floor, the diminutive bail bondsman walked carefully around the furnace, coming to a stop. He could see a bed, drafting table, another table with a chess set, and a refrigerator. A.J. walked carefully across the cement until he reached the bed. A lamp turned down low was next to it, and he recognized Fritz lying under the covers. A.J. shook him.

"Izzat you, Lotte?"

"No, goddamn it, it's me, A.J."

Fritz frowned in puzzlement and sat up. "Gee!"

"Yeah," A.J. said. "*Gee*! Now get up and put on some clothes. We're hauling ass out of this place."

"How'd you get in here?"

"The same way you and me are getting out. That window over there."

"That's kind of high up, isn't it?" Fritz asked.

"I came down on a rope," A.J. explained. "Your old buddy Dwayne Wheeler lowered me, and he's gonna pull us both up."

Fritz broke out into a smile. "Dwayne! God! I haven't

seen him in a long time." Then he shook his head to come completely awake. "How'd you know I was down here?"

"Don't fret yourself about that right now," A.J. said. "And don't talk so goddamn loud."

Fritz pushed the covers off and stood up. "I don't think I can leave."

"I put up your bail, Fritz, and I guarantee that you're leaving," A.J. said. "Now hurry up before I really get pissed!"

"You don't understand, A.J.," Fritz said. "I'm on a secret government project. As soon as it's finished they're gonna pay me off, and the FBI will take care of the bail and the charges against me."

"Yeah, and Santy Claus will bring us all a lot of nice presents and we'll have a big party," A.J. said with a sneer. "Now get your ass dressed!"

"You better leave," Fritz warned him. "If you get caught you'll go to the Federal pen for interfering with an official mission."

A noise sounded from above and Fritz put a finger to his lips. "Shhh! Karlis is coming. He must've heard us."

"Who the hell is Karlis?"

"He's the guy in charge." Footsteps on the stairs could be heard that were growing steadily louder. "Get behind the furnace quick!"

The lock on the door rattled, and A.J. scooted back into the darkness. He pulled his Beretta and stood still; barely breathing. Fritz quickly went over to the drafting table and grabbed a pencil and a piece of paper.

Karlis Gutmanis, with a locked and loaded German Luger pistol in his hand, stepped into the basement. He looked at Fritz who sat hunched over his work area.

At that point the artist turned around. "Who's there?"

"I am, Karlis."

Fritz switched the light fully on. "Oh, hi, Karlis."

"I am hearing strange noise."

Fritz chuckled weakly. "I couldn't sleep so I felt like doing some drawing. I was singing my old East High School song." He took a breath and cleared his throat:

> *"We hail the glory of East High,*
> *her honor shining bright.*
> *In Wichita we proudly raise her banner,*
> *blue and white!*

It's like a national anthem."

Karlis was definitely suspicious. He glanced around the basement, then focused on the furnace. He started to walk over.

"Hey, Karlis. Come look at this."

Karlis took another glance, then went to the work area. "What is it you are wanting?"

"I drew a picture of a dog, see?"

Karlis glanced at the sketch. "Why do you show this to me?"

"Don't you think it's good?"

"Yes. Very good."

The Latvian turned and went to the bathroom, gazing into the interior. He turned and started back toward the furnace, and Fritz watched in fear. A.J. moved slowly around to keep on the opposite side out of sight. He had the Beretta ready to fire if Karlis noticed the open window, but the man's eyes were low as he searched for somebody crouching in a corner.

Karlis, satisfied there were no intruders present, walked toward the exit, leaving the basement. He locked the doors, then his footsteps could be heard ascending the stairs. A.J. left his hiding place. "Let's go, goddamn it, Fritz!"

"I told you I can't."

"Well, they're eventually gonna find that somebody came down here through that window," A.J. pointed out. "All that caulking around the plywood has been chopped out. So you better get out of here or you're gonna be in deep shit."

"There's more caulking on the workbench over there," Fritz said. "And a spatula, too. I can set the plywood back in place and recaulk it."

A.J. knew for sure that the kid wasn't going to leave the basement, and if he kept arguing with him, the risk of his being discovered would increase. "Well, clean up the mess on the floor, too." He hurried over toward the rope.

Upstairs Karlis decided to check outside the house. He grabbed a flashlight, and went out the front door to the porch, pausing to listen for sounds. Then he descended the steps to the yard.

"Excuse me, sir!"

Karlis looked up startled and saw a policeman with a drawn pistol standing on the sidewalk. "*Was*, er what?"

"Drop your gun," Tommy Joe commanded. "Do it now or I'll shoot."

Karlis wisely let the Luger pistol fall to the grass. "I am doing what you say."

"Do you live here, sir?"

"Yes," Karlis replied. "It is here that I live."

"Why are you out in the yard?" Tommy asked. "And with a pistol."

"I am hearing noises," Karlis said. "Maybe some robbers are wanting to get into the house."

"Get back up on the porch," the Wichita cop

commanded. "Stay there 'til I get back. I'll take a look around."

Karlis, still the disciplined SS-soldier, almost clicked his heels and saluted. But he caught himself. "I go on the porch."

Tommy Joe made sure the man obeyed his order, then he started around the house. When he reached the basement window, he saw Dwayne pulling A.J. out. Dwayne looked up. "The bail jumper refuses to go with us."

"Do you want me to let you in the house?" Tommy Joe asked. "I can do it if he's missed court."

Dwayne shook his head. "No. There's something more here. I got to figure out another plan of action."

"Okay," Tommy Joe said. "The guy that lives here is waiting for me on the porch. You guys hurry up. I'm going back to take a report from that concerned citizen." He grinned. "And I'm a slow writer."

Dwayne worked quickly to put the plywood back in place. With that done, he and A.J. gathered up their stuff and headed toward the backyard. They went through the gate into the alley, then hurried toward the coupe. When they reached the vehicle, they wasted no time in getting in. Dwayne fought the throttle and starter, then drove away quickly after the motor kicked to life.

By that time Tommy Joe was in the living room of the house, sitting on the sofa with a clipboard in his lap. He had already entered the date, time and location of the incident, and he began his questioning.

Karlis protested. "Is big mistake. Nobody come. You are not needing to make a report."

"I'm afraid I got to, Mr. Watkins," the young cop said. "It's the law. And you were out in the yard with a pistol."

Karlis sighed, then began answering the questions that

the policeman asked while slowly writing down the responses in a deliberate manner.

———

DWAYNE AND A.J. TRAVELED TOWARD THE latter's place of business, neither one speaking as they rolled through the streets. Dwayne parked in his usual place behind the building, and after the bail bondsman returned the sofa pillows to his Packard, they went inside. A.J. put on a pot of coffee while Dwayne sat down at Jill's desk.

A.J. looked up from his task. "That punk bastard Fritz Harrigan! We should have him in here with us *right now*."

"If we'd rushed that house, we'd all be dead right now," Dwayne said. "And that'd include Tommy Joe." He lit a cigarette. "How come Fritz wouldn't come out?"

"You ain't gonna believe this shit," A.J. said. "He told me he was on a secret government project for the FBI or some such crap like that. He said when the job was over, the Feds'd clear everything up."

"I knew there was something special going on," Dwayne said. "But I don't believe that's it. Too many things don't add up. Just what happened while you were down there?"

"Well, I woke up Fritz and told him to come with me," A.J. said. "That's when I got the bullshit about a government project. Then the guy Karlis came down—"

"Karlis?" Dwayne asked. "What'd he look like?"

"Big and husky with a foreign accent."

"That's got to be the guy Watkins I talked to when I used the telephone repairman scam," Dwayne said.

"Anyhow, the guy nosed around but didn't see me 'cause I got behind the furnace," A.J. said. "He left and

Fritz wouldn't go with me. I pointed out the busted up caulking and he said he'd fix it. So that's it. You pulled me up, Tommy Joe came around, and we hauled ass. So here we are."

"Yeah," Dwayne said. "So the guy's name is Karlis Watkins. He said he was Latvian but I know for a fact that Watkins ain't a Latvian name. But Karlis prob'ly is. That Latvian guy that was killed in the Warehouse District was named..." He pulled out his notebook. "...Mikelis Kilitis. I wonder if there's a connection."

"Just a minute!" A.J. exclaimed. "I just remembered the door to the basement was locked."

"Then Fritz is a goddamn prisoner!"

"I'd say so," A.J. agreed, getting up to check the coffee pot.

A few minutes later both men sipped the hot fresh brew. They had sunk into silence as each sleepily mulled over the evening's events. When Dwayne spoke, it wasn't about the incident. "I broke up with Donna Sue."

A.J.'s eyes popped open. "You're shitting me!"

"She got to be a pain in the ass," Dwayne said. "Or rather, I was the pain in the ass since she wanted a change of lifestyle."

"What'd she expect you to do?"

"Give up betting on the ponies, mainly," Dwayne said. "Then start saving my money and getting a better office...a better car...better clothes."

"What a nag!"

"Well, it did kind of piss me off since our little romance was going along real nice," Dwayne said. "I just don't care about the things she does lately."

"Well, it's best you two ain't together anymore," A.J. pronounced. "Anyhow, the breakup is gonna make Jill happy."

"Your secretary? Why will she be happy about it?"

"She's got a crush on you, man. Ever'time you come in here she gives you googley eyes. Ain't you noticed?"

"I guess not," Dwayne remarked. "How old is she?"

"She's nineteen," A.J. said. "It's prob'ly time she had her first real romance."

Dwayne took a thoughtful sip of coffee. "Mmm. That's a year older than the legal age of consent."

CHAPTER 20

D onna Sue was completely moved into her new apartment by the weekend following the visit to the Royal Arms Apartments. Her boxes were delivered, the gas and lights turned on, the telephone installed, and her name placed on a mail slot in the lobby. The Royal Arms boasted an underground parking garage, and she was assigned space 511, that was the same number as her apartment.

With those preliminary arrangements taken care of, Donna Sue turned her attention to unpacking everything and putting it away. She hadn't realized how few cooking and eating utensils she actually owned until she found she'd used only about a third of the storage available in the kitchen. The cereal boxes, canned goods, coffee and pack-aged foods hardly took up any shelf space at all.

The kitchen finished, and she turned her attention to her clothing. After putting her garments away in the bedroom closet, there was nothing left over for the one in hallway. Her undies and other such items took up only a drawer and a half of the chest of drawers. It was the same for the bathroom, and her few knickknacks in the living room were hardly noticeable. It all seemed like a good excuse to go shopping again.

A late Friday afternoon phone call from Brian Murchison's executive secretary Bess Pusser rounded out the last of her pre-employment information. She would be expected at the Oil Production Division on the third floor of the Murchison Building by eight o'clock Monday morning. Arrangements had already been made for a company-furnished space at the EZ Park lot downtown. Donna would not be required to pay a fee since the parking for employees assigned to the executive wing was taken care of by the company. After hanging up, Donna Sue called Mrs. Thompson at facilities to tell her the empty boxes were ready to be picked up. The lady said for her to place them out in the hall Monday morning, and Henley would be by to collect them.

Donna Sue spent Saturday and Sunday settling in, purchasing some groceries and taking drives in her Chevy sedan. After being limited in moving around the city to Dwayne's coupe, the bus or walking, it was wonderful to be able to get in a car and go directly to any destination she desired. She had never felt so free and liberated in her entire life. It would have been nice if her mother were still alive and could see all these new, exciting things that had unexpectedly transpired in her life.

However, the excitement she felt about all those great changes were dulled a great deal by Dwayne's absence. Saturday and Sunday night had never seemed so lonely, and the melancholy feelings were harder to bear because of her being in a new and unfamiliar place. Even when she admitted they would never find a mutual compatibility; it was sad to think of the relationship ending.

THE EZ PARK LOT WAS ONLY A BLOCK NORTH OF the Murchison Building but she made sure she arrived early on Monday morning. The short walk down to Douglas included crossing only one street, and it was seven-thirty when she walked into the lobby. Donna Sue got on the elevator with a couple of other people, and went up to the third floor. When she stepped out into the hall there was a sign that listed **OIL PRODUCTION DIVISION, MILLING DIVISION,** and **CONSTRUCTION DIVISION.** Each had an arrow indicating which direction to follow to find the offices, and Donna Sue headed toward Oil Production. When she arrived, the door was locked. She felt awkward at being the newbie as well as showing up too early for work. It seemed appropriate to take a slow walk around the third floor. By the time she was halfway through the stroll, the elevators had disgorged more people, and she spotted some going into Oil Production. She stepped up her pace and entered the office.

A receptionist occupying a waiting room was hanging up her coat, and Donna Sue walked up to her. "My name is Donna Sue, er, Donna Connors," she said, remembering what Brian had said about her full name. "I'm reporting for work this morning."

"Yes, Miss Connors," the receptionist said, taking a seat. "We're expecting you. Go down to the end of the hall and you'll find Mr. Brian's office. Miss Pusser, his executive secretary, will be seated at a desk outside the door."

"Mr. Brian?"

The receptionist laughed. "Yes. There are so many Mr. Murchisons around, we use their first names. By the way, I'm Toni Garson."

"I'm pleased to meet you," Donna said, appreciative of the young woman's friendliness.

She went through the door, past other offices with occupied secretary desks out in the hall. Most of the women were busy beginning the work day by opening mail and checking appointment books, and they didn't give Donna much notice as she passed

Donna found Miss Pusser similarly occupied. "Good morning."

"Oh, you must be Donna," Miss Pusser said. "I'm glad to meet you. I'm Bess." She was a thin, middle-aged lady with her gray hair arranged in a simple bun, wearing a plain but dignified dress suit. Despite the outward appearance of sternness, she had a friendly smile.

"I'm glad to meet you, Bess. I'm anxious to get to work."

"I've been told you'll be attending shorthand classes," Bess said. "I've not received your schedule from the business college, but as soon as I do, I'll let you know. Take a seat, please. I must sort all these letters and check Mr. Brian's appointment book, then I'll be with you."

Donna sat down with her purse in her lap. A couple of other women on the staff walked by, each giving her a smile. She immediately picked up on the fact that Brian's method of leadership was easy going.

Bess finished with the mail and took it into Brian's inner sanctum, then reappeared. "Let's go have a look at your office."

Donna stood up, surprised. "I have an office?"

Bess laughed. "It's pretty small, I'm afraid, but it's an office just the same."

They went around the corner of the hallway and down to a door that was similar to others along the way. "This is where the oil production men maintain their places of work when they're in town. They are gone most of the time out in the field, some as far away as South America and the Middle-East. When the company got into the petroleum business about twenty-five years ago, they strictly limited their operations to Kansas, Oklahoma, and Texas. Now they've branched out all over the world."

Bess opened the door and gestured for Donna to precede her. She stepped in and found a neatly arranged work area with a desk, typewriter and stand, file cabinet, and a bookshelf. The window looked down on Douglas Avenue.

"This is quite nice," Donna said.

"I stocked your desk, but if you want more or different items you can contact the supply room," Bess said. "There is a catalog of available material in the top drawer along with inter-company extension numbers. Just dial the number and tell them what you want. You can generally have it delivered within two or three hours. If it's an emergency, let them know and you'll get it right away. That's one advantage of being in the executive wing."

"I'm overwhelmed."

"You'll also find a history of the company on the bookshelf," Bess said. "It would be a good idea to take it home and give it a careful read. They're big on tradition here, and the elder Murchisons are pleased to note employees' interest in the historical aspects of the firm. There is also another book that should have all the information you'll need on the company such as conditions of work, ethics, standards of dress, location of various branches, and other subjects."

"That makes it easier to settle in."

"Believe me, it does exactly that," Bess assured her.

"What will be my main duties?"

"You will maintain communications with the men in the field on behalf of Mr. Brian," Bess explained. "That means you have immediate access to him at anytime they send in their reports. After you log them in, you must not delay in getting them to me. If I'm not at my desk, place them in the box labeled 'field communications'. After Mr. Brian reads them, they'll be returned to you for filing. Have them ready anytime Mr. Brian needs to review a report. He will also transmit messages and memos to the field through you."

"I understand."

"And you have a job title as would be expected," Bess informed her. "You are the operations coordinator."

"Oh, my!"

"And there's one more very important thing," Bess said. "No company information or activities are to ever —*ever*—be discussed with outsiders. And that includes your family and friends. The petroleum business, while seemingly respectable and congenial on the surface, is as cut-throat as banditry beneath that reputable exterior. There are many people in rival companies who are dirty dealing and downright dishonest and will do anything to take advantage of vulnerable situations if it will benefit their firms or themselves. They can only do that with inside information they acquire through careless talk or out-and-out spying."

"I'll remember that."

"Fine," Bess said. "There are some preprinted folder labels in the top right drawer. These identify the various individuals and offices in the field. Put them on your folders in the top file drawers. These are where you will maintain those records. Always leave them there so they will be readily accessible for either Mr. Brian or me." She walked to the door. "If you have any questions, Donna, don't hesitate to call me."

"I will, thank you."

Bess left the office and closed the door, and Donna hung up her coat, and put her purse in a bottom desk drawer. Then she turned to setting up her files.

———

DWAYNE DECIDED TO TURN HIS ATTENTION TO other matters on the Tuesday after the abortive attempt to retrieve Fritz Harrigan. As he dressed he decided to put that caper on the back burner and turn his attention back to the Kilitis murder. After learning that the first name of the man who lived in the Emporia Avenue house was Karlis, a hunch was forming in the back of his mind. Obviously the name Watkins was not Latvian as Mrs. Kilitis had informed him, and Karlis seemed to be a genuine Latvian name. He would have to check that out with her. All these Latvian connections coming together in Wichita could be a coincidence, but on the other hand some sort of conspiracy was also possible.

After breakfasting at the Tip Top Diner, Dwayne drove up toward Wichita University, turning onto Yale Street to visit the Kilitis residence. Mrs. Kilitis seemed glad to see him when she answered the doorbell. "Come in, Mr. Wheeler."

"Thank you, ma'am," Dwayne said. He followed her into the living room and they settled down. He cut to the chase, asking, "Is the name Karlis a Latvian one?"

"Oh, yes," she replied. "It's quite common. The English equivalent would be Charles."

"I see," Dwayne said. "Then you must have known people with that name, correct?"

"Oh, yes, of course."

"Would any of these Latvians named Karlis have been an enemy of your husband during the war years?" Dwayne inquired. "I mean enemy enough to want to murder him?"

"I don't think so," Mrs. Kilitis answered. "Well, there was one who was a Nazi. He was involved in right wing politics before the war and had been arrested by the Soviets. I believe he was scheduled for trial but the arrival of the German Army was so sudden that all the Russians could do was quickly withdraw. They left the jailed political prisoners behind."

"So this guy just walked out of prison, huh?"

"Yes, almost that literally," Mrs. Kilitis said. "He immediately linked up with the Germans since he saw them as liberators. After he joined the SS, he was in command of a unit that hunted down and arrested intellectuals who were anti-Nazi. He had a confrontation with my husband before we were smuggled to Sweden."

"I see," Dwayne said. "What was his full name?"

"Karlis Gutmanis."

"And what are the details about this confrontation you're talking about?"

"Gutmanis was put in charge of a special SS detachment linked to the Gestapo," Mrs. Kilitis explained. "Their main duties were to maintain surveillance on the university faculties. Those activities increased when a movement arose in academia to hinder the rounding up of Latvian Jews to be deported to camps in other parts of Europe."

"That would be the concentration camps, right?"

"Yes," Mrs. Kilitis responded. "But at that time we did not know about the systematic application of genocide against Jewry in gas chambers as was discovered later.

However, there were reports of groups being taken out to remote areas and summarily executed after being forced to dig their own graves."

"So what did you guys actually do?"

"We set up a smuggling system in which Jews were helped to reach hidden places on the coast where they could be transported to Scandinavia. This Karlis Gutmanis had an informer in Riga University who reported my husband and me as part of that underground. He went to my husband's office and accused him of being involved, but offered him a pardon if he exposed others in the plot. Mikelis—my husband—asked to be given some time to think it over. Gutmanis granted him twenty-four hours. We used the time to put ourselves into the pipeline to freedom. Thus, we ended up in Sweden."

"Good thinking," Dwayne said. "So if this Gutmanis happened to see your husband here in Wichita, it would be to his advantage to kill him so he wouldn't turn him in, right?"

"If that could happen," Mrs. Kilitis said. "But we read reports that Gutmanis had died in the last days of the war during the Battle of Berlin. Any SS man who surrendered to the Soviets would be executed, so they fought to the death."

"Yeah. You told me about that. Would there be any chance this guy had survived?"

"Anything is possible, Mr. Wheeler."

He handed her his notebook. "Would you write the guy's name down for me? I ain't sure how to spell it."

Mrs. Kilitis complied. "I hope this helps you."

"Would there be any other of these Latvian SS types who would want to kill Mr. Kilitis?"

"I suppose," she allowed. "But none I can think of with the first name Karlis."

"Okay," Dwayne said. "Well, thanks a lot. I've got something more to work on now." He stood up, putting his notebook back in his pocket.

Mrs. Kilitis accompanied him to the door. "Have you discovered something from the war, Mr. Wheeler?"

"Well, I've discovered something, but I ain't sure what it is."

He stepped off the porch, walking toward the coupe. The people in that house on Emporia Avenue were starting to really piss him off.

CHAPTER 21

After leaving Mrs. Kilitis' house, Dwayne drove over to a nearby Conoco gas station. He parked on the edge of the area by the air pumps, and walked to a payphone on the side of the building. After feeding in a nickel, he dialed a special number he'd committed to memory during the Kansas City caper.

The call was answered by a feminine voice. "FBI."

"Hi," Dwayne said. "I'd like to speak to agent Steve Williams. Tell him it's Dwayne Wheeler."

"What does this call concern, sir?"

"Just tell him it's Dwayne Wheeler like I told you," Dwayne said. "He'll want to talk to me."

In less than a half minute, Steve Williams' voice came on the line. "Hello, Dwayne, what can I do for you?"

"I need to talk to you," Dwayne said. "Is there a chance we could get together in your office PDQ?"

"How about a hint on what we're going to be discussing."

"A Nazi war criminal," Dwayne said. Then he added, "Maybe."

"Okay," Williams said. "I'm pretty much freed up for the next hour."

"I'll see you in a few," Dwayne said, hanging up.

The FBI office was located in the Wheeler Kelly Hagny Building on South Market downtown. Dwayne lucked out by finding a parking place a couple of blocks away, and he hurried over to the FBI office on the third floor. When he walked in, the receptionist looked up from her typewriter. "Yes, sir?"

"I'm Wheeler."

She flipped the switch on the intercom. "Mr. Wheeler is here."

Dwayne walked to the door and entered before the agent made a reply to the lady's announcement. Williams stood up and offered his hand. "It's good to see you again, Dwayne. Sit down. What's this about a Nazi war criminal?"

"I better start at the beginning," Dwayne said. "This is a pretty complicated caper I found myself on. All sorts of weird things keep popping up."

Williams settled back in his plush desk chair.

Dwayne began his story with Fritz Harrigan's arrest and subsequent disappearance when he skipped out on his bail, and how he was hired to track the fugitive down. The pawn shop angle and the trash can hunt in the Emporia Avenue alley were brought into the narrative, and led up to his telephone repairman ruse with Karlis Watkins who lived at the address where Cockroach Cochrane found the illustration. "And this Watkins claimed he was from Latvia."

Williams listened patiently but unenthusiastically until the dissertation turned to the murder of the Latvian Professor Mikelis Kilitis and the subsequent interviews with the widow after she hired Dwayne.

"We've had some inquiries from Washington regarding the case," Williams said. "What info did you pick up from the lady?"

"I got some inter'sting facts," Dwayne said. "Missus Kilitis gave me some dope on a Latvian SS-officer by the name of Karlis Gutmanis. She also told me that during the war the professor had been in conflict with local Fascists after the Soviets' withdrew. Some trouble came out of that, and they had to haul ass to Sweden."

"Ah!" Williams said. "What as the name of that SS guy again?"

"Gutmanis," Dwayne replied. "It's spelled G-U-T-M-A-N-I-S. Mrs. Kilitis showed me how to spell it right. It seems to me that all of a sudden there's a whole bunch of Latvians that dropped in my lap."

"Could be a coincidence."

"But there's something else," Dwayne continued. "There's a woman living at that house with this Watkins character. And she's a Kraut. So we got a mix here, see? There's a murdered Latvian professor and his wife; some guy calling himself Watkins but is Latvian; and the German woman. And she's definitely from Germany, 'cause a German lady who is a war bride working at an art supply store sold her some stuff. She said they talked in German."

Williams flipped on the intercom. "Ruth, bring me the file on the wanted war criminals. The European ones."

The efficient secretary didn't take long to bring in a fat three-ring notebook to Williams. After she went back to her workstation, the FBI man thumbed through the alphabetical list to the G's. He scanned the roster of Nazis and collaborators, then looked up. "Nobody here by the name of Gutmanis. But the guy is probably using an alias if he's wanted. And that's a pretty big 'if'."

"He's calling hisself 'Watkins'," Dwayne said. "I told you that. And Mrs. Kilitis said that wasn't a Latvian name. Which struck me as kind of odd. If he told me he was a Latvian, how's come he's calling himself Watkins?"

"But you didn't see anything suspicious while you were in the residence acting like a phone repairman?"

"I couldn't get to the basement without causing a fuss," Dwayne admitted. "But I solved that problem with A.J. Kessler. He's the bail bondsman that's holding the paper on Fritz Harrigan." At this point, Dwayne did not mention the young policeman Tommy Joe McNeil since he might get into trouble if his participation was revealed. "Anyhow, A.J. got into the basement on the night him and me went to that house."

"How did he get in when you couldn't?"

"We pulled a breaking and entering in the middle of the night," Dwayne said with a grin. "A.J. went in through a basement window. It was easy for him 'cause he's a midget."

"Dwayne," Williams said, "you always seem to hang around with the most exceptional people."

Dwayne chuckled. "I live in Wichita, Kansas."

"And what, if anything, did this bail bondsman discover?"

"Fritz was down there all right, but wouldn't leave," Dwayne explained. "He claimed he was working on a secret government project and that the FBI would clear up everything about the charges against him when it was over."

Williams shook his head. "I can tell you right now that this office has no knowledge of any clandestine projects going on locally."

"That's what I figure," Dwayne said. "And I got a gut feeling that Fritz is in deep shit that's gonna bring him some very bad luck before all is said and done. He's a strange little guy. An artist, y'know? And I think he's been set up for a fall. Maybe framed or maybe bumped off. It don't look good from where I sit."

The FBI agent was thoughtful for a moment, then said, "There's really nothing I can do for you, Dwayne. Unless you can get proof that the guy at the Murdock house is really a war criminal, my hands are tied. I don't care if he says his last name is Magillicuddy."

"Maybe he's in the country illegally."

"Then you'll have to go to Immigration and Natural-ization."

"Shit!" Dwayne snorted. He stood up. "Well, I gave you the story, so at least if something comes along that seems related, you'll know about it. And give me a call, will you? I really want to wrap this up and get Fritz Harrigan back to the world of the living."

"I'll keep my eyes and ears open," Williams said. "And we do get regular reports about wanted Nazis and Japs." He grabbed a pen and pencil. "What was that guy's name again?"

"Karlis Gutmanis," Dwayne answered. "K-A-R-L-I-S-G-U-T-M-A-N-I-S."

Williams wrote it down, then glanced up at Dwayne. "Stay in touch."

DONNA CONNORS HAD BEEN EMPLOYED IN THE Oil Production Department of Murchison Enterprises for a little over a week before Brian Murchison asked her out on a date. It happened on a Friday just before lunch, and he popped his head into her little office. "Hi, Donna."

She looked up from tallying some South American

reports, and gave him a smile. "Hello, Brian. How was the trip to Texas?"

"Beneficial," he replied. "The reason I dropped in is that there's a party over at my parent's place tomorrow night, and I wondered if you'd give me the pleasure of your company at the event."

She knew that meant some extremely wealthy, prominent people, and she thought about her department store off-the-rack clothing. Her garments might be fine for night clubbing, but not for a fancy affair in a mansion. She'd look like Little Orphan Annie next to the other women. "I hope it isn't formal."

"Oh, no, nothing like that," he said. "It's going to be held out on the patio by the swimming pool. It's a catered barbecue actually, and quite informal. I know for a fact my sister Kate will be wearing a blouse, slacks and sandals." He noticed Donna still looked uneasy. "I tell you what. I'll have Kate give you a call and pass on some feminine advice on proper wear for the event."

"That would be nice," Donna said. "And, yes, I would be happy to go to the party with you."

"I'll pick you up at five o'clock," Brian said. He gave her a smile, and went back down the hall to his own office.

Donna turned her attention back to her paperwork, but couldn't concentrate. The idea of going out with Brian disturbed her more than just a little bit. It hadn't been that long since the breakup with Dwayne, and the idea of being with someone else didn't set well with her. She took a deep breath, rationalizing that it was inevitable that she would eventually date someone else sometime in the future. And it might as well be Brian Murchison.

THAT SAME EVENING AFTER SHE'D EATEN A LIGHT supper and was relaxing on the sofa with the radio while doing her nails, the phone rang. Once again she felt a surge of hope that it would be Dwayne. She picked up the receiver, took a breath, then answered. "Hello."

"Hello," a woman said brightly. "Is this Donna?"

"Yes it is."

"Hi, Donna, I'm Kate Woodsley," the caller said. "Brian's sister. Woodsley is my married name."

"Oh, hi," Donna said. "He said you'd call. I was a little worried about what to wear to the affair at your father's house."

"I'm glad he wanted me to call you to put you at ease," Kate said. "Men are so inept in social situations. At any rate, you can wear slacks or a skirt with a simple blouse. Flat shoes are appropriate as well, if you prefer them over heels; and a simple purse will do. We'll be eating barbecued pork and beef, baked beans, potato salad with some other simple side dishes. So, as you can see, it's a very informal affair even if it is catered."

"Brian said it was by the pool," Donna said. "Will I be expected to swim?"

"Not at all," Kate said. "In fact there are never too many people wanting to go for a dip at these affairs. It's too much trouble to dress and become presentable again after diving into water."

"All right," Donna said, relieved. She could swim quite well, but didn't own a bathing suit. "And thank you, Kate, for filling me in."

"You're certainly welcome," Kate said. "I'll see you tomorrow night."

———

ON SATURDAY MORNING, DWAYNE AND OFF-DUTY policeman Tommy Joe McNeil walked into the Wichita Police Department with a very special task to attend to. They went up to the second floor to keep an appointment with the sketch artist. This was the man who drew faces based on descriptions given by witnesses when there were no photos available of the bad players. Dwayne agreed to pay the guy ten dollars for coming in on his day off.

The artist's name was Greg Douglas who had moved down from Hutchinson to take the job with the Wichita Police. He liked the work except when he had to put in time in the fingerprint file room when not required to sketch suspects' features. When Dwayne and Tommy Joe entered his tiny studio, which also served as a storage area for cleaning supplies, Greg was ready with pencil and pad as he sat in front of his drawing board.

He did his sketches from a special FBI manual that was filled with illustrations showing head shapes and different sorts of eyes, mouths and noses. The examples also included hair styles along with moustaches and beards. The procedure began with a witness first picking out these various characteristics so that Greg could make his preliminary sketch. When that was done, the witness would have the artist alter the drawing until he was convinced it was an accurate portrayal of the criminal involved in the case.

"Okay, listen up, guys," Greg said. "The best way to do this is for me to sit with each of you alone. That'll get us two sketches, then we'll finish up by having both of you sit together and discuss how they look, so any disagreements of the likenesses can be straightened out."

"That seems like a waste of time," Dwayne complained.

"Believe me," Greg said. "It's the best way. I've done

this on a couple of hundred cases when more than one person was involved in the procedure. When two or more people give their impressions together, there are disagreements, and someone ends up giving into the others to avoid getting into an argument. But if I keep the witnesses separate, then let 'em compare what they did individually, accuracy is practically a sure thing."

"Okay," Dwayne said. "How about if I go first?"

"That's fine with me," Tommy Joe said. "I ain't had lunch, so I'll run across the street to Dockum's for a sandwich and milk shake."

After Tommy Joe left, Greg turned to the pages of the head shape samples, and Dwayne carefully studied them, picking out one.

"Okay," Greg said. "Now we're cooking. Go to the hair style section and from there we'll work down the face to the eyes, nose and mouth."

Dwayne was methodical as he slowly and carefully scanned each example. Greg was patient as the private detective made his choices. Within an hour the drawing was completed. Dwayne then suggested that the eyes be put closer together and the chin made a bit squarer in appearance.

When those modifications were made, Greg sat the likeness down. "You're sure now, right?"

"It's dead-on," Dwayne assured him. "I'll run across the street to Dockum's and send Tommy Joe over. When you're finished with him, he can come get me."

Dwayne went downstairs and crossed William Street to the drug store on the corner. When he walked in, he spotted Tommy Joe seated at the counter reading a copy of *Sport* magazine as he slowly sipped at his milkshake through a straw. The empty plate that had held his chicken salad sandwich and potato chips was pushed off to the side.

"Okay, Tommy Joe," Dwayne said, taking the stool beside him. "It's your turn."

"I'm on my way," Tommy Joe said, putting a half dollar and a couple of dimes on the counter. He slid the magazine toward him. "Here's something to read while you're waiting. There's a good article on Ralph Kiner of the Pirates. It looks like he might win the home run race this season." Then headed for the door carrying his milk-shake with him.

In ordinary times, Dwayne would have gone down to the Jayhawker Restaurant for a bite to eat, but those days were gone forever. When the waitress came up for his order, he requested a grilled cheese sandwich. Unfortunately, he had to settle for potato chips since French-fries weren't available.

———

IT TOOK TOMMY JOE AN HOUR AND A HALF TO enable Greg to produce a likeness he approved of. With that done, he went to fetch Dwayne as the artist put the two sketches together for a team effort at producing the final version.

When the pair sat down together, Greg waited patiently as they discussed the project. Dwayne disagreed with Tommy Joe on the nose and mouth mostly, and also thought he had picked eyes that were slightly too wide.

"Well," Tommy Joe conceded, "you're prob'ly right, Dwayne. I can't really argue with you 'cause the only time I talked to that guy was out in his front yard at night with the porch light on about twenty feet away. When we went into the house so I could write out my report, there was only a small table lamp turned on."

"Okay then, fellahs," Greg said. "I'll make up a final sketch. I'll work on it over the weekend to provide some enhancement for reality's sake, and you can pick it up Monday."

"Great," Dwayne said. "The big test is gonna be if Missus Kilitis recognizes who that son of a bitch is."

"And if she does?" Greg asked.

"Then the shit's gonna hit the fan over on Emporia Avenue," Dwayne replied. "And that can't happen too soon."

CHAPTER 22

D onna Connors sat in front of the small dresser that was a recent, heady purchase she had made in the furniture department of Buck's. There had been a spot for it next to the west wall of her bedroom, and having one was more convenient than standing in front of the bathroom mirror.

She was busy applying her makeup for the soiree at the main Murchison mansion, and was being extra careful since the evening would be spent in the company of Wichita's most socially elite which included some very important people from Murchison Enterprises. At least much of the nervousness she had initially felt had been allayed by the kindness shown her by Brian's sister Kate.

But as she dabbed rouge to her cheeks, Donna was aware that her emotional state was slowly sinking into a morass of melancholy in spite of the upcoming gala. These were the occasional feelings that crept into her consciousness since the break-up with Dwayne. He had simply walked away from her without declaring his intentions, but somehow she knew he wouldn't be coming back. Although her relationship with him had been relatively short, it had turned out to be more meaningful than she realized, and each time he entered her reveries, she felt a sad sense of loss. And there was also the matter of no longer being able to enjoy all that great sex with him.

———

WHEN DONNA SUE'S TWO MARRIAGES ENDED there had been no regrets on her part. Her first husband, a truck driver much older than she, had offered an escape from a dreary life of drudgery and poverty as she worked at menial jobs with her mother to help provide food and shelter after the father deserted them. The trucker's name was Jim and his idea of sex was to come home drunk from an evening out with his buddies, and rape her while calling her "whore" and "bitch." He rarely provided much money for the household, and Donna Sue had been forced to take a waitress job at the Jayhawker Restaurant downtown to make ends meet.

Most of the time, between his trips, Jim sat around the apartment intoxicated to the point of angry stupidity, telling her how the women he screwed on the road gave him a better time than she did. They were experienced and willing, while she was no more than an awkward teenage girl. He also ordered her around with insulting comments, and found fault with her housekeeping and cooking. His displeasure was often accented with cuffs and slaps, and one time he had thrown her across the room to crash into the opposite wall. That mistreatment was the result of her having served undercooked green beans to him.

Donna Sue's relief from the hell-on-earth came a couple of years later when he simply disappeared. She was able to get a divorce on the grounds of desertion, but the horrible marriage had left her wondering what the rest of her life would be like.

Donna Sue met Archie her second husband after the war started and she had obtained employment as a welder at the Boeing Aircraft Company. Archie was not drafted into the Army because he had a critical job skill as a tool and die maker. They began dating not long after meeting in the company cafeteria, and the marriage occurred after they developed a habit of having sex following evenings out. Archie ended up being a pretty decent husband, and even allowed Donna Sue to handle all the family finances after they moved into one side of a duplex on Pawnee Street near George Washington Boulevard. They got along great and jokingly said the best part of their relationship really began when they were assigned to different shifts.

But the marriage ended when she came home early from work one afternoon. A delay in the delivery of materials to the airplane factory brought production to a halt. When she walked into the house, she caught Archie in their bed with the woman who lived in the other side of the duplex. Donna Sue was furious and went berserk, creating such a scene that the neighbors called the police. The end result was a divorce, this time the grounds were adultery, and Donna Sue found an apartment downtown to begin yet another phase of her life.

A year after the divorce, she realized that she hadn't been in love with Archie, and her attraction to him was that he was so different from Jim. Then she met Dwayne Wheeler not long after the end of the war brought about layoffs of the women workers at Boeing.

She had gone back to the waitress job at the Jayhawker, and Dwayne had just gotten out of the Army.

He had begun coming into the Jayhawker because of his connections with certain individuals across the street at the OK Barbershop. Dwayne was a handsome guy with a cheerful way about him, and she was attracted to him at first because of those male attributes. And as she got to know him better, she recognized that he was extremely smart and seemed rather dashing since he was a private detective. Donna Sue also eventually learned that he was generally financially strapped, drove an old car and like to bet on horse races through the bookies at the barbershop. All this while living in a crummy little bedroom in a rooming house.

Their relationship did not start at the Jayhawker; rather it occurred almost by chance when she was out with her girlfriend Wanda Riley on a Saturday night. The two had gone to a redneck nightspot called Western Danceland. Dwayne spotted her from the bar and came over to say hello. The girls invited him to join them, and the evening began when another guy was allowed to join the group by Wanda after she had danced with him a couple of times.

As the evening progressed the guy ended up taking Wanda home, and Dwayne offered to give Donna Sue a ride back to her place. They made a date for the following Saturday night; then another and another until they began going out together regularly.

A couple of weeks went by before they had sex, and the first coupling occurred when some predate necking got out of hand, and they ended up in her bedroom for a quickie before going out. By then they had developed a habit of going to Western Danceland. Donna Sue liked the place because an evening of fun and dancing there made her forget the previous week of waitressing.

Eventually, Donna Sue realized that her attraction to

Dwayne, while not serious, was because he was perfect for her. He made no demands, was nice, good looking and the sex was fantastic as far as she was concerned. Even though his personal life was less than desirable, she didn't care as long as he was there for Saturday nights. Donna Sue's affection for him was genuine, and she hadn't realized how intense it was until that evening when he walked out of her apartment.

But Dwayne would always be Dwayne, and she had to move on no matter how painful it was.

———

BRIAN MURCHISON ARRIVED AT THE APARTMENT to pick Donna up at a quarter past six. He was casually dressed in a sports shirt, slacks and loafers. His attire made her feel comfortable in the blouse, skirt and ballerina shoes with bows at the sides that she had donned for the occasion.

Brian gave her a warm smile. "You look real cute, Donna. You're a credit to Kansas womanhood."

She smiled back. "Well thank you; I'm glad you think so. Would you care for something to drink before we leave? I don't have any liquor but there's Royal Crown Cola in the fridge."

"That's okay," he said. "There's plenty at the party, believe me. The last thing we'll lack this evening is something to drink."

She got her purse, and they left the apartment, and went down to the building lobby on the self-service elevator. Brian had parked his Packard a half block down the street, and, after going out on the sidewalk, they strolled toward it in the evening air that was still dominated by the day's earlier warm temperatures. Brian walked slowly, casting a casual glance at the traffic on North Market Street. "It'll be a lot cooler on the patio at the party. I guess I forgot to tell you that you could go swimming in the pool if you wanted to."

"I've already discussed that with Kate," Donna said. "She advised it's best to forget the swimming at these functions."

"You'll get good counsel from her," Brian said. "I know I always did."

"You talk like you're younger than she."

"By seven years," he said.

Donna laughed lightly. "I find it hard to imagine you as a little brother."

"Oh, I was certainly that," Brian said. "And Kate referred to me as a sassy brat countless times over the years. I guess I was especially annoying when one of her boyfriends came over."

Brian unlocked the passenger door and opened it for Donna. After going around to get in on the driver's side, he started the powerful engine. "And with that mighty roar, we hie ourselves to the festivities." He pulled away from the curb and merged into traffic, heading north. Brian looked straight ahead as he drove. "I've heard nothing but the best about you at work. How do you like being a coordinator?"

"I enjoy my job very much," Donna said. "It's actually fun to talk to those oil production guys on the out-of-town projects. They're always cracking jokes."

"They're a varied bunch," Brian said. "Some are college graduates with degrees in petroleum engineering, paleontology, and geology and others are former rough-necks who came up the hard way in the business."

"Roughnecks?"

"The name describes them to a 'T'," Brian said. "Those are the muscle boys on the derricks."

"Well, they're all characters."

"That they are," Brian agreed with a laugh. "They're the guys on what you might call the front lines. A work environment like that makes even a college boy a robust sort of individual after a few months in the field."

They chatted as he continued driving up north on Broadway. When the car passed Thirty-Seventh Street, Donna recognized it as where Mrs. Davies' mansion was located. That was where Dwayne had hidden her away after the Kansas City gang threatened to kidnap her. They had wanted to get even with him for beating up a couple of their thugs. Mrs. Davies was the premier madam of Wichita, and provided Donna with a luxurious bedroom suite. During her stay there, the lady's secretary had taught her to type, and this had led Donna Sue's quest for a high school certificate and attendance at the Keystone Business College.

Brian drove farther out into the country, then turned off on a well-maintained gravel road. After passing several large, well-appointed residences, he turned into a gate, continuing up to a rambling two-story mansion. Numerous late-model automobiles were parked along the drive. A trio of well-dressed but tough-looking men were standing around the area. One waved at Brian.

Donna asked, "Who are those guys?"

"Well," Brian said, "back in the old days when Wichita was a cow town, they would be called hired guns. They're a bit similar to Dwayne, except they're not detectives."

The men made Donna feel uneasy. "I suppose they're necessary."

"They can be at times."

Brian went past the guests' cars and pulled into a

driveway that led to the back of the house. After braking to a stop, he got out and once more walked around to tend to the door for her. She was getting used to the courtesy and rather enjoyed the extra attention.

The sound of people laughing and talking could be heard as Brian took her arm and escorted her to a hedged entrance leading into a patio. As they walked onto the scene, several people in what appeared to be a crowd of thirty or so, turned toward them. Donna's first priority was to see what the women were wearing, and she was relieved to finally know that she fitted in.

Brian nodded greetings to everyone as they crossed the area to an elderly couple who were seated near the swimming pool as if they were holding court. Brian leaned down toward Donna's ear, whispering, "I'm about to introduce you to my parents."

A flash of nervousness went through her, but she maintained her composure. Since the Murchisons were a powerful local family that wielded strong commercial and political clouts in the Wichita area, she figured the patriarch and matriarch must be rather imposing and unpleasant people.

The old man's eyes fell on Brian and he laughed aloud. "So you finally got here, hey?"

"I had some work to clear up, Dad. But more importantly, I had to pick up this very attractive young lady."

The old man beamed at Donna. "And she certainly is very attractive." He stood up. "Hello, my dear, I'm Ted Murchison, this fellow's father, though I try to keep that a secret."

"How do you do," Donna said, easily determining he was joking.

"And this is my better half," Mr. Murchison said.

"Mrs. Murchison, of course, whom everyone calls Miss Dolly."

Brian finally got a word in. "Mom. Dad. This is a new employee, Donna Connors. She is the operations coordinator in the Oil Production area."

Dolly Murchison laughed loud and lustily. "I'm really impressed! You got the position awfully quick, Donna. I never got above secretary in that joint." She emitted another burst of laughter, nodding her head toward her husband. "O'course I married the boss."

Donna immediately liked the woman.

"All right," Brian said. "Now that I've tended to the social duty of introducing this guest, I shall take her over to the bar for a libation."

Mr. Murchison said, "If you see one of those lazy waiters stumbling around out there, send him over here with two vodka martinis."

"Will do, Dad," Brian promised.

He offered his arm to Donna, and she slipped her own around it. Most of the crowd were seated at patio tables with umbrellas while a few were in the usual cocktail hour poses of standing in small groups and chatting. The trip to the bar was interrupted when he steered her over to an attractive middle aged woman who was standing with a dignified man with silver hair.

"Kate!" Brian said.

Kate Murchison Woodsley turned toward her brother. "Hello, Brian."

"Hi," Brian said. "Hello, Ned."

"How are you, Brian?"

"I'd like you guys to meet Donna Connors," Brian said. "I think Kate has already met her over the phone."

"Yes!" Kate said. "It's nice to see you, Donna."

"Thank you," Donna said. "And another thank you for your kind counsel."

"My pleasure."

"We're on our way to the bar," Brian said. "And Mom and Dad need a couple of more martinis. Excuse us."

The couple's trek across the patio was interrupted yet again when Brian spotted another couple, and guided Donna toward them. "Here's someone else for you to meet."

A rugged looking old man wearing a western-style shirt and pants accented by an obviously very expensive pair of cowboy boots, glanced over at them as they approached. The woman with him had the look of a farmer's wife with a wide, smiling face showing wrinkles that were as much from exposure to the sun as age. She was clad in a simple cotton frock.

"Hey there, Brian!" the guy called out.

"Hi, J.T.," Brian said. He nodded to the woman. "Hello, Bertha."

The woman beamed. "Hey, Brian. Who's that cute li'l thang a-hangin' on your arm?"

"It's somebody J.T. doesn't know that he already knows," Brian said.

"If I knowed a perty gal like her, I'd sure be aware of it," J.T. said with a loud guffaw. "These spectacles on my nose don't mean I'm completely blind."

"Well, you've talked to her on the phone," Brian informed him. "This is Donna Connors."

"Then you must be J.T. Turner," Donna said, having been in several conversations him with him since starting the new job. "I'm the operations coordinator."

"Why you're as perty as you sound," J.T. said.

Brian looked at Donna. "J.T. has come up from Texas for that meeting with the Louisiana Cartel."

"By Gawd, Donna!" J.T. said. "Yo're gonna have to have lunch with us while we're here." He nodded to Bertha. "Ain't she, honey?"

"Sure," Bertha said. "She can help me make you watch your table manners." She turned to Donna. "This man o' mine is an ol' roughneck who wildcatted 'til he was past fifty years old. It tuck him that long to find a decent well. Me and him raised six kids in the oil fields of east Texas, and not even making a shitload of money could turn him into a gennelman."

Donna's mood was improving as she began to realize that while most of the people at the gathering were moneyed, they had worked their way up through being focused on their ambitions; like she was doing.

After a brief conversation with the Turners, Brian conducted Donna through the crowd, pausing only long enough to send a waiter with a couple of martinis over to his parents.

During the remainder of the evening, she met three more men out of the oil fields who were also in Wichita for the meeting with the Louisianans, but these were paleontologists and petroleum engineers with degrees. Their wives were also well educated, but the couples all had down-to-earth attitudes and were friendly. Donna felt they were sincerely glad to make her acquaintance.

She had a few drinks like she would have done at Western Danceland except that these were mixed by a bartender and the liquor in them was of a superior quality. As drinks were consumed and she was introduced to more people, Donna became quietly buzzed, and her thoughts turned to what it would be like for her to be married to Brian.

She would have to quit work of course, but she would be a well-to-do housewife with plenty of time on her hands. She could join the Prairie Wind Golf and Tennis Club and take up one or both of the sports between card games; meaning she would have to learn bridge and canasta in order to fit in properly. And there would be countless social events she would dress up for, wearing garments purchased during weekend shopping trips to Kansas City or Dallas with girlfriends who would also be wives of wealthy businessmen.

Donna stood by the pool with Brian, looking out over the crowd of the elite and privileged; the luxuriously appointed patio area and pool; and the mansion that overshadowed the scene. She had already taken a big step from waiting the counter at the Jayhawker to her present existence. Now, for the first time in her life, Donna was truly optimistic about her future.

———

THE PARTY BEGAN BREAKING UP AT ONE A.M. Brian had been drinking steadily through the whole affair, but showed no affects from the alcohol other than a slightly exaggerated joviality. Donna now knew he would never be a mean drunk, and that was a strong indication he was not the sort to abuse or brutalize the women in his life. By then his aged parents had gone to bed, and she and Brian had another drink to allow the guests time to vacate the driveway.

———

THE RIDE BACK TO THE ROYAL ARMS Apartments was interrupted by the flashing red lights of a police car. Brian pulled over, fetching out his wallet from his pants pocket. As he rolled down the window, the cop walked up. "You were going a little fast there, buddy."

"Sorry, officer," Brian said. "Here's my license. And my courtesy card."

The cop ignored the license and took the card. "Okay, Mr. Murchison. I'd appreciate it if you'd slow down a bit."

"I sure will," Brian promised.

"Good night." The cop handed the documents back and returned to his patrol car.

"What's a courtesy card?" Donna asked.

"It's just a piece of cardboard," Brian replied with a grin as he replaced the wallet in his pocket. "Of course it has my name on it and the signature of the chief of police. It's like the 'Get Out of Jail Free' card in Monopoly."

"I'm impressed!" Donna said. "How do you go about getting one of those?"

"One must be acquainted with the right people," Brian said.

They continued down the street, and Donna turned her slightly buzzed mind to what might happen when they got back to her apartment. Brian might have ideas of getting her into bed, and she gave the matter some quick thought. It took a moment or two to come to the conclusion it would probably not be the best thing to do. It could be he was after a quickie one-night stand, and that would be the last time he took her out. And Dwayne Wheeler was still dancing through her heart and mind.

Fifteen minutes later, Brian had taken her up to her apartment, and unlocked the door when she handed him the key. He returned it after turning the knob and pushing the door open. "Well, good night, Donna. I enjoyed the evening with you."

"Thank you, Brian," she said. "I had a good time, too."

He walked down the hall and she went inside. After closing the door, she stood pensively for a moment, then walked over to the window. She looked down and watched him stroll down the sidewalk toward his car.

Once more the thought of being married to Brian Murchison entered her thoughts.

Hang, you blind fate," she said. "I had a good time."

He walked down the hall and then went to the door, sitting on a wood frame just on the other side of it, and waited over to the window. She seized the handle mostly half and down the sidewalk from her as a car...

Once more she stepped into the house before Samuel washed one out of the room.

CHAPTER 23

Dwayne parked his old coupe in front of the Kilitis home, and cut the chugging motor. The final police sketch of the Latvian who lived on Emporia Avenue was in a manila folder on the seat beside him. He pulled the likeness out and gave it another scrutiny. He was more than satisfied with the accuracy of the drawing; this was definitely the guy. He got out of the car and walked up to the front porch and rang the bell.

Mrs. Emilija Kilitis peered through the curtains on the door, then opened it. "Please come in, Mr. Wheeler."

"Thanks," he said, entering the house. "How are you today, Missus Kilitis?"

"Fine," she said. "Do you have any news for me?"

"I got something else, ma'am," Dwayne said. He pulled out the drawing and handed it to her, then waited for her reaction.

She took the art paper and looked at it, her eyes opening wide. "Where did you get this?"

Dwayne ignored the question. "Do you know that man?"

Mrs. Kilitis took a deep breath. "This is Karlis Gutmanis. He looks almost the same as when I last saw him. But there is no doubt." She repeated in a low voice, "This is Karlis Gutmanis."

"You're positive?"

"Yes, Mr. Wheeler."

"And what was he doing exactly the last time you saw him?"

"He was in our apartment in Riga," she replied, "dressed in an SS uniform. I can recall the skull insignia on the band of his cap."

"All right," Dwayne said. "And just what was he doing at your apartment at that particular time?"

"He had come to question my husband about several things. He wanted the names of faculty members of Riga University who had been participating in anti-Nazi activities."

"What did your husband answer?"

"He lied, of course," she responded. "Mikelis said he had no idea of any such movement going on." She paused and her voice quavered. "Gutmanis bellowed loudly, calling him a liar, and struck him hard across the face, knocking him to the floor." After taking a deep, calming breath, she said, "Let's sit down." She walked over to the sofa and took a seat.

Dwayne settled on the far side, taking out a notebook and pencil. "I know this is tough for you, ma'am. But I've made contact not only with the Wichita Police but also the FBI. Both outfits said they can't do nothing without facts. And they mean all the facts I can dig up."

"I understand," Mrs. Kilitis said. "I'll do my best."

Dwayne made some preliminary notes before speaking again. "Okay. After he knocked your husband down and yelled at him, what else happened?"

"He grabbed Mikelis by the collar and dragged him to the dining room table and forced him to sit down," Mrs. Kilitis said. "Gutmanis placed a list of professors' names in front of him, and ordered him to make a mark by the ones who were plotting against the Germans or Adolf Hitler." She began sobbing. "Mikelis insisted he had no such information...then Gutmanis pulled a pistol from his holster and pointed it at Mikelis' head...he threatened to shoot him then and there unless he began cooperating immediately."

Dwayne wrote rapidly in the notebook.

"Mikelis decided he had the intellectual capacity to deceive his tormentor since the man was obviously a brute," Mrs. Kilitis continued. "He said that he was not interested in politics and so never discussed such things with any of his colleagues."

"Did that satisfy Gutmanis?"

"Of course not, Mr. Wheeler. He hit Mikelis again, this time with the pistol barrel. Gutmanis began to shout that he knew my husband was deeply involved in the movement. He said a Gestapo informant employed at the university had seen him at a meeting of the anti-Nazi members of the faculty. By then Mikelis was bleeding from a cut on his forehead. But he insisted he was innocent and had never attended any such sessions."

"What were you doing at this time?" Dwayne inquired.

"I was weeping and begging Gutmanis not to hurt Mikelis. Of course it did no good. And I was frightened almost witless. It was obvious the SS knew the truth about our activities. I fully expected that we would both be dragged from the apartment and taken to Gestapo headquarters to be tortured until we told all we knew."

"Did Gutmanis arrest you?"

Mrs. Kilitis shook her head. "He did not do so at that time since he thought it unnecessary. The Nazis had no knowledge that we could be smuggled out of the country by the underground, thus they thought escape was impossible for us. After all, we were hemmed in by enemies. The Soviets were to the east, and the Nazis to the west. At any rate, I think he preferred to frighten us into cooperating. This would be more advantageous to his superiors than having us physically and mentally tormented. But, of course, there was always a chance he might put us in custody. That is what Mikelis and I feared would be our unhappy fate."

"Uh huh," Dwayne acknowledged. "So then what happened?"

"Gutmanis stopped talking about naming professors who were political enemies of the occupation. He now wanted to know about those among them who were Jews. And, of course, Mikelis continued his denials in order to protect his colleagues. Then the Nazi said he wanted names of private citizens in Riga who were Jewish. He stated that intellectuals like us and Jews were running dogs in the same pack. For the next half hour or so of questions and accusations, he slapped my husband instead of hitting him with his fists or that pistol. When he left, he said we were to stay in Riga and be confined to the apartment. If we were spotted on the street, we would be immediately arrested."

"So that's when you made your getaway to Sweden, right?"

"Yes," Mrs. Kilitis said. "We had a special number to call and code words to indicate we were in danger. The underground came to our house in the middle of the night and took us to a special place to hide. A week later we were rowed out to a Swedish ship. You know what happened after that."

"Yes, ma'am," Dwayne said, replacing his notebook in his pocket. "This is gonna help a lot, Missus Kilitis." He stood up. "Is it all right if I use your phone?"

"Of course. It's in the hallway."

Dwayne went to the telephone and dialed the FBI office. He made an appointment for a quick meet with Agent Steve Williams, and hung up. He walked back to the living room. "Okay, Missus Kilitis. I'm moving along good on the caper now. I'll see you later."

"Goodbye, Mr. Wheeler. And thank you."

———

DWAYNE, HOLDING ON TO THE MANILA FOLDER with Gutmanis' portrait, rode the elevator in the Wheeler Kelly Hagny Building up to the third floor. When he walked into the reception area, the secretary on duty quickly spoke into the intercom, then gestured for him to go right in. Dwayne found the agent waiting for him.

"Okay," Dwayne said, sitting down without being asked. "I got a witness who made that guy who was calling himself Karlis Watkins. His real name is Karlis Gutmanis."

"Fine," Williams said. "Who's the witness?"

"She's the widow of the WU professor who was murdered in the Warehouse District," Dwayne reported. "You said the office in Washington had shown some interest, right?"

"Yeah," Williams said. "And I also read about it in the *Eagle*."

"The dead guy knew the SS criminal during the war," Dwayne continued. "And the widow Missus Kilitis told me about what went on back there in Latvia." He pulled out his notebook and slowly and deliberately gave an oral report on his interview with Mrs. Kilitis. It took Dwayne a full twenty minutes with embellishments and side comments of his own. When he finished, he leaned back in the chair. "That ought to wrap it up with a bright red ribbon."

Williams was not too impressed. "It will be just her word against his, Dwayne. The three of them were the only people in the room."

"I would think a damn good Federal prosecutor could make a case out of this," Dwayne insisted. "She made a positive ID from that police sketch. So it's for sure he was in the SS." He handed the manila folder over. "There's the drawing of the guy's features in there. Right now I don't want to discuss how I got it, but Missus Kilitis said it was him."

Williams looked at the likeness. "His name, as you well know, isn't on the list of wanted war criminals. And let me tell you something else in confidence as one professional to another. There are a lot of former Nazis who are in the employ of the United States Government. Their rocket scientists, for example. The Soviets got some and we got the rest. And our intelligence community is using ex-SS and Gestapo who know a lot about Russian spying and espionage operations and methods. They learned all this from interrogating compromised Communist spies."

"I guess that makes sense."

"Those guys are now cooperating with us to avoid being prosecuted for what they did during the war, and it doesn't matter if they killed thousands of people. They have too much to offer; and that includes helping us in the FBI." Williams paused and lit a cigarette. "And there's another even more important thing. If this Gutmanis murdered the professor, it's a case for the Wichita Police Department not Federal law enforcement."

"Okay," Dwayne said. "Facts are facts. So I'll go to Lieutenant Forester in homicide and give him the information. He'll be able to build a case on it that'll satisfy the Sedgwick County prosecutor's office."

"I hope you succeed," Williams said. "Because if the guy gets convicted for murder, he may roll over and give up some useful information on fugitive Nazis to get a life sentence instead of hanged. We just went through that with your old bookie buddy Arlo Merriwell, didn't we?"

"You're right, Steve. We're definitely gonna be winners in this. And it'll get a guy punished who's really got it coming." He stood up and walked to the door, speaking over his shoulder. "I'm on my way."

The FBI office was close to police headquarters, and Dwayne hoofed it over to the cop house. He went directly upstairs and headed for Lieutenant Ben Forester's cubby hole of an office in homicide. He opened the door without knocking, and announced, "I got the guy that killed the professor."

"Sit down," Ben invited. He knew enough from their long friendship to take the private detective seriously. He had solved a puzzling case involving a dead bookie not long before, and there had been other incidents in the past when he'd scored some impressive investigative coups.

Once more Dwayne dipped into his pocket for the notebook and went through his interview with Mrs. Emilija Kilitis. When he finished, he gave the police sketch to Ben. "Here's what he looks like."

"Mmm," Ben mused. "This seems to be Greg Douglas' work."

"That's beside the point. You got the motive right there, Ben. Gutmanis killed the professor because he could finger him as a war criminal. D'you think you can run with that?"

"I need to put Gutmanis in the Warehouse District at the same time as Professor Kilitis' murder," Ben said. "I take it that the widow will be happy to testify against the guy."

"She hates his guts."

"Okay," Ben said. "And her ID-ing that sketch should be the icing on the cake. I'll put Gallagher on it."

"Oh, no!" Dwayne insisted. "I got a job to take care of before you guys move in."

Ben didn't like the sound of that. "What the hell's going on, Dwayne?"

"An old school buddy of mine is being held prisoner in the basement of the house where Gutmanis is living," Dwayne explained. "If the pressure is put on that Latvian son of a bitch, he's gonna kill Fritz."

"Who the hell is Fritz?"

"He's my little bitty buddy from my school days going from Willard through Roosevelt and finally East High. He even lived close to me when we were kids. His full name is Fritz Harrigan."

"And how do you know he's a prisoner in that house?"

"Because me and A.J. Kessler busted into the place and found him," Dwayne said. "Well, actually it was A.J. I couldn't fit through the basement window." He related the happenings on that particular night, being careful not to mention Patrolman Tommy Joe McNeil.

Ben was silent for a moment or two, drumming his fingers on the desk. "And, pray tell, what was the reason for that breaking-and-entering—and that's exactly what it was—where Fritz Harrigan was allegedly being held against his will."

"He jumped bail, and A.J. wanted him back," Dwayne explained. "But Fritz claimed he was on a secret government project and that the FBI would clear that all up when the time was right. But I was just talking to Steve Williams, and he said there wasn't no Federal projects going on."

"Okay."

"Anyhow, Fritz wouldn't come out of the basement with A.J. And, o'course, we didn't have a lot of time to start an argument that might have got real loud."

Ben took a deep breath then muttered, "How in the hell do you get into these crazy-ass situations?"

Dwayne grinned. "Just lucky I guess."

"Well, you ain't too lucky," Ben said. "I got to act on this and do it quick. You've just brought me information that you have proof that would solve a murder, and you've also thrown in a kidnapping on top of everything else. I'm putting Gallagher on the case."

"Shit!" Dwayne complained. "Fritz is gonna get killed. If Gutmanis don't do it, then that Kraut broad living with him prob'ly will."

"A Kraut broad? What's this all about?"

"I don't know for sure," Dwayne said with a shrug. "And I wouldn't want Gallagher in on this no matter what. Something like this is gonna take some finesse; know what I mean? That fucking Gallagher would fuck up a train wreck."

"I know you two guys hate each other. And maybe Gallagher's rough around the edges, but the guy's a damn good cop. He's like a stubborn bulldog when he gets on a case. If anyone can find evidence against Gutmanis, it's him, so I'm giving him the assignment."

"The minute Gallagher goes over to ask questions; Fritz is dead."

"I can give you a week before I sic Gallagher on the guy."

"Two weeks, Ben, please. None of the people involved in this caper are going anywhere."

"Oh, hell. All right you got two weeks."

"Starting tomorrow, okay? Most of this day is shot."

Ben had enough faith in Dwayne's ability to bring things to a satisfactory close, that he relented. "This is a big favor I'm doing you, Dwayne." Then he added, "And I want that sketch of the Latvian."

"Thanks," Dwayne said, handing him the folder and portrait. "I'll see you later, Ben."

———

PATROLMAN TOMMY JOE MCNEIL ROLLED INTO his watch area at eight p.m. Rather than begin his regular patrol duties, he had a special job to tend to for Dwayne Wheeler. Dwayne wanted to make sure that Karlis Gutmanis alias Karlis Watkins was still in residence at the Emporia Avenue house.

After parking in front of the target location, Tommy Joe gave the area a thorough scrutiny to see if anything had changed since the exciting night of little A.J. Kessler's one-man infiltration of the place. It all looked the same, and Tommy Joe left his car to walk up to the porch. He knocked on the door, and a somewhat attractive woman appeared. The young cop figured she was the female the guys on the other watches had noted. Her face flinched slightly at the sight of his uniform, but she maintained her composure.

"Yes?"

"How d'you do, ma'am," Tommy Joe said. "I'd like to speak to Mr. Watkins."

"What is this about?"

"Is he home?" Tommy Joe asked curtly.

"I'm not sure, I'll have to look."

The young cop grasped the screen door handle and pulled it open. He stepped inside. He expected some protest from her, but she seemed to accept his boldness as standard police behavior. Tommy Joe kept the expression on his face serious. "Tell him I'm the policeman from the other night when he heard prowlers."

Lotte wordlessly left the front room and went into a hallway. A moment later Karlis Gutmanis appeared barefoot, wearing an undershirt and khaki pants. "What it is?"

"Hello, Mr. Watkins," Tommy Joe said. He noted the man's brawniness and heavy shoulders and arms. If Watkins had gotten his hands on A.J. the night of the break-in, he would have torn the little guy to pieces. "I'm the officer who was here the night you had a prowler."

"*Ja?*"

"Yeah," Tommy Joe said. "I'm doing a routine follow-up on the incident, and wanted to find out if you had any more problems."

"No," Karlis said, shaking his head. "No more problems do I have."

"Now that's real good," Tommy Joe said, deciding he would like to take a look around. "I'd be glad to check out your house to see if there's weak spots for burglars to break in."

"No need," Karlis said. "Everything is fine."

"It's a free service for honest citizens from the Wichita Police Department."

"I am fine."

"Okay, Mr. Watkins," Tommy Joe said. "If it happens again, let us know. We'll deal with any troublemakers in the neighborhood."

"Thank you."

"And don't go running around outside with a pistol again."

"I will not do that," Karlis promised.

Tommy Joe left the house, thinking that Dwayne would be glad to learn the man was still in Wichita.

———

DWAYNE HADN'T HAD SEX SINCE THE LAST TIME with Donna Sue. He had even thought about asking Maisie Burnett from the Jayhawker Restaurant for a date since he knew for certain she was putting out. But since Donna Sue would hear about it, he decided to try A.J. Kessler's secretary Jill Stuart. A.J. had already told Dwayne she had a crush on him.

Jill was a cute girl, about eight years younger than he, and Dwayne had decided to ask her out with the intention of beginning a new romantic and sexual relationship. Their age difference could well mean that she would adapt quickly to his lifestyle with an acceptability that would prove long lasting.

———

IT WAS THE MORNING AFTER HIS VISITS TO MRS. Kilitis, Steve Williams, and Ben Forester when Dwayne went up to his office and dialed A.J.'s phone number, then leaned back in his chair and waited for an answer.

"Kessler Bail Bonds," Jill announced.

"Hi, Jill, this is Dwayne. How're you doing?"

"Pretty good," she replied. "A.J. is out on business and won't be back for a couple of hours."

"I didn't call to speak to him," Dwayne said. "I wanted to talk to you."

"Really?"

"You bet," he said cheerfully. "Would you care to take in a movie with me this Friday night?"

"Well, sure, Dwayne!" she answered happily. "I'd love to."

"Is there a particular picture you'd like to see?"

"Yeah!" she responded. "A Doris Day movie is showing at the Miller."

"Sounds good to me," Dwayne said. "Where do I pick you up?"

She gave an address of a house on Wellington Place.

"Okay," he said, after writing it in his notebook. "How does seven o'clock sound?"

"I'll be waiting, Dwayne."

———

IF DWAYNE HAD ANY SECOND THOUGHTS ABOUT taking out a girl who only recently graduated from high school, he smothered them. But when he went to her house on that Friday night, he immediately perceived that the whole idea might have some awkward drawbacks.

Her father answered the doorbell.

Dwayne was taken aback by the sight of a middle-aged man. When he learned Jill lived in a house, he assumed she shared the rent with one or more female roommates. "Uh...is Jill in?

The man gave him a suspicious look. "Yeah. She is. I'm her dad. What can I do for you?"

"Well, we're going out tonight."

The man hesitated, and it appeared he was about to slam the door shut, but after a moment's hesitation, he growled, "Wait." With that, he disappeared into the interior of the house.

Dwayne, at that point, experienced a strong feeling of indecision. Now he could hear loud voices—one male and the other female—that gave strong indications that a vigorous argument was in progress.

The quarrel eased down into dead silence, and a moment later Jill appeared at the door, stepping out onto the porch. "Hello, Dwayne."

"Hi. Is ever'thing all right?"

"Sure," she replied brightly. "Shall we go?"

As they walked toward the street, Jill slipped her arm in his. When they got inside the car, he started the engine but glanced over at her before driving away. "You're sure ever'thing is all right, huh?"

"Don't worry about Daddy. He complained you're too old for me to go out with." She rolled her eyes. "God! He thinks I'm still in junior high!"

Dwayne put the coupe into gear, and headed out into the street, thinking that a Wichita father could shoot an older man who seduced his innocent daughter as dead as dead could be, and there was no local jury that would convict him.

"I thought after the movie, we'd go out for something to eat," he suggested.

"I should tell you that Daddy wants me back home before midnight."

"I don't think we're going to disappoint your daddy," Dwayne said glumly, as he headed downtown.

The date began with the movie at the Miller Theater. It was a new Doris Day flick called *Romance on the High Seas*. It was a musical about two people—Doris Day and Jack Carson—getting in the middle of a married couple's quarrel. When

Doris Day sang *It's Magic*, Jill reached over and took Dwayne's hand.

Afterward they went to Armstrong's Ice Cream Parlor across from Roosevelt Junior High School for a snack. Normally, Dwayne would take their banana split special and devour it all, but that evening his stomach was too nervous. All he could manage was a couple of scoops of chocolate ice cream in a bowl, as pictures floated through his mind of Jill's father sitting out on the front porch with a shotgun.

It was 11:30 when Dwayne walked Jill up to her house. She quickly grabbed him, looking up into his face with a sweet smile. He gave her a peck on the cheek and fled.

CHAPTER 24

The conductor walked through the cars announcing that the train was fifteen minutes outside of Chicago, and Dwayne snapped himself out of a shallow nap and prepared to get off. The package he carried was similar to the last one in size he had delivered, but was a great deal heavier. Just to reassure himself, he checked his valise to make sure it was still nestled safely within his underwear and socks. This trip Dwayne was armed, and he patted his shoulder holster under his jacket. Pete Van Dyke had given him a serious warning that what he carried was valuable, and there were certain people who would kill to get their hands on it.

Dwayne hadn't wanted to make the trip when Pete called him to the suite in the Riverview Hotel the day before. He still had a week left on the time Lieutenant Ben Forester had given him before storming the Emporia Avenue house to rescue Fritz Harrigan. He was anxious to wrap that up and get his little chum away from the bad guys, and back to safety. Unfortunately he was obligated to Pete because of the previous agreement to keep himself available for that clandestine project. On the other hand there was the matter of the hundred dollars he would earn on the errand to consider.

Now, with the train halted, Dwayne stepped from the passenger car and moved with the crowd into the terminal. Within ten minutes he spotted Paul Jabaran; the big guy with the unusual jaw. There were no smiles in their greetings; only businesslike nods. Dwayne noted that Jabaran looked around the area carefully, then gestured that all was well. They walked together outside to the street where the same 1940 Desoto from previous trips was waiting. The guy at the wheel had also driven it the last time.

Nods were once more the accepted form of greeting, as Dwayne settled in the back seat. The car immediately moved into the late evening traffic, but this time, however, he noticed they were following a different route from his last visit. Rather than the parkway, they went through a seedy neighborhood before hitting a two-lane macadam road that was a state highway. At that point they headed westerly for three-quarters of an hour, then the driver turned off onto yet another highway to go in the opposite direction.

They went about five miles and reached an area that was familiar to Dwayne. This consisted of large, expensive homes that were widely spaced. He remembered the area from before, and when the car reached a gate, it was also recognizable to the shamus. The driver came to a stop and dimmed the lights. Two men walked into sight from somewhere nearby; one kept a lookout while his buddy opened the barrier. With that done, the car moved forward up the tree-lined drive and stopped at the side of the recognizable large one-story bungalow.

"C'mon," Jabaran said curtly.

They went inside to the same parlor that Dwayne recognized. The somber elegance was as it had been, and he took a seat on the plush sofa, holding on to his valise while Jabaran went through another door. In less than five minutes the disgraced British ex-captain Nigel Hawthorne appeared with Jabaran on his heels.

Hawthorne showed a toothy grin. "Hello, Wheeler, old boy," he said brightly.

"Howdy," Dwayne replied.

"I believe you have something for me, do you not?"

Dwayne opened his valise and pulled out the package. "Here you go."

"One moment, if you please, old boy," said Hawthorne, going over to a table. He turned his back to Dwayne to hide his actions, and fumbled with the parcel. "Jolly good! Just what we were waiting for." He looked over at Jabaran. "Do fetch some drinks, will you? The usual, of course."

Jabaran went to a sideboard to pour a couple of stiff Irish whiskies.

"I sense the proper moment for a toast," Hawthorne said. "This package may be quite small but its importance is considerable. This delivery is most significant, and will now permit our little organization to move into high gear. In other words; we are in business. And, of course, that means that a bloody good amount of money will be in our greedy hands within a very short time." He raised his glass. "Here's to scads of money and those chaps smart enough to get more than their fair share of it."

Dwayne stood up. "And the quicker the better."

Hawthorne laughed. "Right you are, old chap!"

———

PETE VAN DYKE HAD BEEN WAITING FOR DWAYNE at the Newton train station when the shamus returned from the errand. Now, traveling south toward Wichita, the two men were both in a relaxed mood. Dwayne pushed in the cigarette lighter, then pulled it out and touched it to his Lucky Strike. "Hawthorne was extremely happy to get that delivery."

Pete chuckled. "Not as happy as I am to hear he's in possession of it."

"So it means we've moved from the starting line out on the track, right?"

"That's it," Pete said.

Dwayne took a drag of the cigarette and exhaled. "When am I gonna get filled in on the facts of this operation?"

"It won't be long," Pete assured him. "Things are still a bit risky right now until the European side of the situation is firm and under control. As a matter of fact, it's better for you that you're kept in the dark."

"D'you think I'll be making any more trips soon?"

"Not for two or three weeks," Pete replied. "It'll probably be more like a month."

"That's good," Dwayne said. "I've got some real important work that needs my undivided attention. I've struck a deal for the homicide squad of the local cops to back off their investigation in one of them so I can get some work done."

"What's this all about?"

"A murder that occurred in the Warehouse District," Dwayne replied.

"What was your leverage?" Pete asked.

"I not only know who killed the guy, I can prove it."

"You were always a top notch investigator, Dwayne. I remember that from our army days."

"Except when I got carried away with living high on the hog."

"Not to worry," Pete said. "It's obvious you're a lot more mature now."

Dwayne snuffed out the cigarette in the ashtray. "Don't forget you're gonna be dropping me off at my rooming house."

"Oh, yeah," Pete said. "It's a good thing you reminded me."

He took a left turn at the location of Central and Broadway, heading east.

———

DONNA'S SECOND DATE WITH BRIAN MURCHISON was not a weekend affair. It was a special dinner on a Wednesday evening to celebrate the wrap up of the conference with the Louisiana Oil Cartel. All the Murchison field supervisors and their wives would be there along with the group from New Orleans.

It was strictly formal, and since it was a business gathering, Brian signed an authorization for Donna to be given funds to purchase a complete evening outfit; including a ball gown, shoes, small purse and accessories. The latter were earrings, a necklace and bracelet with small but not inexpensive diamonds. The authorization statement he put on the voucher was that she needed to be dressed appropriately while socializing with the field representatives who sent in their reports to her. Naturally the finance manager signed off on the document without argument.

All that had been a very pleasant surprise for her, but not half as much as when she was informed she would be flown down to Dallas, Texas to an exclusive woman's boutique to pick out what she wanted. The Murchison Enterprise's assistant protocol officer Marilyn Owens accompanied her to provide advice and to sign the bill that came to over two hundred dollars. Marilyn worked for the son of Brian's sister Kate who was the chief protocol officer. But his title was just a formality. He had been shuttled off to the position since he had made a mess not only of his studies in college, but also had several arrests for drunk driving, disorderly conduct and one instance of assaulting a law officer. To make things worse, he had gotten a girl into trouble, and that had cost plenty of money not to mention some difficult negotiations before it was settled. Not much was expected of the dissipated young man, and he only showed up at the office once or twice a month, and the visits were mostly to flirt with company stenographers. Thus, Marilyn actually ran the department.

When Donna returned to Wichita, she followed her usual practice after any shopping trip, by trying on her latest purchases for a slow and thorough study of her choices. She felt like a movie star as she studied herself in the dresser mirror. The cost of the gown had been more than she earned in three weeks working at the Jayhawker restaurant, and when the evening purse, shoes and jewelry were thrown in, the whole package amounted to four month's salary of a waitress.

———

ON THE EVENING OF THE GALA, BRIAN SHOWED up at her place in the Royal Arms Apartments, and his reaction to her appearance had been one of astonishment. He didn't say a word for a moment, then spoke under his breath. "You're always attractive, Donna, but right now you are positively beautiful!"

"Thank you, Brian," she said, smiling at him. "I'm glad you think so."

"Oh, believe me, I think so. C'mon, I want to show you off."

His comments made a sudden realization form in her conscious mind. There were no doubts whatsoever that her assent in the world had now evolved into a rapid climb upward, and it would be up to her how high she would fly.

A big surprise also awaited Donna when they went downstairs and walked out of the building. Rather than Brian's Packard, a limousine with a chauffeur waited for them at the curb. The driver opened the rear door, and Brian allowed Donna to precede him into the interior. When he joined her on the seat, he grinned. "Murchison Enterprises has rented limousines for all the guests tonight. Some had to be brought up from Oklahoma City so there would be enough. Impressive, no?"

"Impressive, yes!" Donna said, delighted. "I just hope this one doesn't turn into a pumpkin after midnight."

"Not to worry, darling. None of this is an illusion."

The fact he had addressed her with such an endearment caught her by surprise. She glanced out the window, not thinking of where she was going, but how far the trip would take her.

The arrival at the Prairie Wind Golf and Tennis Club brought the couple into a whirl of social activity. Chauffeured limousines were pulling up to the front of the building forming a line, and each in its turn disgorged the elegant passengers who walked under a canopy into the main entrance. A liveried doorman greeted each with a salute, holding the heavy glass portals open for them.

There were ushers stationed inside who directed the partiers toward the immense Chisholm Trail Ballroom.

When Brian and Donna entered the chamber, they adhered to what Donna now understood was a serious custom that had to be complied with at any company gala. They went directly to where Ted and Dolly Murchison were seated at the table of honor. Brian's parents were affable as ever, and Miss Dolly was especially friendly toward Donna. Mr. Murchison gave Donna a bold perusal, and his wife remarked how beautiful she looked.

After a brief chat, hurried by the line that was forming behind them, Brian and Donna broke away. As they worked their way to their table, Donna held on to his arm. "Your mother is very nice."

"She likes you," Brian said. "I got that from the horse's mouth; which is Dad, of course. You must remember she was a secretary for the company when she met him."

"And he was quite cordial, too."

Brian laughed. "The old man was lusting after you. I'm just glad he didn't reach out and grab you."

When they reached the table, they found that the other two couples seated there were J.T. and Bertha Turner, the redneck pair who had come up the hard way in the oil fields of east Texas; and a sophisticated man and wife from Louisiana by the name of Raymond and Pauline Robichaux who Donna had also met at the Murchison mansion patio party. Although both were college educated—Ray was a petroleum engineer and Pauline had majored in English—they had a southern friendliness about them that Donna appreciated. Once more her growing ego was fed by a flow of compliments.

The crowd was allowed a half hour of socializing as wine was served, and J.T. Turner had just explained to

everybody that the ballroom was named after the trail that
Jesse Chisholm, a half-Cherokee Texan had blazed from
San Antonio to Wichita back in 1864. Before he could
elaborate more, the master-of-ceremonies—a senior vice
president who was Brian's cousin Harold—quieted them
down with the announcement that dinner was about to
be served.

The meal started out with Waldorf salads. The main
course was a choice of roasted chicken and rice pilaf or
broiled sirloin with baked potatoes. The oilmen went for
the meat while most of their wives preferred the chicken.
The vegetables were the same for each; servings of
asparagus and squash. The dessert was a chocolate mousse
topped with whipped cream and a cherry, while the
gentlemen enjoyed an additional treat of Napoleon
Brandy that would be sipped when they lit up their after
dinner cigars.

The waiters cleared the tables as quickly as possible
so that a short program could be presented. This
consisted of cousin Harold Murchison announcing the
number of barrels that each location had produced over
the previous year. It was noted—and applauded—that
the Louisiana fields had increased their output by
twenty-six percent, and plans were being made to apply
new technology to begin searching for oil beneath the
waters of the Gulf of Mexico. More applause. Several
personages were recognized for their good service to the
various projects, with J.T. Turner honored for his
successful efforts in foiling a unionizing attempt at an
oilfield northwest of Houston.

With all the formalities taken care of, the orchestra
filed in to take their seats on the raised dais at the open
end of the room. The musical program began with a
medley of Glenn Miller hits, and the ladies quickly led

their reluctant men out to dance. Half-finished brandy snifters and smoldering cigars were left back on the tables.

Brian, unlike the other males, was looking forward to taking a few turns on the dance floor, and he took Donna out to begin what would be a full evening of swaying to the rhythms as they glided across the room. Donna noticed that on this occasion, he held her close to him and they danced cheek-to-cheek. And during the times they sat out the dances, his arm was draped across the back of her chair with his hand gently touching her shoulders.

And so the evening went.

———

LEAVING THE DANCE WAS THE REVERSE OF THE arrival. The limousines began showing up, but no one worried about riding in the same one they came in. They simply stood in a disorganized line, and each couple entered one of the luxury vehicles as they worked their way to the front. Brian and Donna were among the last to be taken from the grounds for the return ride to the city.

When they arrived in front of the Royal Arms Apartments, Brian got out and dismissed the limo. When the chauffer drove off, Donna gave him a puzzled look. "How are you going to get home?"

"I'll call a cab," he said, taking her by the arm and leading her into the lobby. During the elevator ride up to the fifth floor, Brian had his arm around her waist, pulling her close to him. Then he gave her a lingering kiss. Donna felt a nervous chill with the thought that this was the evening. He obviously expected to spend the night; the problem was that she might not be quite ready for their relationship to reach that point.

She took out her key at the door and opened it. Brian

followed closely as she went in. Donna looked at him. "Would you like a cup of coffee?"

Brian responded by taking her in his arms, holding her firm and close to him. He put a hand under her chin, and lifted it up. This kiss was not persistent, but it was fixed. At first she felt like resisting, then gave in and their lips were pressed against each other as she responded.

Then Donna broke away as thoughts of Dwayne Wheeler once more slipped into her emotional state. She spoke softly, saying, "Brian."

He didn't seem upset. "Yeah?"

"I'm not...not ready."

He slowly let his arms loosen, then he smiled. "Okay. Then how about that coffee?"

CHAPTER 25

The deadline for Dwayne's planned raid to rescue Fritz Harrigan was nearing. He had talked with A.J. Kessler about it after his meeting with Lieutenant Ben Forester. He emphasized to the small bail bondsman that he wanted to move on it as quickly as possible. A.J., however, had some prior commitments that would delay the operation until just about the last minute. Dwayne would have to wait for him, since A.J., as a bail bondsman would have a lawful right to break into the house since they knew that one of his errant clients was either hiding there or being forcibly held by others. If Dwayne tried the forced entry with anybody else, there would be all sorts of unpleasant legal ramifications. He might even end up charged with breaking and entering. That would bring about the loss of his private investigator license.

The delay irked Dwayne somewhat, but as long as the police didn't make any moves he could afford to wait. But if the law beat him to the Emporia Avenue house, it would tip off the Latvian and his German wife that they were under suspicion for the murder of Professor Mikelis

Kilitis. And Fritz Harrigan's life wouldn't be worth a plug nickel after that. The couple would murder the artist before fleeing Wichita.

Since he had some time to spare, Dwayne decided he'd gone long enough without sex. His plans to romance Jill Stuart had turned out to be a bust. He never dreamed she was living with her parents. She was over eighteen, but dating under the circumstances was not appealing, even if they did become intimate. Any sort of long term relationship would mean having to sneak her into motel rooms, and that was strictly illegal. If they were caught, their relationship could be declared a common law marriage. And there would be the matter of a furious Wichita father who would have a choice of shooting him or forcing the couple into a wedding. Dwayne pretty much figured Mr. Stuart would choose the firearm route.

Dwayne had gone into A.J.'s place of business a couple of times to stay up-to-date on the little man's availability, and each time Jill had been sullen about the fact he hadn't asked her out on another date. He told her he was busy day and night with a couple of cases, but she was suspicious of his excuses. After she burst into tears during his last visit to the office, he decided to handle all his communications with A.J. over the phone. Later, when things had settled down, he would have a quiet talk with Jill and explain the situation kindly and fully.

———

DWAYNE REACHED A POINT WHERE HE COULD barely control his natural urges. His sexual state of mind and frustrations were male phenomena that would not be easily understood by women. Even after the break-up of a relationship, females were dismayed learning that their former lovers were quickly dating again. This was simply because men's sex drives don't slip into neutral even when their hearts are broken. And Dwayne's certainly hadn't; even though he missed Donna Sue a great deal. He, like other males in that same predicament, had become physically frustrated and was ready to seek female company to satisfy those urges. In such situations men are not thinking with their brains. It is another part of their anatomy that drives their behavior.

———

IT WAS ON A FRIDAY NIGHT WHEN HE swallowed his pride and opted for an evening at Western Danceland to see what sort of woman he could pick up. This was the redneck nightclub just across the city limits on Highway 81. It had been established during the war when a local entrepreneur by the name of Jessie Pickens saw the advantages to setting up a dance hall for the defense plant workers who had flooded into Wichita for the available jobs.

The employment was a Godsend for most of these people who came from Oklahoma, Arkansas and Texas. They had suffered long months of unemployment and hard times through the Great Depression and the Dust Bowl. But after President Roosevelt declared war on the German Reich and the Japanese Empire, there was work available with plenty of overtime in Wichita, Kansas. They left their home states to toil faithfully and hard, building airplanes at the defense plants to support the war effort. And those workers needed a place to play just as enthusiastically on their evenings off.

Their idea of blowing off steam was raucous to say the least, and more than just a little violent. Fights were common during their revelry, and most of the conflicts in the club were over the available women. But when some guy's wife was involved, the incident could turn deadly. Knifings and even shootings occurred in such cases that would bring out the homicide detectives of the Sedgwick County Sheriff's Department. Generally it was only a matter of finding out from witnesses who the killer was, then going out to pick him up in Planeview. This was the town established southeast of the city to house the influx of out-of-staters working in the aircraft plants.

Dwayne prepared for an evening that guaranteed an absolute certainty of a sexual encounter. He donned his special sports jacket with rodeo pockets and shoulder patches that gave him a western look. It would fit in well in the atmosphere of the night club, though he didn't go far enough to wear a Stetson hat and cowboy boots. Thus, with his hair slicked down and a generous splash of Old Spice aftershave lotion, Dwayne stuck a pint bottle of Jack Daniels Whisky in his inside jacket pocket. He had a backup he kept in the trunk of his old Pontiac coupe. A quick check showed a couple of condoms in his wallet, and with that final touch, he was fully prepared. Thus girded for a *rencontre d'amour*, Dwayne Wheeler sauntered out of his rented room in happy anticipation of getting his ashes hauled that evening.

Dwayne drove down Douglas to Broadway where he turned south and headed toward the city limits. After leaving Wichita proper, it was only another ten minutes to Western Danceland, and he pulled into the parking lot. Even though it was only eight o'clock, there were so many cars that he could only find a place in the outer reaches of the area. For what Dwayne wanted, it was just as well since it offered a greater potential for privacy. He parked and made his way through the rows of vehicles to the front door, and strode purposely into the establishment.

"Hey, Dwayne!" greeted Benny Gordon. He was the husky bouncer of the place and an ex-paratrooper. Dwayne often hired him to help out in strong arm assignments he had from time to time, and Benny had lent a hand not too long ago when a couple of Kansas City pimps needed their asses kicked.

"How're you doing, Benny?"

"Not bad," Benny answered. "Where's Donna Sue?"

"Aw, we broke up," Dwayne said.

"No shit? I figgered you two was together for life."

Dwayne shrugged. "Well, at times things don't always work out the way you want 'em to."

"Ain't it the truth?" Benny remarked. "By the way, there's a pretty good band tonight."

"I ain't thinking about doing a lot of dancing."

Benny laughed out loud. "Horny, huh? There's the usual available women, but none of 'em are ever gonna be movie stars. Fact is, some of 'em got faces that'd stop a Sherman tank going full speed."

"It ain't their faces I'm inter'sted in," Dwayne said with a wink. He walked farther into the place, and paused to study the layout.

A long scarred and scuffed bar went along one entire side of the interior while booths dominated the other. The center of the building was the dance floor, and at that moment there were close to a couple of dozen people dancing to music from the juke box. A raised stage was at the north end where the bands played. It was covered by a heavy gauge steel screen to protect the musicians from flying debris that would be hurled at them by the drunken critics in the audience.

Dwayne took a deep breath, then headed directly for

the bar. He slid onto a stool and signaled to the bartender. "Soda."

The bartender pulled a bottle of Canadian Club soda water off the shelf behind him, and poured some into a glass. He sat the mixer in front of Dwayne and picked up the dollar laid out for him. Dwayne pulled his bottle out of his pocket and poured himself a generous shot.

"Hey, Dwayne."

He turned around and saw the owner Jesse Pickens standing behind him. "Hey, Jesse. What's the good word?"

"I got three good words," Jesse said with a grin. "Friday—night—crowd. Where's Donna Sue?"

"We ain't going together no more."

"Damn! I never thought I'd see the day," Jesse said. "Women is fickle, ain't they?" He had a promiscuous wife who would disappear for a week or so at a time. He'd hire Dwayne to track her down, and the shamus would usually find her drunk and alone in a hotel room where some guy had left her. Jesse's teen-age daughter was showing the same tendencies, but she preferred truck drivers. Jesse took it all in stride, showing a tolerance that amazed all the men he knew.

"Things change between two people," Dwayne said. "And they just drift apart."

"Yep," Jesse said. "Well, I got to go mix with the customers. See you later, Dwayne."

Dwayne finished off his first drink and ordered another set-up. He turned around on the barstool, gazing out over the scene before him. It was hard to believe, but before the evening was over, the place would be packed almost wall to wall with people. But that wasn't what concerned Dwayne at that moment. He continued looking around, until he found what he was looking for.

A couple of women were sitting together in a booth. They wore summer print dresses, and were a bit on the plump side. Both were large breasted with wide, plain faces. He watched them for five minutes until he was certain they were alone. With that established, he got up and walked across the floor, threading his way through the dancers, until he reached them.

"Hello, ladies."

They both looked up, then smiled. The pair liked what they saw in the good looking man who had just greeted them. He seemed the sort of guy who could take care of himself as well as any lady he might be with. One of them gave him a bold look. "And hello to you."

"You wouldn't mind if I joined you, would you?"

The one who spoke quickly scooted over. "Just slide on in here, honey."

Dwayne responded to the invitation, and sat down. "My name is Dwayne."

"Hi," the woman said. "I'm Helen, and this is my friend Dora."

Dora seemed to concede that Helen had laid claim on the stranger. "Hi."

"What're you ladies drinking?" Dwayne asked.

"Just Cokes right now," Dora said.

"Well, we can do better than that," Dwayne assured. He glanced around and caught a waitress' attention. When she came over, he asked Helen and Dora what kind of set-ups they wanted.

"It depends on what we got to put into it," Helen said.

"I got some Jack Daniels right here in my pocket," Dwayne said. "And when that's gone there's a spare in my car. And I don't mean the tire."

The two women laughed and ordered set-ups of

ginger ale. Dwayne laid out two dollar bills, then reached over and took Helen by the hand. "Let's dance."

They went out on the floor, and swung into the rhythm of the country-western music. Dwayne pulled Helen close to him, and she didn't resist. "I don't think I've seen you here before," she said.

"I used to come out here all the time. But I been busy." His right hand was around her waist, and when he slid it down he could feel the full feminine flesh beneath the skirt. He began to erect and within a moment she felt it. She gazed into his face with a smile and a wink.

Dwayne generally didn't like to dance, but he stayed out on the floor through three songs as he and Helen gave silent sexual signals to each other. Finally she said, "I could use a drink."

"The set ups are waiting," he said.

They walked over to where Dora sat, and slid back into the booth. Dwayne produced his whisky and poured strong shots into the ginger ales. Then he slowly sipped his drink while Helen and Dora took deep swallows of their libations.

After an hour of drinking and dancing, another guy showed up having obviously noticed that Dora was alone. Within five minutes they were linked up, and Dwayne and Helen could give each other their full attention. The evening became one of dancing, drinking and necking. By eleven o'clock, Helen allowed Dwayne's hand to wander up under her skirt. When he tried to get into her brassiere, she resisted. Unlike the skirt, people could see that bit of hanky-panky. Dwayne concentrated his efforts on getting feels between her chubby thighs.

IT WAS FIFTEEN MINUTES BEFORE ONE A.M. WHEN
Dwayne and Helen walked together through the cars in
the parking lot. They reached his old Pontiac and she took
note of the coupe. "No back seat, huh?"

"Nope," he said. "Sorry."

"Oh, hell, that's okay," Helen said, waiting for him to
open the door. "I done it on a tractor once when I was a
young gal down in Texas."

They got in the car and turned their attention to
much more serious petting than could be done inside the
club. Within five minutes her blouse was open from neck
to waist, and her brassiere was off, revealing ponderous
breasts with large nipples. A little more necking ensued
and her passions rose. She doffed her panties and pulled
her skirt up.

Helen lay back with her head crammed against the
passenger door, her left leg up over the seat and her right
on the dashboard. Dwayne slipped on a condom and got
into position with his shorts and trousers pulled down to
his knees. He humped away and Helen gasped in time
with his thrusting. He ejaculated with a near violent quiver-
ing, then relaxed, almost collapsing on top of her.

"Damn, Dwayne!" Helen said. "You ain't had any for
awhile, have you? It felt like you busted a crate of eggs in
there."

———

IT WAS NINE O'CLOCK ON SATURDAY MORNING
when Dwayne walked into the OK Barbershop. He had
brought his trusty old valise with a change of clothing, a
towel and soap. He stopped at Ernie Bascombe's chair,
dropping off a quarter. "Shower."

"Sure," Ernie said, pausing at his haircutting chore. "You look like you had quite a night, huh?"

Dwayne grinned. "Yeah."

Ernie started cutting hair again. "You got a call from Lieutenant Forester about an hour ago. He wants you to call him back."

Dwayne was mildly curious as he went to the front payphone. He put in a nickel and dialed, then waited for Ben to answer. When the lieutenant replied, Dwayne spoke in the husky voice of a hangover. "This is Dwayne. What's up?"

"I got bad news for you," Ben said. "I can't hold out on that professor's murder any more. The pressure is on from W.U. to find out who did in their guy, and the chief is leaning on me. I'm sending Gallagher over to that Emporia address this afternoon to serve some papers."

"Hey, what the shit, Ben!" Dwayne said, snapping out of his semi-stupor. "You promised me two weeks! This is gonna shake up that Latvian son of a bitch and put him on guard."

"Sorry," Ben said.

"That means Fritz Harrigan is up to his neck in shit!"

"Look, Dwayne, I feel bad about this, I really do."

"Goddamn it, Ben!" Dwayne said. "Why don't you let it slide? You can come up with some excuse, can't you?"

"Goodbye, Dwayne." It was apparent Ben didn't want to have a lot of conversation on the subject.

Dwayne slipped the receiver back on the hook. He had to see A.J. Kessler immediately if not sooner, and he headed for the door. Ernie looked up from his work. "Hey! I thought you was gonna take a shower."

"That's all right," Dwayne said over his shoulder. "I just had some cold water thrown in my face."

―――――

Sergeant Al Gallagher, homicide squad of the Wichita Police Department, pulled up to the curb in front of the Emporia Avenue residence. He picked up the 10 x 14 envelope on the seat beside him, and got out of the car. The house to his direct front seemed perfectly normal for the neighborhood; it was well kept and the small front lawn was mowed and trimmed.

The plain clothes detective walked up to the front porch and ignored the doorbell. He banged heavily four times on the door. After a brief pause, he repeated the pounding. It was Gallagher's style to be as aggressive as possible before he entered a target residence. It helped set a proper tone with the people inside.

The door opened and Karlis Gutmanis, his eyes narrowed with irritation, glowered at the caller. "What is it you are wanting?"

"Sergeant Gallagher, Wichita Police," he said, showing his badge. "Are you Karlis Watkins?"

Karlis nodded. "I told other policeman is no need to look at house."

Gallagher frowned as he opened the screen door. "What other policeman?" he asked, pushing Karlis back into the living room.

"Somebody sneak around house one night," Karlis said, immediately worried by the assertive cop. "He come here and can't find nobody. Then come back later and ask if he can check the house. I tell him I don't need that."

"Well, that's got nothing to do with me," Gallagher said, irritated by the foreign accent. "Does anybody else live here?"

"My wife."

"Call her," Gallagher ordered. Karlis called out Lotte's

name, and she came into the living room from the kitchen. She looked at Gallagher, then to Karlis, noting he was very uneasy.

"Is police sergeant," Karlis explained.

Gallagher scowled. "You two go over and sit down on the sofa." He waited until they settled down, then he opened the envelope and pulled out the morgue photograph of Mikelis Kilitis. "D'you know this guy?"

Karlis shook his head.

"What about you, lady?"

Lotte looked at the photo that showed the dead man on a gurney. "I do not know him."

"He's Latvian," Gallagher said. "And you're Latvian, ain't you?"

"I am Latvian," Karlis said. "My wife is German."

"Okay," the sergeant said. He looked at Lotte. "Where's your passports?"

"They are in the bedroom."

"Fetch 'em quick."

Lotte gave Karlis another look, then got up and left the room. When she came back she handed the documents to Gallagher. He took them from her hand, turning to the first pages. "It says here that your name is Gutmanis. How's come you're calling yourselves Watkins?"

Lotte decided to answer, since Karlis' English was wanting. "We only use it with strangers," she explained. "We are not hiding who we are. The name 'Gutmanis' is sometimes difficult for foreigners to remember."

"*You're* the foreigners, lady!" Gallagher snapped. "And what're you doing in Wichita?"

"We hope to open a restaurant," Lotte said, falling into a preconceived cover story. "I was a chef in Germany before the war. I have much experience. We are in Wichita to see if the opportunity is right in this city."

"Listen to me good," Gallagher said. "This dead guy here was shot in the Warehouse District. We can't find any connection between him and nobody else. And it looks like whoever offed the guy did it for personal reasons. The date of the guy's death is on the photo. Where were you two that night?"

"At home here," Lotte said. "All evening. We did not go out."

Gallagher knew he couldn't disprove the alibi at the moment. He reached into his jacket pocket, pulling out a paper. "This here's a court order saying you can't leave Wichita. You do that and you're fugitives, understand? The name on it is Watkins, but it has your address." Next he got a pen and wrote on the document. "I just scratched out 'Watkins' and wrote in 'Gutmanis' and initialed it. And them passports won't do you no good if you try to leave the country. This information is gonna be sent out on the teletype and that means it'll go all over the U.S. of A."

Karlis swallowed nervously. "Are you thinking I killed the Latvian man?"

"At this point, I got no idea whether you did or not," Gallagher said. "But let me tell you something, buddy. I'm gonna act like you did it, understand? And that's bad news for you." He turned and walked to the front door. After opening it, he spun around on his heel once more and glared at them. "Remember, you ain't supposed to leave Wichita. You're under suspicion of first degree homicide, and that's official. Got it?"

Karlis and Lotte watched him exit the house. He left the door open, and Lotte walked over and shut it. "Sometimes you go out," she said.

He shrugged. "That means nothing."

Lotte took a deep breath, then asked, "Did you kill that man, Karlis?"

"Of course not," Karlis insisted. "He is a stranger to me."

"I have never been to Latvia," Lotte said. "I have no knowledge about that part of your life." Lotte was silent for a moment, the softly said, "We must inform Nigel about this."

Karlis gave her a furious glare. "That's not for you to worry about!"

CHAPTER 26

I t was one o'clock in the morning and Karlis Gutmanis sat alone at the kitchen table. Lotte had gone to bed an hour earlier after an entire evening of fretting about the police detective who had come with the picture of Mikelis Kilitis lying dead on a gurney. The not quite veiled accusations of the policeman and the court order he brought with him had disturbed Lotte. After the detective left, she had gotten so upset that Karlis had slapped her hard across the face couple of times to shock her into calming down.

The ashtray in front of him was filled with cigarette butts as he smoked heavily and drank the potent clear whisky he purchased during his excursions to that part of Wichita called the Warehouse District. As he sat there sullen and growing drunk, Karlis' mind drifted back to how he came to develop a habit of visiting the neighborhood.

THE PRELIMINARY OUTING HAPPENED SHORTLY after he and Lotte had arrived in Wichita. On that evening he had fallen into one of his frequent black moods and left the house for a solitary walk. He strolled slowly down to Douglas Avenue with no particular destination in mind. After going a few blocks he noticed a taxi coming toward him, and Karlis raised his hand to signal for the cabbie to pull over.

"Where we headed, buddy?" the driver asked.

Karlis, being used to Europe, spoke plainly. "I want to go to woman. To whore."

"Sure," the driver said. "It ain't far."

They drove a half mile, then the guy turned north into a dimly lit area of warehouses and other drab buildings. A quick swing down an alley brought them to a wire fence in back of an obviously empty building with boarded up windows. The driver stopped and honked twice, and a man appeared from the shadows. He exchanged some words with the cabbie, and handed him a dollar.

The driver glanced at Karlis in the mirror. "Here you go, buddy. This is a swell guy, and he can take you to some really good-looking women."

Karlis was skeptical and suspicious, but he had his Luger pistol with him, so he decided to take a chance. He paid the fifty cents shown on the meter to the driver, and got out of the cab.

The stranger walked up to him as the vehicle drew away. "C'mon, buddy. I got what you're looking for."

Karlis stuck his hand over his waistband and felt the pistol as he followed after the man. They went inside the fence and down to the building. His escort knocked on the door and opened it. Karlis could see four or five women inside in the illumination of a bare light bulb. They were seated on a wooden bench in some sort of queue. The one nearest the door spotted Karlis and got on her feet, walking up to him. "Looking for a good time, honey?"

"Yes," Karlis replied, his uneasiness fading away.

The whore took him by the hand and they walked down to Douglas, heading toward a block where several cheap hotels were located. He was led into a lobby of the nearest one, and she got a key from the desk clerk. They went up to a rear room on the second floor, and the whore unlocked the door, leading the way in. There was nothing there but a bed with a dirty mattress. The woman looked at him. "Okay. Five bucks."

Karlis paid, and was rewarded when she took off her coat and unbuttoned the top of her dress. She was braless and when she pulled up her skirt and lay down on the mattress it was obvious she had no other underclothing. Karlis disrobed the minimum amount, then mounted her and did his business. It didn't take long and in less than five minutes, they had both put themselves back together again.

"You was real good, honey," she said. "Go ahead and leave now."

Karlis walked out of the room and down the stairs. He stepped out onto the sidewalk to amble slowly back to Emporia Avenue.

That was the first of dozens of jaunts to the area for sex with the slatterns that were available there. The only time he had taken a taxi was the first incident, and after that he always walked the distance from the house. The last visit was the most memorable, and afterward Karlis knew he could never return to the neighborhood. It was summer by then, and the long days lit the area until a bit past eight p.m. He had been walking down the familiar alley and stepped through the gate toward the building where the pimp kept his whores. As he approached, he could see the man talking with someone else whose back was toward him. When the Latvian walked up, the stranger turned and they locked eyes, and both gasped. It was Professor Mikelis Kilitis from the University of Riga.

"Gutmanis!" Kilitis exclaimed under his breath.

Only the discipline of serving in the SS kept Karlis from panicking. He thought fast, then smiled. "I never thought I would see you again, Professor."

"Nor I you," Kilitis said. "What are you doing here?"

"The same as you," Karlis said. He grinned. "What's the matter? Isn't the wife satisfying you?"

Kilitis ignored the brazen question, asking, "How did you come to America?"

Karlis used a cover story he had composed months before in case he ended up in an awkward situation such as this one. "I am working for U.S. intelligence of course. Many of us are who fought for the German cause have been offered opportunities to serve the Americans."

"You did not fight," Kilitis said with a sneer. "Doing police work for the Gestapo in the rear areas was your method for serving the Nazis."

Karlis displayed a friendly smile. "See here, Professor. The war is over, is it not? Your side was victorious, and I congratulate you. But I am still in the struggle, you see. And my enemy is the same; the Soviet Union." He looked around. "It is best if we do not attract attention. Come with me to the end of the alley where we may speak privately. After all we share a common foe now. I believe you might be interested enough in my current situation to want to give some support."

"Very well," Kilitis said. "But frankly I have my doubts."

They walked out of the fenced-in area to the alley and made their way down to an area containing numerous trash bins. By then the sun was down enough that the shadows offered a covering of darkness. Karlis carefully pulled his Luger pistol from his waist band, then turned to face the professor. He fired a head shot, then put two quick bullets into Kilitis' chest.

The victim crumpled to the alley's surface, and Karlis needed no more than a quick glance to see the man was dead. He hurried out of the area to take a long, round-about way back to Emporia Avenue.

NOW, IN THE KITCHEN, HE LIT A CIGARETTE OFF the butt of another, then took a swallow of the whiskey. He lost track of how many times he'd gone to the area for women. That was also where he learned there were no liquor stores in this strange place halfway around the world from Europe, but he could purchase alcohol in the form of a locally made distilled spirit called moonshine. It was sold in fruit jars for a dollar a pint.

Karlis didn't search out the prostitutes because of pure carnal desire. He and Lotte had sex on a regular basis, and she never refused him anything. What he sought from the street whores was a sort of revenge against his wife for all the times she went to bed with other men to bring money into the house.

Now his mind turned back to the worst days of his entire life.

It all began in desperation during that chaotic period right after the war. At first he had thought himself fortunate not to have died in those last bitter battles as had many of his Latvian comrades who served on the front lines. He even managed to surrender to a British unit in the west of Germany.

After a couple of months in a POW camp, he was repatriated and rejoined Lotte in Frankfort. But they faced a life of deprivation that bordered on starvation. That was when she began selling herself.

Karlis could remember sitting at home waiting while she was out. No matter how hard he tried, he couldn't keep his thoughts from turning to images of her performing all sorts of sex acts on common foreign soldiers of the occupation. She brought back money and cigarettes and soap that could be traded on the black market for food.

Later, as months passed and a semblance of order was established in Germany, her good looks gave her an opportunity to move up to a better class of clientele by servicing officers. And she did it for cash and at times she could earn a great amount by going to parties at army officers' clubs for all night sessions in which she entertained as many as a half dozen horny rankers. It was one of those that gave her gonorrhea; and, of course, Karlis had become infected, too. After the next session of work, they used her earnings to purchase some penicillin on the black market, and took it to a doctor for injections.

The entire state of affairs humiliated Karlis Gutmanis to the point that at one time while she was out, he had taken his pistol and stuck the barrel in his mouth with a genuine intention of blowing his brains out. But somehow he resisted the temptation of blessed death with a wild hope that better days were on the horizon.

It was almost one year after the German Reich surrendered, that Lotte came back mid-morning from a private party at a night club. She had met a British banker with an interesting proposition involving a trip to America. It would involve her once more in selling herself, but this time it would be to only one person. And, better yet, after she told the man about her ex-SS husband who was a pretty tough guy, the Englishman wanted him to go, too. The pay would be fantastic; enough for them to realize their dream of opening a restaurant, and perhaps even going to Switzerland to begin a new life. When he heard the news, Karlis was glad he hadn't put a nine-millimeter bullet in his skull.

Now Karlis poured the last of the jar of moonshine into the cup and lit up a cigarette. He quickly downed the liquor, then got up and went to the cabinet for another pint. After he returned to the table, he began thinking dark thoughts about Fritz Harrigan down in the basement. The little swine had been having sex with Lotte just like the soldiers in Europe, and he hated the young artist with as much intensity as he had her other customers. But at least he would end this present episode with a fulfillment of complete vengeance. It would be even more satisfying than killing Mikelis Kilitis.

Lotte suddenly appeared in the kitchen door. Karlis looked at her. "Want a drink?"

"Yes," she replied, sitting down. "Even if it's that cheap American stuff."

Karlis forced a grin. "One could strip paint off military trucks with this whisky." He grabbed a cup for her from the cabinet, and returned. After he served her, Karlis shoved the pack of cigarettes across the table.

Lotte took one and lit up. "The plates Fritz is working on are finished, are they not?"

Karlis nodded. "As soon as the last batch he made is

approved, we will be returning to Europe. They have already been delivered to Chicago."

Lotte picked up her cup and forced herself to take a swallow of the moonshine. "And what becomes of little Fritz at that point?"

"We've discussed the subject before."

"I ask again; what becomes of little Fritz?"

"He gets a shot of sodium pentothal as he did when he came here," Karlis said. "But this time it will be lethal since you cannot seem to stand the thought of him getting shot."

Lotte looked down in her cup. "Another killing, Karlis?"

Karlis grinned. "This will be the second here in Wichita. I killed that Latvian in the photograph the police sergeant showed us. There is a long story involved that I will tell you later."

Lotte's face tightened into an expression of despair.

"And after I dispose of your young friend in the basement, we will catch a train for Chicago," Karlis stated.

"How can we do that?" Lotte fearfully demanded to know. "We have official orders to stay in Wichita. The police sergeant told us so."

"Bah!" Karlis said. "It will be easy to get to Chicago and then to New York without the police realizing we have gone. You forget that we are working for clever and powerful people. When we reach New York we can easily get forged passports with new names. Then we go all the way to Germany."

Lotte remained silent, and when she spoke again her voice was strained. "Why must Fritz die? He knows nothing."

"Orders."

Lotte laughed without humor. "Ah! The answer each

SS soldier gives as to why certain peopled must be killed or outrages committed. Orders." She raised her cup. "Here is to obedience. Blind, stupid obedience! It makes the perfect excuse to be a complete barbaric swine, does it not?"

Karlis growled, "I'm not giving you any more whisky."

CHAPTER 27

A.J. Kessler lived on Menlo Drive in the Schweiter Edition on the south side of Wichita. Dwayne Wheeler drove up A.J.'s street at nine-thirty p.m., noting there were a lot of cars in front of the bail bondsman's house with a couple in his driveway. It looked like he might be having a party. Dwayne had to park a half block away, and he hurried to the residence, almost trotting in his haste. He went up the porch step in one springing leap, and punched the doorbell.

The ringing was answered by a little blond woman who appeared to be a shade more than four feet tall. She looked up at Dwayne with an expression of annoyance. "Yes?"

Dwayne looked over her and could see about a dozen other little people sitting around the living room. One of their number was standing as he addressed the others who listened closely to some sort of oration or report.

"Hey!" the little woman said, breaking into Dwayne's thoughts. "Whattaya want?"

"Uh...I gotta talk to A.J. It's real important."

The woman turned and went to where A.J. was seated on the sofa. She whispered in his ear and he glanced at the door, seeing Dwayne. He stood up, interrupting the speaker. "Let's take a break in the proceedings. I got some business that just showed up. You'll find snacks and drinks in the kitchen."

His guests wasted no time in heading for the refreshments, and A.J. came to the door. "What's up?"

"We gotta crash into that Emporia house now," Dwayne said. "The cops moved ahead of time, so the people there know the shit's about to hit the fan. That's bad news for Fritz."

"I don't know about going back to that house," A.J. said. "We was lucky to get out of there the last time."

"Yeah," Dwayne agreed. "But tonight we're gonna charge straight through the goddamn front door."

A.J. was still hesitant. "There ain't a lot of money involved in Fritz's bail, and I was only going after him on account of my reputation. That's real important in—"

"I know that, but this is a special situation," Dwayne interrupted.

A.J. shook his head. "Looky here. If something happens to him, the court returns my money, and that's the end of it."

"Aw, c'mon, A.J.!" Dwayne begged. "He's a buddy of mine. If I make the move without you, I get arrested and Fritz still gets messed up anyhow. I'm talking about him getting killed."

A.J. hesitated. "This is a goddamn dangerous thing to do. You said yourself that the guy living there will shoot to kill."

"It's something that's gotta be done."

Every ounce of common sense A.J. possessed told him he should tell Dwayne to take a hike. But there was a male bond—a code of honor—between them that presented undeniable commitments. And Dwayne had always been more than fair and square with him. The bail bondsman showed an expression of acceptance, and shrugged. "Okay. Wait here. I gotta get my heater and cuffs." He hurried away, going toward the back of the house.

The woman who answered the door walked over with a bottle of pop in one little hand and a sandwich in the other. She wore her blond hair like Veronica Lake the movie star, with part of it over one eye. "You're Dwayne Wheeler, aren't you?"

"Yeah," he answered, thinking she was kind of cute and sexy.

"A.J. told me you broke up with Donna Sue. Is that right?"

"Yeah," he replied puzzled. "D'you know her?"

"You bet I know her," she said with a grin. "Me and Donna Sue worked at Boeing together during the war. I was a welder, too. I got the job 'cause I could fit into small spaces in the bomber fuselages. I'm Irma Dwight."

"Are you and A.J. going together?"

"Yeah," Irma replied. "We been dating about two months now."

They were interrupted by A.J.'s appearance. He kissed Irma. "I got some work that's popped up. Tell the others, okay, honey?"

"You bet, sweetie," she said.

A.J. turned to Dwayne. "Let's roll, buddy."

Dwayne had to slow his pace so A.J. wouldn't have to run as they made their way down the block to the Pontiac coupe. They got in quickly, and Dwayne fought the starter and choke with angry impatience until the elderly motor deigned to start.

A.J. shook his head. "You should get a new car. Or at least a newer one."

Dwayne ignored the advice as he headed for George Washington Boulevard. "What the hell was going on at your house?"

"It was a meeting of the Wichita Chapter of A.A.L.P.," A.J. answered. "That's the Association of American Little People."

"You guys don't like to be called midgets, right?" Dwayne asked artlessly.

"No," A.J. responded firmly. "And that includes dwarfs, runts, shrimps, gnomes, and other crap-ass names."

"Right."

Dwayne eased off George Washington Boulevard onto Kellogg, going all the way east to Emporia Avenue. A quick turn north, and the Pontiac sped toward the evening's destination. In ten minutes Dwayne pulled up to the curb a few yards down from the target house.

A.J. glanced around. "Quiet as a tomb, ain't it?" Then he added, "But it won't be for long, huh?"

"Okay," Dwayne said. "This is a fucking attack, okay? We pussyfoot up to the door and open the screen. I'll give a hard kick to the doorknob and we'll charge in."

"Have we got Tommy Joe for backup?" A.J. asked.

"This is a night off for him and he's out of town," Dwayne answered. "We're on our own."

A.J. already had his pistol in his hand. "I'm ready for one hell of a shootout, ol' buddy."

They got out of the car and, after careful glances up and down the street, walked up to the house that showed a light in the living room. When they reached the door, A.J. deftly cut a hole in the screen with his pocket knife and unlatched it. He stood back and nodded to Dwayne.

The shamus didn't hesitate as he drove his foot straight into the doorknob. The old device gave way and the door crashed open, and Dwayne led the way in with his .45 Colt chambered. The pair went only a couple of steps before coming to an abrupt halt.

A blonde woman sitting in an easy chair with her face in her hands, leaped up startled. Tears shown on her cheeks and it was easy to see she had been crying. Before Dwayne could speak, she said, "He is dead."

"Shit," Dwayne said, looking at A.J. then back to her. "Where's Karlis, goddamn it!"

"He is in the bedroom," she said, pointing.

A.J. covered the woman in the living room while Dwayne cautiously went down the short hallway. He took a quick glance inside and saw the Latvian lying on the bed. He eased in the room, then stopped. The left side of Karlis' head was blown away and the gore was splattered on the wall. Dwayne noticed the Luger pistol on a nearby dresser. When he returned to the living room he saw that the woman was seated again and sobbing in quick breaths.

Dwayne walked over and shook her. "Who shot that guy in the bedroom?"

"I did it," Lotte said. "He was going to kill Fritz and I could not let that happen."

"Where is Fritz?"

"In the basement."

"Is there anybody else here?"

Lotte shook her head. "Just us. And Fritz. The keys to the basement door padlocks are on the counter in the kitchen."

A.J. was becoming agitated. "What about the fucking guy in the fucking bedroom?"

"He's dead," Dwayne said. "I'm gonna check on Fritz."

He went into the kitchen and picked up the key ring, then went down the basement steps. He unlocked the first door, then stepped into the small space between it to open the second. After the final unlocking, he entered the basement. Fritz Harrigan was seated on his bed, a nervous expression on his face.

"Hi, Fritz."

"Dwayne!"

"Yeah," Dwayne said. "C'mon. It's all over now."

"I heard a shot awhile back," Fritz said, standing up.

"Karlis is dead."

"What about Lotte?"

"The blonde woman? She's okay."

"Thank the Lord," Fritz said.

He followed Dwayne up the stairs, through the kitchen and into the living room. Fritz rushed to Lotte, kneeling down in front of her. "Are you okay, Lotte?"

Lotte nodded. "He was going to kill you, Fritz."

"You mean Karlis? Why?"

Before she could answer, Dwayne interrupted. "This'll all get covered later. And, by the way, this wasn't a secret government project." He put his pistol in the shoulder holster, and got out a notebook and pencil. He pulled Fritz away from Lotte, looking down at the woman. "Listen here. I'm gonna ask questions. You're gonna answer 'em. And I ain't standing for any funny business. D'you understand?"

"Yes, sir."

"Okay," Dwayne said. "What's your name?"

"Lotte Gutmanis."

"What's Karlis to you?"

"He is my husband," she replied, and began weeping again.

"He *was* your husband, lady," Dwayne said. "Now

explain to me what's going on here and why you two had my buddy Fritz locked down there in the basement."

"May I have a cigarette please?" Lotte asked, wiping at her tears.

Dwayne obliged with one of his Lucky Strikes, lighting it for her. "Now start talking, lady, and I ain't kidding around."

Lotte took a drag. "We were working for some people who were going to counterfeit German military scrip. Fritz was brought here to engrave the plates for printing it."

Dwayne frowned in puzzlement. "German military scrip? You mean the money Kraut soldiers used in occupied countries? What the hell good is that stuff now that the war is over?"

"I have no knowledge of that," Lotte said.

Dwayne glanced over at Fritz. "What do you know about this?"

"I was told it was a secret government something or other," Fritz said. "And don't be mean to Lotte. She's been nice to me."

"That's right," Dwayne said. "She saved your ass, little buddy." He shifted his eyes back to Lotte. "What do you know about a Latvian guy who was murdered here in Wichita?"

"My husband did it," Lotte said. "He told me about it last night."

Dwayne wasn't surprised, so he changed the subject. "Who're you working for?"

"He was a British banker I met in Germany," Lotte said. "His name was Nigel Hawthorne."

"Holy shit!" Dwayne exclaimed in absolute shock.

A.J. asked, "D'you know the guy?"

"Yeah," Dwayne said. He walked over and sat down next to Fritz. "Have you met this Hawthorne?"

"He's never been here that I know of," Fritz said.

Dwayne gestured to A.J. "Come out to the kitchen with me." He led the way with the little bail bondsman following. "Listen, A.J. Right now the murder of that Latvian guy in the Warehouse District is solved. I got all the information. Now I'm gonna make a phone call, then we're going into the bedroom and make it look like the dead guy in there committed suicide."

"How the hell are we gonna do that?"

"The weapon that killed him is on the dresser," Dwayne explained. "We're gonna put it in his hand."

"Okay. Now *why* are we gonna do that?"

"To clear the woman," Dwayne said. "She saved Fritz's life so I'm gonna get her out of a murder rap. And it makes things easier all around, get it?"

"I suppose."

"Good!" Dwayne said. "Now wait here. I'm gonna send Fritz and the woman in here. You make sure they stay."

"Okay."

Dwayne went out and ordered Fritz and Lotte to go into the kitchen, then he went over and picked up the phone book, looking for a number. He dialed it and waited for an answer then said, "Gimme room 406."

"Hello," came Pete Van Dyke's sleepy voice after several rings.

"Pete, this is Dwayne. You gotta haul ass."

"What the hell are you talking about?" Pete replied, now wide awake.

"I'm over on Emporia Avenue," Dwayne said. "Karlis Gutmanis is dead. His wife shot him and I got Fritz Harrigan out of the basement. In other words, ol' buddy, you are compromised. And that would include Hawthorne and ever'body else."

"Goddamn it!"

"I'm giving you a running start for old times' sake, Pete," Dwayne said. "I'm gonna call the cops next and it'll take 'em awhile to put two and two together; if they ever do. I'm not gonna say a word about you, and the woman prob'ly won't either. I'm gonna get her out of a murder rap, so she'll do as I ask her."

"Murder rap?" Pete queried.

"Yeah," Dwayne replied. "She killed Karlis. I ain't got time to jaw, Pete. You gotta get outta town, ol' buddy. Pronto!"

"Why am I not surprised you can handle this situation, Dwayne?"

"Save the compliments. Now what about Wichita's esteemed lawyer Carl Banter?"

Pete snorted. "Wichita's esteemed lawyer Carl Banter is in the clear. And he knows absolutely nothing anyhow. He only handled some routine legal matters."

"I did find out about the German military scrip, but the woman didn't know nothing about what it would be used for," Dwayne said.

"Okay, Dwayne," Pete said. "Let me think a minute... okay, now listen. Be in your office Monday morning. I'll be giving you a phone call. And thanks."

Dwayne hung up and went into the bedroom. He wiped down the Luger pistol, then went over and placed it as best he could in Karlis' right hand, making sure his index finger was within the trigger guard. With that done, he walked into the kitchen. "Listen up, ever'body. Here's the deal and stick to it. Karlis Gutmanis committed suicide."

"But I shot him," Lotte said.

"No, you couldn't have," Dwayne said. "He's got the gun in his right hand. He's right handed, ain't he?"

"Yes," she acknowledged.

Okay," Dwayne said. "I'm getting you out of trouble, lady. So you owe me big time. Understand?"

"Yes, sir," Lotte said, beginning to realize that Dwayne was going to help her out of the mess she was in.

He went back to the living room and picked up the phone. He dialed the operator and said, "Give me the police department."

CHAPTER 28

The Wichita Police Department homicide squad led by Lieutenant Ben Forester with his second-in-command Sergeant Al Gallagher, arrived on Emporia Avenue practically *en masse* twenty minutes after Dwayne's phone call. Uniformed officers were called in from their beats to surround the place even though it was still dark and no one was on the streets.

Inside, Ben and Gallagher had Dwayne Wheeler, A.J. Kessler, Fritz Harrigan and Lotte Gutmanis gathered together in the living room for interviews. Karlis Gutmanis was also there of course, but since he was dead in the bedroom the only attention he received was from the Sedgwick County coroner's assistant. This learned man spent ten minutes with the corpse and came walking out of the bedroom declaring the victim's death was an undeniable suicide. Period.

"Okay," Ben said. "I can go along with that. He knew he was gonna be collared for the Kilitis murder."

Gallagher turned his attention to getting simple statements of facts from Messieurs Wheeler and Kessler who both stated they were operating as bail bond bounty hunters with the mission of bringing a bail jumper by the name of Fritz Harrigan into custody.

"You guys are lucky," Gallagher said. "That's pretty much already on the record so there won't be no charges laid against you."

At that point, Dwayne loudly declared, "And I was also here to put a citizen's arrest on Karlis Gutmanis for the murder of Professor Mikelis Kilitis."

Gallagher growled. "Knock off the bullshit, shamus. That's a Wichita Police Department case, and you know it."

"Fuck you, Gallagher," Dwayne growled back. "I was hired by the victim's widow to find the killer. And it was your boss Lieutenant Ben Forester who recommended that she hire me. And I solved the case, so you pull your nose out of the caper, or I'm gonna bend it."

Ben quickly spoke up. "He's right, Al."

Gallagher glared furiously at Dwayne, then turned his attention to Lotte Gutmanis. "That's your dead husband in the bedroom, right?"

"Yes," Lotte responded. She, being an intelligent woman with a shrewdness developed from living by her wits at the end of the war in Europe, had wisely decided to take Dwayne's advice to not confess to killing her husband. "He went into there and shot himself while I sat here in the living room." Then she added, "He knew he would soon be arrested for the murder of the professor."

Gallagher knew there was no murder case against the woman to build on since the county coroner's office had already backed up her avowal. "You still ain't off the hook, sister. You can be charged with being an accessory to the fact in counterfeiting."

Dwayne chimed in again. "There ain't no counterfeiting. They was reproducing German military scrip down in that basement. You prob'ly forgot the Krauts lost the war, Gallagher, but that stuff belonged to an army that don't exist no more. It can't be used for purchasing anything and wouldn't have no value."

Gallagher snarled, "Then why was they gonna print 'em up?"

"For collectors, dickhead," Dwayne said. "Ain't you heard of war souvenirs and mementos? It's a big market now."

Gallagher's temper flared. "Your big mouth is gonna get your ass slammed up between your ears, Wheeler."

"Anytime you wanna try, you—"

"Knock it off, both of you!" Ben roared. "We've still got this thing with Fritz Harrigan. He was either a kidnap victim or a fugitive and part of whatever was going on here."

Now it was A.J. Kessler's turn to crow. "You cops got nothing on the kid. His attorney Carl Banter had made arrangements with the D.A. for him to make restitution and serve a period of probation. He says he was kidnapped, and you can't prove he wasn't."

Gallagher whipped around and faced the little man. "Shut up, shorty!"

A.J. charged, but Ben jumped in the way and blocked him. "C'mon, A.J., you don't want to be charged with assault on a cop, do you?"

"Assault, hell!" A.J. declared. "I wanna murder the son of a bitch."

By then the new day's dawn was pinking over the horizon, and an ambulance had arrived to cart off the corpse of Karlis Gutmanis, ex-*sturmbannführer* of the Latvian SS. With that detail taken care of, Ben supervised the final wrapping up of the investigation at the scene of the incident.

———

ON THE FOLLOWING MONDAY MORNING, Dwayne sat in his office in the Snodgrass Building, staring at his telephone. Peter Van Dyke had said he would call, and Dwayne was curious about what he wanted to talk about. It was a little after ten o'clock when the phone finally rang.

"How're you doing, Dwayne?"

"Okay, Pete. How're you?"

"Fine, thanks," Pete said. "I really appreciate what you did."

"I owed you, Pete," Dwayne said sincerely. "You got me out of a hell of a jam over there in Europe. I could've ended up doing five to ten in Leavenworth. Man, I would have still been in the slammer with a lot of years to go yet."

"Well, we're even," Pete said. "I'd like to get together with you for a final time. It's important. Do you know where Chanute is?"

"Sure," Dwayne replied. "It's a little place east of here."

"Okay," Pete said. "There's a roadside café on the north side of town on U.S. 169. That's a little less than twenty miles south of U.S. Fifty-Four. It'll be easy for you to find, and you can get here in around three hours. The name of the place is the Sunflower Café."

"I can do that."

"Okay," Pete said. "Leave right away and I'll be waiting for you."

———

IT WAS A LITTLE AFTER ONE P.M. WHEN DWAYNE pulled off U.S. 169 into the small parking area of the café. He drove slowly up beside some other vehicles in the parking lot and came to a stop. Dwayne trusted Pete Van Dyke, but he wasn't sure of anyone else his buddy worked with, and he had arrived armed and ready for trouble. A quick eye-scan of the area showed it to be empty, so he got out of the coupe and walked toward the entrance of the small eatery.

When Dwayne stepped inside, he noted several farmer-types in bib overalls drinking coffee and chatting at the counter. He glanced along a line of booths and saw Pete sitting in the last one. Dwayne walked over and slipped into the opposite side.

"So what's going on, Pete?"

"I'm getting ready to go to Europe," Pete replied. "So I had some things to settle with you."

"Such as?"

"Such as finding out if you still wanted to work with me," Pete replied. "Thanks to you, we're all getting a free run out of the country with no problems. We'll be back in Europe in a week. You can still make some big bucks sometime in the future. So are you game to continue?"

"Sure," Dwayne said. "You know where to find me."

The waitress, a thin bespectacled young woman, came up to the booth. "What can I get you?"

"Well, I ain't had lunch," Dwayne said. "How's about a grilled cheese sandwich and French-fries? And an Orange Crush."

"Coming up," she said, then smiled at Pete. "What about you mister? More coffee?"

"Sure," Pete said. "And another piece of this apple pie."

"Get one for me, too, please," Dwayne said. The

woman walked away, and he turned to Pete. "What's this German military scrip shit? You can't do nothing with that. Right?"

"Wrong," Pete said. "And it's the sweetest little deal I've ever been involved in, and that includes the black market right after the war."

"But scrip ain't worth nothing, is it?"

"Oh, yes it is," Pete said. "You see that's what the German forces used for money in the countries they occupied. The people under their control were forced to accept it. And, of course, when the war ended, there was a hell of a lot of French, Belgium, Dutch and others who had piles of the paper. And it couldn't be cashed in. Then our friend Nigel Hawthorne got word about an unexpected development while working at his job in the British Bank in Frankfort."

"And what was that?"

"He learned that as part of the unconditional surrender of the German Reich, the Allies insisted that Germany make pay offs on all that scrip that was out there. And they would be required to pay cold hard cash in the form of American dollars."

"I'm beginning to understand," Dwayne said. "So you guys printed up a bunch of it to put in the pipeline, right?"

"We developed the right contacts through Nigel," Pete explained. "It would all be printed on stressed paper stock to make it look like it had been in circulation for awhile. We've got several million dollars' worth of the stuff being run off in Luxembourg on those plates that Fritz Harrigan made for us. And we have solid arrangements to have it integrated with the scrip going into German banks to be cashed in. It's an eighty-twenty split in our favor. Very, very profitable."

They were interrupted when the waitress arrived to serve them. "Can I get you fellahs anything else?"

"No, thanks," Pete said. He waited for her to return to the counter before speaking again. "So, Dwayne, as you now know, we are in the chips. Big time."

"But how did Fritz Harrigan get involved in this?"

"We had heard about his engraving and prints through a girlfriend of my wife Sybil who works in a New York City art gallery," Pete explained. "We went there and checked out his work and recognized his great talents. He was just the artist who could take samples of the scrip and cut plates for reproduction."

"Yeah," Dwayne remarked. "He was the right guy for the job, no doubt about that."

"We did some more digging to get personal information on him," Pete continued. "We needed to investigate his sex habits. He might have been queer for all we knew. A lot of artists are. When it was determined he liked girls, Hawthorne arranged to bring in Lotte to provide him with sex. That way he wouldn't mind being cooped up in that basement against his will. And that meant he would have quite a bit of enthusiasm for his work assignment."

Dwayne chuckled. "I guess he would. So where did Karlis come in?"

"As a tough guy," Pete said. "It was a load off my mind when you told me Lotte had killed him. But you didn't tell me why."

"Lotte said Karlis was gonna kill Fritz, and she didn't want him to," Dwayne explained. "I guess she had grown fond of the kid."

"That would be Karlis' idea and his alone!" Pete strongly pronounced. "Nobody in the organization had any intention of harming Fritz Harrigan. As a matter of fact, a cashier's check for five thousand dollars has been drawn up and sent to him. He should get it in the next couple of days."

"I'm glad to hear that, Pete," Dwayne said. "I'd hate like hell to think you'd do a lowdown thing like that."

"Anyhow, when we tried to contact Fritz, we learned he had gone back to Wichita."

"I see," Dwayne said. "So you didn't come here especially to contact me, huh?"

"Actually, I'd forgotten you were from Wichita," Pete admitted. "Seeing you at the Roadhouse that night was an unexpected bonus."

"And you obviously found Fritz, too."

"Yeah, after looking around," Pete said. "We located his house where he lived with his mother through the East High Class of 'thirty-eight's alumni committee. We followed him and finally made contact in that warehouse area where there weren't many people on the street. A quick stab of sodium pentothal in his ass got him drowsy and that night we took him to the house on Emporia. That's when we discovered he had pawned his engraving tools."

"Were you the guy who redeemed the pawn ticket?"

"Yeah," Pete said. "By the way, what's the upshot on Lotte?"

"She's being deported back to Germany as an undesirable alien," Dwayne informed him. "They really couldn't pin anything on her, so Immigration and Naturalization just wanted to get her out of the country."

"She's better off," Pete said. "She'll get a big payoff, including Karlis' share. The lady wants to go to Switzerland and open a restaurant." He finished off his pie. "Who convinced the Wichita Police the scrip was keepsakes for collectors?"

"Me," Dwayne replied. "It seemed that would have

been the only reason for printing it. And to tell you the truth nobody really gave a shit."

"By the way," Pete said. "I have something for you." He reached into his shirt pocket and pulled out a document. "This is the title to that 'forty Buick. I've filled it out and all you have to do is sign it and go down to the motor vehicle department and it's yours free and clear."

"Oh, man!" Dwayne exclaimed. "Thanks a lot, Pete."

"Here're the keys," Pete said. "You'll find it in valet parking at the Riverview Hotel." He reached beside him on the seat and pulled up a small canvas briefcase. "And there's one last item I have to give you."

"What the hell is that?"

"This is your share of the profits to be made," Pete said. "There's some extra included as a bonus for your 'special' services. If you hadn't called me, our entire operation would have collapsed. Not only would we not have succeeded, but we would have lost our entire investment. I'm talking about thousands of dollars, Dwayne. The best we could have hoped for in the situation was some limited freedom as fugitives. Not—I say again—*not* a happy situation."

"Yeah," Dwayne said. "So what's in the canvas doodad?"

"Five big ones," Pete replied.

"Five hunnerd dollars?"

"Five *thousand* dollars," Pete replied. "I told you big money was being made here, and our business partners thought it would guarantee your continued loyalty to the cause. And you deserve it. Don't forget we'll be involved in other, shall we say—opportunities—and will be in touch when we need you."

"But five thousand dollars!" Dwayne said. "You guys can't be *that* grateful."

"There's a bit more to it," Pete said. "If you accept this, you also accept an obligation to continue your association with the organization." He gave him a serious look. "And it's an obligation you should never—I say again—never betray."

"What's the name of this group?"

Pete shook his head. "No name. No information. Just the 'organization'."

Dwayne shrugged. "That's good enough for me."

Pete stood up and offered his hand. "I'll be seeing you, Dwayne." He started to walk away, then stopped and turned back. "You know what, Dwayne? Your sense of morality is tempered by a levelheaded dash of malfeasance."

Dwayne grinned and watched him leave the café.

———

IT WAS THE BEGINNING OF A NEW WORK DAY when Donna Connors walked into her office and hung up her hat and coat. A quick check of her **IN** box showed she had a few reports to process with none being marked as rushes. With the pressure off, she walked down the hall to the break room to get a cup of coffee along with a sweet roll. She also grabbed one of the copies of the morning's *Wichita Eagle* that were available for the executive staff. When Donna got back to her desk, she sat down and took a sip of coffee. After a small bite off the roll, she unfolded the paper. An article on page one caught her eye.

**Murder of WU professor solved;
killer commits suicide before arrest**
By Bud Terwilliger, Eagle Police Reporter

The case of the slaying of Professor Mikelis Kilitis, an instructor of European History at Wichita University has been solved through the efforts of local private investigator Dwayne Wheeler. He had recently been a principal participant in the crushing of a Kansas City crime cartel's plans to move into the city.

The professor's widow, Mrs. Emilija Kilitis, hired Wheeler to take over the investigation of the murder after the local police department was stymied. Wheeler's investigation led him to a Nazi war criminal living in Wichita by the name of Karlis Gutmanis. Gutmanis was a member of the infamous SS storm trooper units of the German armed forces. His motive for killing Kilitis was to prevent him from revealing his past atrocities to authorities. However, a scant hour before Wheeler moved in to make the arrest, Gutmanis committed suicide. (More of the story and photos inside on page 5A.)

Donna quickly flipped to the indicated page and saw a two column photograph of Dwayne standing with Lieutenant Ben Forester of the Wichita Police Department on the porch of a house on Emporia Avenue. A second photo showed a Mrs. Lotte Gutmanis, the widow of the murderer being escorted to a police car by Sergeant Al Gallagher.

Donna gave her attention to the rest of the article which told of how Professor Kilitis and Gutmanis had known each other in their native country of Latvia, and that Gutmanis almost turned over Mr. and Mrs. Kilitis to the Gestapo for anti-Nazi activity in 1941. However, the underground was able to smuggle the couple to neutral Sweden, thus saving them from certain death in a Nazi concentration camp.

A rapping caught Donna's attention and she looked at the door to see Brian Murchison. He smiled at her. "Ah! You must be reading about Dwayne's latest exploits."

"Yes," Donna replied.

"One thing can be said for Dwayne Wheeler," Brian remarked, "he most definitely is a remarkable and capable guy."

"In some ways," Donna commented.

Brian leaned across the desk, and Donna stood up. They kissed, holding their lips together for a moment before parting. He pulled back. "Don't forget our date Saturday night."

"I'm looking forward to it," Donna said.

Brian left, and Donna picked up her cup of coffee and walked over to the window. She glanced down at the motor and foot traffic along Douglas Avenue. It was a time for a complete break from Dwayne, and that could only be done by going to bed with Brian. Giving herself to him would be a special gesture as the final big step away from her old life.

EPILOGUE

Dwayne went up the back steps of the rooming house, pausing at the second floor porch to look down at the curb where his newly acquired 1940 Buick was parked. He had sold the old 1935 Plymouth Coupe to his bootlegger buddy Elmer Pettibone for twenty bucks. Elmer planned on replacing the engine with a souped up V-8 to use for deliveries of his illicit liquor.

Dwayne went into the house, walking down the hall to his room. He carefully checked the scotch tape he had put on the door near the top, noting it was unbroken. He had placed it there after leaving to sell the Pontiac and pick up the Buick.

Satisfied that no one had broken in, he used his key and entered his simple abode. The first thing Dwayne did after tossing his hat on the dresser, was fetch a pint bottle of Jack Daniels from the top drawer. He poured a half a glass, took a deep swallow, then went to the closet to fetch the hidden canvas briefcase that Pete Van Dyke had given him. He took it to the bed and opened it, pouring the contents over the spread.

A quick inventory showed five packs of ten one-hundred dollar bills each. Dwayne examined them closely, happy to note that all had separate serial numbers and had obviously been in circulation for some time. No counterfeits here. This was an untraceable five thousand dollars of cash money, ready to spend as he desired.

After getting himself another drink—this one poured to the top of the glass—he returned to the bed to gaze down at his treasure. "Self," he said aloud to himself, "you are at a crossroads here. What to do?"

The thought of making some bets on the ponies seemed sour to him. This situation called for a complete turnaround in his usual conduct. A mental picture of handing over dough to Longshot Jackson in the OK Barbershop was almost obscene. If he placed any bets, the inclination to gamble was sure to continue until he was broke again.

Sudden thoughts of Donna Sue brought a feeling of loss and sadness. "Y'know, Self, maybe if you used the money in a smart way..." Dwayne stopped speaking and downed half of the whiskey in a couple of swallows.

This was a windfall that would never happen to him again even if he lived to be a hundred. In less than twenty-four hours he had acquired a luxury automobile and enough legal tender to live on comfortably for the next seven or eight years even if he never worked again.

Dwayne drained the glass, feeling the liquor ease into his consciousness. He went back to the dresser for a third go at the whiskey. He turned and looked at the money again, and once more spoke his thoughts aloud to himself.

"Listen, Self, d'you think you might just once in your life make a choice about something that would at least show enough logic and intelligence to benefit you; even if just a little bit?"

He laughed, raising the glass in a toast. "Well, I reckon that's gonna be something for me and Jack Daniels to work out."

A Look At Book 3:

Wichita Undercover

1940s Wichita, Kansas

Only Private Detective Dwayne Wheeler is capable of submerging himself deep into a gang war among Irish thugs, a Sicilian mob and two different Mafia families—in the middle of the Kansas prairie.

As a powerful criminal operation from the east coast moves in on a rural area of Kansas for unknown reasons, the FBI enlists Dwayne as an undercover operative.

But it isn't long before a complicated crime operation shakes up the Wheat State—or for Dwayne to become embroiled in a desperate fight for his life.

Wichita Undercover is book three in a historical private eye series that follows Dwayne Wheeler—a tough and hardboiled detective.

AVAILABLE OCTOBER 2022

About the Author

Patrick Andrews was born an Army Brat on January 14, 1936—his sister's arrival just two years later. His father was a paratrooper in the 82nd Airborne Division during World War II. His mother was a good army officer's wife, who, like several of her lady cousins, wrote short-stories and poems.

After the war, Patrick's father transferred into the Army Reserves, and they moved to Wichita, Kansas—where Patrick caught the scribbling bug. When Patrick got a job as a copy boy at the *Wichita Eagle* newspaper, he was ecstatic.

A few years later, Patrick got a yen to be a paratrooper. He enlisted in the Army and took basic training in Camp Chaffee, Arkansas, soon after being transferred to the 82nd Airborne Division in Fort Bragg. His career with the 82nd was rewarding—being promoted to sergeant and tasked with training cadets in West Point before retiring.

When Patrick read James Jones' *From Here to Eternity*, he appreciated the pride and struggling of soldiers. Soon after, he moved to San Diego, California and began writing and mailing manuscripts while working at a union typesetting company. He married and had one child, named William Patrick.

One pivotal night, Patrick was with a couple of his writing buddies, drinking scotch whiskey and playing at writing the *Sixgun Samurai* series. The next day, they drove up to Pinnacle Books in Los Angeles, where they walked out with a book deal. Patrick and his friends went on to write the series' twelve novels—which were also printed in the U.K. by Star Books, the paperback division of W.H. Allen & Co.

From then on, Patrick started writing and selling western, men's adventure, and military fiction. Years passed, and he had 24 published e-books with Piccadilly Publishing in the U.K.

Today, all six of Patrick's Wichita Detective books are getting another chance to see the light of day—with Rough Edges Press—and find refuge on a cozy shelf in Ocean Hills, California where Patrick and his beloved wife, Julie, live.